last will and
TESTAMENT

DAHLIA ADLER

LAST WILL AND TESTAMENT
Copyright © 2014 by Dahlia Adler
Cover design: Maggie Hall
Interior formatting: Cait Greer

ISBN-10: 0990916812 (paperback)
ISBN-13: 978-0-9909168-1-9

Other books by Dahlia Adler

Behind the Scenes
Under the Lights (coming soon)

I, Dahlia Adler, being of vaguely sound mind—
depending on whom you ask—hereby declare this to be
my in-no-way-legally-binding Last Will and Testament:

To Gina, chocolate macarons and a filthy mention in
every book;
To Marieke, a key to Nijkamp Hall for always;
To Katie, doughnuts, ballet dancers, and a swipe to the
right;
To Sara, all the salad, none of the bacon, and half my
Gushers;
To Becks, all my copy editor empathy;
To Lindsay, a hoodie of terror with mini vodka bottles
in the pockets;
To Maggie, the perfect mimosa...*after* you delete your
inbox;
To my family, anything you want if you please stop
reading this book right now;
and to Yoni, all my love and all that I am. Plus flat-
front pants.

chapter one

Supposedly no one even answered the front door when they first started knocking. No one could hear it over the music blasting from the speakers, the Sigma Psi Omegas chanting around keg stands, and Jessica Fiorello singing loudly along with some song no one else seemed to hear. (She got admitted to the hospital that night for alcohol poisoning, but nobody really talks about that. It kinda got lost in what came next. Lucky me.)

I didn't hear the knocking either. The tightly closed door of Trevor Matlin's room made sure of that. Even if it hadn't, Trevor's moaning in my ear as he begged me to get down on my knees probably would've drowned it out. He's never been very quiet. Kinda makes me wonder how we got away with it for so long.

The knocking was impossible to miss when it sounded on Trevor's door, though. And once Trev and I were silenced by it, it was almost as easy to hear Sophie Springer yelling, "Why the hell would you think she's in there? That's my boyfriend's room."

"Shit," Trevor mutters, yanking his pants back up as I straighten myself out. "Who the hell is that?"

"Well *I* obviously don't know," I whisper back, snatching my black-framed glasses from his nightstand and sliding them on. "Am I zipped?" I show him the back of my sleeveless top, then check my fly.

"Yeah," he says. "Me?"

"Yeah. Wait, no, your buttons are off."

"Trevor Matlin? Are you in there?"

"Who wants to know?" he calls back as we both scramble to fix his shirt.

"This is the Radleigh Police Department. We're looking for Elizabeth Brandt. We have reason to believe she may be with you."

Trevor and I both freeze, eyes widening in a panic. "Why the fuck are the cops after you?" he whispers fiercely.

"I have no idea! Just tell them I'm not here."

"I can't lie to the cops!"

"Your girlfriend is standing right outside that door," I remind him. I have no love for Sophie Springer—not since she "accidentally" spilled her beer on me last year when she spotted me talking to Trevor

2

for the first time—but that doesn't mean I want her seeing me with her boyfriend, in the flesh.

As if on cue, Sophie yells, "That slut better not be in there, Trevor Matlin!"

"Ma'am, please," I hear an officer say, his voice muffled. I wonder how many of them there are. What the hell are the police doing after me? I wouldn't say I'm a model citizen, but they just walked through an entire house of underage drinkers, so…. Then the same officer says, "Mr. Matlin, I'm not going to ask again. Open this door."

Trev and I exchange one more quick glance and then I dash under the bed, squeezing in as much of my body as possible. I'm not tiny, but sadly, this isn't my first time in a similar predicament, though this *is* the first time the cops are involved. I've learned how to get decent coverage under Trevor's full-size mattress.

I pull the blanket down enough to cover me but still allow me to see feet, just as Trevor pulls open the door. "Sorry about that," Trevor says with the same charismatic smoothness that allows him to be president of Sigma Psi Omega, date the campus princess, and bang a random nobody on the side. "How can I help you, officers?"

"We're looking for Elizabeth Brandt," one of them replies. I count shoes. Six, including Trev's. They're all men's, but I know Sophie's lurking there somewhere. I can feel her silent fuming. "Her roommate said she was

3

probably here with you."

Fucking Cait.

"Sorry, officer—I don't even know who that is, or why her roommate thinks she'd be here."

"That's what I've been trying to tell them," Sophie says, her voice steel-edged.

"Are you certain about that, son?" the other officer asks. "It's very important we speak with her."

"Very certain," Trevor says. Hell, I'd believe him with that confidence in his voice, if I didn't know way, way better. "I'm sorry I can't help you gentlemen. Whatever this girl did, I hope you catch her."

"She didn't do anything, Mr. Matlin. There's been a family emergency. If you find—"

I whoosh out from under the bed like a tidal wave; I'll deal with Sophie later. "What family emergency?" I demand, getting to my feet on wobbly legs. "What happened?"

The officers don't even look amused at the fact that they've caught perfect Trevor Matlin cheating on perfect Sophie Springer, and that's when I know this is really, really bad. My brain starts to go fuzzy and my hands clam up, my heart turning over in my chest. Sophie's screeching at Trevor somewhere in the room, but it's barely penetrating my consciousness.

"Elizabeth Brandt?"

"Yeah. Yes, I mean. That's me. But…Lizzie. It's Lizzie." My tongue feels enormous as it struggles to work with my lips and teeth to form words.

"Lizzie." The lighter-haired officer's face falls, and I can tell he's wishing I'd never slid out from under that bed, that he'd never found me at all. "I'm so sorry. There's been a terrible accident. Your parents…they didn't make it. I'm so sorry."

I know the words he's saying are horrible, life-altering ones, but I can't seem to assign them any meaning right now. Because he can't be saying what I think he's saying. I wonder if it's his first time delivering news like this. It certainly sounds like it is. The double apology—that's the giveaway. He's new at this, new to the force. Looks it, too, all young and covered in shaving nicks.

"Lizzie?" I'm not even sure who says my name. It might be one of the officers. It might be Trevor. Hell, it might even be Sophie. I'm so far away, I swear it could be fucking Santa Claus. I shouldn't have had those stupid Jell-O shots. They're just confusing everything right now.

"Lizzie?"

"Miss Brandt?"

I blink. I'm not sure why it's "Miss Brandt" that does it, but it is. "I'm sorry, did you just say that my parents are dead?"

"Yes, ma'am. I'm so sorry."

"You apologize a lot."

"I'm sorry."

I smile, just a little, and it briefly occurs to me I must look deranged. I *feel* deranged. "You're still doing it."

"Miss Brandt—"

"Please don't call me that." I hold up a hand. "My parents are dead. Yes? That's what's happening here? That's *actually* what you meant to say?"

"Yes."

It feels like I've swallowed a blade and it is slowly but surely shredding my insides with every word. "My parents were in an accident, and they were alive, and now they're dead. My parents, like, the people who raised me. Edward and Manuella Brandt. Tall lawyer guy with a mustache? Filipina high school history teacher? Those parents?"

"Miss Brandt—"

"*It's Lizzie.*"

"Lizzie, then. Do you have a counselor on campus? Someone you can speak to? A family member we can reach out to?"

It's like having salt rubbed in an open wound the size of my entire chest cavity. "Didn't you just tell me my parents are dead? Who the fuck in my family would I want to reach out to if my parents are dead?"

Blondie wants to melt into the floor; I can see it. I should feel bad, I know, but also, apparently my parents are dead, and I don't give a fuck how he feels.

"We've spoken to your grandmother—"

"Fantastic. She won't remember in the morning."

"And your aunt—"

"Well, I'm sure that stopped her drinking for a whole thirty seconds."

Dark Hair sighs again. They really should've introduced themselves. If you're going to tell an eighteen-year-old college sophomore that her parents are dead, don't you think you should at least open with an "I'm Officer So-and-So" first? "Yes, we gathered that the rest of your family is...not in a position to assist you with this news. Is there anyone else?"

And then it hits me like an actual punch to the gut. Of course there's someone else. There are two someone elses. "My brothers," I whisper. "Where are my brothers? Are my brothers okay?"

"Your brothers are being taken care of," Blondie assures me, confident again now that he actually has something to offer other than my name and an apology. "Your neighbor has them right now. We're working on other arrangements."

"But...permanently. Who...? What...?" I don't even know what I should be asking. This is an insane amount to process for someone who *isn't* half-drunk and wasn't interrupted mid-sex haze, let alone me, right now. "I need to sit."

I forgot Trevor was even standing there, but suddenly, he gets his ass in gear and brings me a chair. I drop into it like a lead weight.

"Miss Brandt—Lizzie—your brothers will ultimately need to be cared for by a long-term guardian, whom your parents have presumably designated. Once you're with your family, a lawyer and a social worker will help you through this difficult time."

But I stopped listening after "guardian." Because I know exactly who my parents designated. And it's someone who can barely handle her own life, let alone that of a thirteen- and seven-year-old.

"Me," I blurt out. "It's me. I'm their guardian now. I'm the one in the will."

The officers exchange a look. "If you, and a judge, feel that you're equipped to serve in that capacity." It's pretty clear from their demeanors that they possess no such feeling about me.

"And what happens if I—we—don't?"

"You really should talk to your lawyer and social worker, Miss Brandt," says Dark Hair.

"It's going to be a little while before I get to do that, considering I don't have either one right now." Is someone reaching into my skull and squeezing my brain? It really feels like it. But at least discussing logistics is keeping me from losing it outright. "Please just tell me what you know. Generally."

"Generally, either they'll go to another family member—"

"I think we've already established that won't be happening."

"Or they'll enter foster care," Dark Hair finishes.

"No."

"No, what?"

"No, you're not making my brothers into foster children. They're my brothers. I'll do it. I'll take care of them. I can. I promise." This is sort of a lie, but it's all I can say right then.

"Lizzie, come on," says Trevor.

"Fuck you, Trevor. No one asked you." I turn back to the officers. "How does this work? What happens now? When can I see them?"

"First, let's get you back to your room," says Blondie, shooting a glare at Trevor. "We can talk there, or you can come to the station."

"Yeah, sure, whatever." I've had enough of Trevor's room anyway. I need to get out. I need to breathe fresh air. "Let's go."

I'd completely forgotten that there was an entire frat party taking place in the house until I followed the officers downstairs and found myself being stared at by every single resident of Greek Row. It's hard to tell what people know; some faces are disgusted, some sympathetic, and some are just curious. I focus on the back of Blondie's head as we walk out the door. It isn't exactly how I'd imagined my first time in a police cruiser would be, but there really isn't anything about this night I'd pictured happening as it does.

Only when we pull away from the house, and Trevor and Sophie are gone, and I can hear the music blast from the house once again, do I fall apart in the backseat and cry.

chapter two

"How long are you going home for?" Cait perches on her bed to watch me pack, her green eyes wide with curiosity, her sharp little rodent teeth going to town on a Twizzler.

"I don't know." *Where the fuck is my black dress with the belt?*

"Are you coming back?"

"I don't know." I need that black dress. My brain's been running like a hamster on a wheel to nowhere since I got back from the police station, and focusing on an appropriate outfit is the only thing helping me keep my shit together.

"Are you really gonna be your brothers' guardian?"

"I don't know, Cait. I don't even know where my fucking black dress is."

"I think Frankie has it. She wore it to that thing."

Fucking Frankie. "That thing?"

"That history department thing."

Oh, right. I'd skipped that history department thing. I'd gotten a C on my Byzantine History quiz that day and decided my talents were better spent elsewhere, like in the back of Trevor's BMW, with a bottle of Maker's Mark.

I step out of my closet and into the common room. "Frankie?"

"Yeah?" she calls back from our suite's other bedroom, which she shares with a Greek pre-med named Stamatina whom I probably see once a week at best.

"Do you have my black dress? The one with the belt?"

"Umm...I think it's in my hamper? Lemme check."

"It's dry-clean only. It better not be in your hamper."

She pads out of her room a minute later, carrying the dress in hand. It's got a small but glaringly obvious stain on it I can see from a few feet away, and it had better not be what I think it is. "Here you go." She tosses it at me.

I toss it right back. "First of all, what the hell is that stain, Francesca? Did you *have sex with someone* while wearing *my funeral dress*?"

She hollows out her cheeks, the Frankie Look of

12

Contrition I've come to know well since we first met during freshman orientation last year, and she lost my pen two seconds after borrowing it. "I'm so sorry, Lizzie. I didn't realize it was your funeral dress."

I still can't believe I even *need* a funeral dress. I shake my head. Or maybe it's the rest of me that's shaking. "Well it isn't gonna be now. Who the hell did you screw at the department thing?"

She snorts. "Please, like there was anyone fuckable at that thing. I went to the Sigma party after and hooked up with James Nagawa."

"That would explain why this *also* smells like beer and smoke," I murmur. "Dry-clean it, Frank. Seriously. And you better have something to lend me instead."

"Oh, actually, you know who looked *really* fuckable at the thing? Your Byzantine TA. What's his name? Connor?"

"I don't care who looked fuckable at the stupid department thing, Frankie. I need something to wear to my parents' funeral."

She exhales sharply, as if my not wanting to discuss the fuckability of Connor Lawson is an inexplicable offense to her very existence. In fact, Connor Lawson's the one who gave me that C, and I don't think any woman could turn him on harder than Alexios Komnenos does; even if I *could* think about sex right now, it would not be with my history TA.

Unfortunately, the mention of his name *does* make

me realize that I need to get in touch with him. My professors have all been notified about my parents' death, but Connor's the one who takes attendance. I've got a paper due tomorrow, and if Professor Ozgur didn't tell him I won't be there and why, I really don't feel like dealing with the consequences.

I head back into my room, followed by Frankie, who promptly receives a whisper-scold from Cait about saying "completely inappropriate shit" to me right now. Cait's not wrong, but the truth is, I appreciate the predictability of Frankie's inability to keep her thoughts to herself. It's a grounding comfort now that everything else has been thrown into upheaval, and it stops my hands from shaking as I compose my quick e-mail to my TA.

Hi, Connor,

Don't know if Professor Ozgur filled you in, but I had a family emergency and I won't be in class tomorrow. Sorry about the paper.

Lizzie

I hit Send and then head back to my closet, where Frankie is knee-deep in discarded tops and skirts. Everything I own is too dirty or short or low-cut or...I don't know what. Wrong. Wrong in that my mother, who was raised staunchly Catholic in Manila, would hate it, even though she hasn't been to church in at least a decade. Wrong in that my father, who always called me his little girl, would think I looked too old in it.

Wrong for a funeral that shouldn't be happening in the first place.

"What about this?" Frankie holds up a gray dress with pearl buttons and white lace trim. "I've never even seen this before."

"My grandmother made it," I say flatly, taking from her hand and hanging it back up. "It's not for this." Not that my grandmother would recognize it, or remember she made it, with the way Alzheimer's has completely eaten her brain. But I still can't wear it to her daughter's funeral.

"Okay." She digs back in. "What about a plain shirt and this skirt?" She bends down to pick up a skirt I've already discarded.

"Too shiny."

"Just stop, Frank," Cait says. The crinkling of plastic suggests she's having yet another Twizzler. She's freaking addicted to them, though they're the only candy I've ever seen her eat. "She's not going to agree to anything. She's been doing this for like six hours."

I open my mouth to snap at Cait, and then shut it. She's right. I don't want to wear anything I own to the funeral. Whatever I wear, it's pretty guaranteed I'll never be able to look at it again. I don't want to wear anything I'm not ready to throw in a bonfire as soon as the last lily's been laid on the caskets.

I'm not sure if she gets it or what, but Frankie just

15

tosses the skirt back on the floor and says, "Hang on, I think I have something that'll work."

While she goes back to her room, I sit back down at my computer desk, and see I've got a reply from Connor.

Elizabeth,

Nice try. I believe you used the "family emergency" excuse to get an extension for the first paper. I'll see you at 9:00 a.m.

Connor

Fucking. Asshole.

I click reply and type back my response, my fingers flying as I stab at the keys.

Connor,

Unfortunately, I'll have to miss yet another enthralling session of talking about ancient buildings because I'll be at my parents' funeral. Perhaps if they were a thousand years older and lived on the other side of the world, you'd actually give a shit.

Lizzie

P.S. Research lover that you are, feel free to contact Professor Ozgur for copies of their death certificates.

"How's this?" Frankie returns with a black turtleneck and a surprisingly sedate gray kilt-like thing.

"Perfect," I say gratefully. "Thank you."

"Who were you just eviscerating via e-mail?" Cait asks as I slip on the kilt to make sure it fits.

Of course she was reading over my shoulder. I must've been typing so loudly it covered the sound of her licorice-chomping. "Just my TA. He thought I was making up having a family emergency."

"Ooh, the hot TA?" Frankie asks as she gives the kilt a thumbs-up.

"He's so not hot." I unzip the kilt and let it drop to the floor, then pack it and the turtleneck. "He's a prick, and he lives in stupid striped button-downs. And pleat-front pants. What the hell kind of man still wears pleat-front pants?"

"Lizzie has *standards*," Cait informs Frankie, throwing her dirty-blond hair up into a bun on top of her head. "She only screws fraternity presidents who already have girlfriends and drive Mercedes."

"It's a BMW," I correct her as I toss in a few more T-shirts and some jeans. No one's told me how long I'm expected at home, and I'm not sure what's still in my old dresser. "And I don't screw them anymore, after last night."

"He's always been a complete asshole," says Cait. "Just the fact that he's been cheating on his girlfriend the entire time should've tipped you off. Glad you finally figured out that he isn't worth your time. Though, obviously it'd be nice if it were under…better circumstances."

Understatement of the century, but I just nod. Both Cait and Frankie have been trying to be there for me in the best ways they know how, but that's mostly involved trying to take my mind off things and using euphemisms to dance around what's happened. As if talk of clothes and hot guys will help distract me from the fact that when I go home to Pomona, I won't be greeted by one of my father's woodsy-aftershave-scented hugs or a plate of my mother's lumpia. Just thinking about it makes me wish I hadn't told Cait and Frankie not to come down for the funeral, but I need to focus on my brothers when I'm down there, and I'm afraid I won't be able to with my friends around.

"Thanks for small favors, I guess. At least Sophie can't kick my ass under these circumstances."

"I heard she threw a crazy shit fit on the quad this morning, though," says Frankie, helping herself to one of the after-dinner mints I keep in a bowl on my desk. "There's a rumor she slashed Trevor's tires, too, but that one's unconfirmed."

"Whatever. They deserve each other. I haven't heard from Trevor once since I left the Sigma house in a cop car." As if on cue, my cell phone starts ringing from my desk. My first thought is *Mom*, because she's the only one who ever calls me instead of texting, and then I remember that it can't be her and will never be her again and oh shit I need to throw up.

"Is it Trevor?" I hear Cait ask as I run out to the bathroom and drop to my knees in front of the toilet.

"Nah, random number. Who do we know with a

five-oh-four area code?"

"No idea. Here, bring it to her."

Frankie comes into the bathroom with my phone, ignoring the fact that I'm dry heaving to the porcelain gods. "Phone call from a mysterious stranger."

"Can you get it?"

She does. "Lizzie Brandt's phone." Pause for response. "Who?" Another pause. "Oh! This is Frankie Bellisario. We met at the history department party." Another pause, and then her face sours. "She's here. Hold on." She hands me the phone, despite the fact that I'm waving my hands in the air and mouthing *hang up*.

I give her a demonic glare before taking the phone. "Connor." I turn around and rest back against the toilet, wiping a thin sheen of sweat from my forehead. "How'd you get my number?"

"It's on the sheet I passed around on the first day. Listen, Elizabeth, I just spoke with Professor Ozgur—"

"Wait. You seriously *checked up on me*? You thought I would *lie* about my parents getting killed?"

He chooses to sidestep that one. I don't blame him. "I just wanted to say that I'm sorry for your loss, and of course you are excused from the paper."

"Thanks so much for that. Means a lot that you'd let me out of homework so I can bury my parents."

"Yes, well, I've been known to be rather saintly in my time," he replies just as dryly, and I'm so shocked at his attempt at humor that I actually laugh for the first time since the cops showed up the night before.

I decide to be straight with him. "Look, I don't know if or when I'm coming back, so, it probably doesn't really matter if you just fail me or whatever." *Not like I still have parents to care.*

"I'm not *looking* to fail you. I don't teach with the hope everyone will play games on their phone during lectures and then skate by with Cs."

"If you did, you'd probably be much happier."

"I'm going to ignore that."

"Probably for the best."

He sighs. "Please let me know if there's anything I can do."

"I don't suppose you want to drive me back to Rockland County, do you? I really hate the bus."

"Oh." He pauses. "Well, I guess—"

"I was kidding, Connor. I mean, not about hating the bus, but about you driving me five hours, yes, I was definitely kidding."

"Thank God."

"Maybe when we're on better terms. Appreciate the check-in, Connor. I'll see ya when I see ya." I do him the favor of hanging up before he can respond. Then I pick myself up, wash off my face, and go back to my room.

I have a bus to catch.

chapter three

"I'm so sorry for your loss, dear." I accept my millionth cheek-kiss of the day from a woman I don't even recognize, who reeks of Pond's cold cream and cheap perfume. "Goodness, you look so much like your mother. She was such a lovely woman."

Where my parents picked up all these devotees, I have no idea, but other than my grandmother, the neighbors, a couple of coworkers, and maybe two or three friends, I don't recognize anyone at the funeral, or anyone who files into their house afterward, bearing casseroles and lasagnas. My aunt didn't even show up.

Thankfully, I hear a familiar clacking just then— my parents' best friend and neighbor, Nancy, hopping over on her crutches, her prosthetic leg concealed by a pair of somber black pants. "One of your mom's co-teachers. They never actually got along," Nancy whispers to me. "That woman complained about everything. Nice that she's here."

"Yes, we're so lucky," I reply dryly, and Nancy smothers a laugh as I get intercepted with yet another tin of something that undoubtedly contains pasta, sauce, and cheese. "How much longer do I have to nod and smile at these people?"

"Hey, at least they're bringing free food," she murmurs back. "Go put that in the fridge and check on Ty and Max; I'll handle the pleasantries."

I smile gratefully and head into the kitchen with my newly accumulated pile of foil dishes. The idea of eating any of them makes me sick to my stomach. All I really want to do right now is break into my dad's liquor cabinet, but I suspect even Nancy would frown upon that. Anyway, there'll be plenty of time for that once the boys are asleep.

"Hey, guys." I ruffle Tyler's hair, but he's thirteen, that way-too-cool-to-acknowledge-his-big-sister age. Apparently the day of our parents' funeral is no exception. Max is stuffing cookies in his face, the natural seven-year-old response to tragedy. "Hope you like lasagna."

"Mom likes lasagna," Max says, licking the cream off the center of an Oreo.

"*Liked*," Tyler corrects harshly.

Happy Hour can't come fast enough.

"Yes, well, then we can eat it vicariously for her," I say. "Did you guys talk to grandma?"

"She keeps calling me Abe," Max says sourly. "Who's Abe?"

"Grandpa's name was Abe," I remind him. "Grandma gets confused."

"She asked me where Mom was. Like, four times," says Tyler. The words come out bitterly, but I can tell he's trying not to cry. I don't blame him; that combination sums up how I've felt all day. Maybe I'll share the liquor stash with him. Thirteen's probably old enough for a couple of shots of Jack. Or scotch. My dad always had good scotch. I was never allowed to touch it, for obvious reasons. No stopping me now.

I excuse myself to my dad's old study. It smells like rich leather and musty books. He loved that smell, almost as much as he loved the smell of cigars. I close my eyes and inhale deeply, remembering the way I used to play with the globe in the corner while he would read in his chair and randomly announce facts, like, "Did you know the male seahorse carries the baby?" I can still hear ice cubes clanging in his highball, and when I open my eyes, they're burning with tears, and I need to taste that scotch ASAP.

I don't even bother filling a highball, just chug straight from the bottle. It burns like hell on the way down, but it feels purifying, like liquid fire. After a while, tears spring to my eyes and my stomach turns and finally I have no choice but to pull the bottle away from my lips. I'm not even sure how much I drink before I finally put it down, but my first thought when I see that the level has conspicuously lowered is *shit, Dad's gonna kill me.*

And then the laughter starts. Loud, hysterical laughter that brings footsteps running toward the study. I've locked the door, but someone knocks anyway, and says, "Honey, you all right in there?"

I have no idea who's talking, only that it isn't Nancy, Tyler, or Max, so I say, "Just peachy!" until I hear a deep sigh and then footsteps retreating.

I never was a favorite of the neighbors.

I take the bottle and wedge myself into the big leather seat. I expect it to be warm and somehow feel like a hug from my dad, but it doesn't even mold to my body; it just kind of sticks. It's so depressing, I take another drink. And another.

By the time Nancy comes to shake me awake, the house is empty.

• • •

I hate being in my old room again. The last time I was here, I was home for the summer, and constantly fighting with my mother over my grades. She wasn't even really pissed at me; more like concerned. I'd gotten into Radleigh with an academic scholarship that depended on my keeping an A-minus-or-better average, and I was hovering around a solid B.

She insisted she wasn't upset because of the potential loss of scholarship money, though she would've had a right to be. She "just wanted to make sure I was okay." The truth was, though, that I didn't know how to explain my decline. College was just...*hard*. Harder than anyone had said it would be. And full of people who'd known what they wanted to study from birth, rather than having vague notions of this or that before settling on law school for lack of a better plan.

So rather than try to be something I couldn't, I just let myself spiral into being a raging letdown.

If only she could see me and my C-minuses now. Not to mention the awesome homewrecker reputation I'm sure I've got on campus.

I wish Nancy'd stuck around to talk to me for a while, but she has her own shit to take care of, which is hard enough for her since the cancer that took most of her leg. She used to be the one set to inherit Ty and Max if anything happened to my parents, but I was sixteen when she got sick and my parents changed their will pretty much the second I turned eighteen.

Nine months ago.

There hasn't been any talk of what'll happen with the custody arrangement. A lawyer's coming to the house tomorrow, and I guess we'll figure it out then.

For now, I need to...something. Sleep feels out of the question. Instead, I crack open the window over my old bench seat, light up a cigarette, and text Cait. *I should've let you come with me. This is horrible.*

Her reply comes less than a minute later. *I'm not sure I would've made your day any better, but I'm sorry it was difficult.*

What the... Oh. Shit.

Connor.

I'd put him in my phone so I could let him know when I'm coming back to school, and of course he's right under Cait, and of *course* in my stupid scotch-y haze I'd miss it by one. *Of fucking course.*

I start to reply that the text wasn't meant for him, but beyond the fact that it's just telling him what he already knows, I know that'll be the end of the conversation. As much as I hate to admit it, I could really use the company. *You might've made the bus ride more entertaining,* I write back, squinting to check for spelling mistakes. *You could've described the Hagia Sofia the entire way down.*

His response comes far quicker than I expect. *If I thought there was a chance you'd listen, maybe I would have.*

Touché, I think but don't type as I stare at the screen. This is by far the greatest number of semi-friendly words Connor and I have ever exchanged. It's almost...nice.

Except Connor's probably one hundred percent serious about the fact that he would've turned the ride into a lesson and then been disappointed in me when I failed to pay attention. He's not exactly known for his sense of humor around class. Even now, I know he's only being remotely nice to me because of my parents. Still, it makes me feel a little less lonely, and I stick my cigarette in my teeth and start to type back, when suddenly, my phone beeps with another text.

Sleep well, Elizabeth.

Oh. So much for continuing that conversation. I put my phone down on my nightstand, stub out the cigarette on the brick exterior of the house, and slip into bed. I curl up with Taco, my old teddy bear, trying to think about anything but where I am now and why, and praying for morning to come soon.

• • •

"Lizzie? Are you in there?"

I jolt out of bed at the sound, thinking it's my mother, but then reality crashes in through my sleepy haze and I recognize Nancy's voice, fuzzy as it is through the door. Of course it's not my mother. It's never going to be my mother.

I slip on my glasses and glance at the clock. Naturally, I overslept. Not like I had anything important to wake up for. Just a lawyer coming to the house to determine everything about my future from here on out.

I wonder if I can get away with a breakfast tequila shot.

"Liz, the lawyer's here."

Oh, shit. I'm even later than I thought. Not even time for a breakfast cigarette. "Just give me one second," I call back, glancing down at my tank top and boxers. I know there are a few dresses in my closet, things my mom bought that I hated and had no interest in bringing with me to college, and I grab one now and throw it over my pajamas. I skip the shoes—not like I'm leaving the house—and brush my teeth so hard I probably take off a layer of enamel.

Within five minutes of the knock, I'm seated downstairs at the dining room table. Tyler's with us; Max isn't.

"Max is playing in his room," Nancy responds to the question I didn't ask.

Personally, I think Max should be here, but if even Ty doesn't object, I'm just going to keep my mouth shut.

"Lizzie, John Burton. It's nice to see you again," the lawyer says with a grim smile. It takes me a few seconds to realize I have in fact met him before, at my parents' fifteenth anniversary party. I'm pretty sure he's wearing the same sweater vest today he was wearing then. "I'm so sorry for your loss."

I just kind of grunt in response. I don't have the energy to pretend that anyone's being sorry fixes anything. Whose idea was it to have this meeting at 9:00 a.m.? How am I supposed to pretend I can handle this conversation without caffeine?

As if on cue, Nancy says, "I put on a pot of coffee, but I'm not sure how hot it still is."

Right, because I overslept. I'm already rocking this responsibility thing. I mumble my thanks and shuffle into the kitchen, the bitter smell of my mother's preferred dark roast coffee assaulting my nostrils. I grab a mug from the cabinet, then flinch when I notice it's the NYU Law one my dad used religiously on the weekends. I exchange it for a more innocuous one, pour myself a cup with plenty of sugar, and sit back down.

Fortunately, John Burton is the get-down-to-business type. "You'll be glad to know your parents were in good standing, financially. As per their will, equal shares have been placed in trusts for each of you, which Nancy will control, and which you'll receive upon turning twenty-one. Your tuition is paid through the semester, and your scholarships and life insurance should help with the rest."

At the word *scholarships*, my stomach clenches, and I instinctively let go of my mug as if even thinking about consuming coffee will make my insides erupt. The merit-based scholarships I'd busted my ass for in high school aren't going to be renewed next semester, not with my GPA as it stands. If those are necessary for me to continue at Radleigh, I am fucked.

Then the deeper meaning of the discussion hits me. "Wait, I'm going to back to school? What about...?" I glance at Tyler, who hasn't said a word, who isn't even making eye contact with anyone.

"Your parents would want you to finish, more than anything," Nancy says quietly. I know she's right, because when we had this discussion about my becoming the boys' guardian—this conversation I thought was a joke—they said as much. But still....

"Ultimately, it's up to you," says John.

"What would happen to my brothers if I went back?"

"If you agreed to remain their guardian, at least until the hearing determining whether a judge sees you fit, then they would come with you. Nancy's already spoken to their principal here; she's been very accommodating."

"She says she's ready to transfer their records to the schools closest to Radleigh as soon as we give her the word," Nancy adds.

They go back and forth, sharing more information, but my eyes are strictly on Tyler. He isn't saying a word, isn't looking up, isn't anything. I have no idea what he wants me to do. What I *should* do. I can barely even take care of myself. What the hell would I do with my brothers? Where would they even sleep? On Cait's and my floor? Using a pile of shoes as a pillow?

"What happens if I can't...if I'm not...you know." I nod at Tyler.

"Then we'll look into alternatives," says John, but his voice is wholly lacking in confidence. It's obvious to me as I watch him exchange glances with Nancy that they've already done this. There are no real alternatives. There isn't really a question here.

Well, just one. "And if I don't go back? I just...move in here?"

"Then you'd lose your deposit for the semester, lose your scholarships, and honestly, it's unlikely you'd ever be able to go back, sweetie," says Nancy. "You'd get a job, I suppose."

It's both easy and impossible to picture the rest of my life if I choose door number two. With all of a year under my belt, I'd probably end up going back to my old retail job at Banana Republic, at best. Not exactly what Kendall High had anticipated for their former valedictorian, I imagine.

Or my parents, either.

"This is so massively fucked-up," I say without thinking, then immediately regret it when I hear John suck in a breath, and see Nancy's lips press into a thin line. Then I see the corners of Ty's lips turn up in a little grin. Totally worth it.

I take a deep breath, his tiny nothing of a smile giving me confidence. "Okay. So, let's say we do this. I go back up to school to finish out the semester, and Ty and Max come with me and finish their semester up there?"

"Exactly," says John. "You'd have to get an apartment, and a social worker will come and interview you, check out the place, and make sure you have suitable arrangements for the boys."

"And then what?"

"Then it depends on the court. And it depends on Ty."

Ty's head jerks up. "What depends on me?"

"Well, you'll be fourteen in December, right?" Ty nods. Our birthdays are a week apart, but I'm the one who has to share with Jesus. "Once you turn fourteen, you'll have the opportunity to voice your opinion regarding your guardian. If you don't want your sister as your guardian, you'll be able to tell the court as such, and your preference will be considered, even though she was named in your parents' will."

"But I don't get any say now?"

Ouch. "I'm listening to you, Ty," I say, fiddling with a strand of long black hair that's escaped my half-assed ponytail. "I swear. If you don't want to come up with me, I won't make you. We'll figure something out." It's an empty, bullshit statement, but I have to say it. We've had enough taken from us this week; I can't take this choice away from him too.

"Nah, I'll go. Whatever," he mutters. "Not like I really wanna stay in this place now."

I just nod, but in reality, I'm shocked to hear it. Ty's a sullen teenager, same as I was—am—but I thought he'd put up more of a fight. He's got friends, he's always trying to start a band…he's got roots here. And unlike me, he's not trying to yank them out of the ground as swiftly as possible.

Or maybe he's more like me than I think.

We let Ty bike over to his best friend's house to tell him the news. Then it takes another few hours to discuss bank accounts, the house, and a million other things that require multiple cups of coffee and frown-inducing smoke breaks. John leaves just as it's time to serve Max lunch—casserole, obviously—and then I get the dubious honor of explaining to Max that in another day or two, he's going to have a new home.

"Are we living in your room?" he asks, not sounding concerned. God bless seven-year-olds.

"I'm gonna get us our own apartment," I tell him. "Isn't that fun?"

He shrugs and takes another bite of his casserole. "Am I gonna have my own room?"

"I don't know, sweetie."

"Will—"

"I don't know," I say, more forcefully this time. I can't take any more questions. I can't take any more unknowns. I don't know what I'm doing, and I don't know how to make anyone else feel better about my ability to do this when I'm pretty sure I'm going to fail at it as hard as I'm failing at everything else.

I have to do something. I need to fix my life up at Radleigh, or it's over. If I lose my scholarships, or my brothers, or both…. I just can't.

I need help.

And there's only one person I can think of right now who can provide it.

chapter four

Two soul-sucking days later, I'm back at Radleigh with my dad's car and two underage kids in tow. Thanks to Nancy, Max and Ty are enrolled in Sweetwater Elementary and Edmund J. Barrington Junior High, respectively. What used to be my emergency credit card is now my for-everything credit card, with Nancy setting the budget and paying the bills. It's what I'm using to put the boys and me up in a motel until I can find something more permanent. All of our crap is filling my side of my dorm room, but Cait's such a pack rat she probably doesn't even notice.

All that's left to take care of right now is making sure I don't fail out. Which brings me here.

"You did ask if there was anything you could do," I remind him.

Connor Lawson nods, a world of regret etched on his face that almost makes me laugh, except I'm here to ask a rather big favor, and he doesn't seem like the type of guy who enjoys laughter. Or impertinence. Or much of anything, really. "I did," he says slowly. "What kind of tutoring did you have in mind?"

"What kinds of tutoring are there?"

"Well, are you just looking for some guidance with the research papers, or…." He trails off, obviously hoping I'll pick door number one.

"I'll take whatever will make me not fail this class and lose my scholarship." Bluntness has always been a strong suit of mine. "And obviously I'll pay you and stuff. I have money. My parents, they left me money."

Connor furrows his brows, drawing attention to the dark-blue eyes beneath them. They're actually sort of gorgeous, which just gets me annoyed at Frankie for making me contemplate his fuckability. Thankfully, his atrocious corduroy pants are quite the ladyboner-killer. "I can't take payment for any assistance. But I will help you, as I'm able, provided you're willing to do the work."

"I am." My head bobs up and down as if on marionette strings. "I promise." My palms are itching for a cigarette, but something tells me Connor won't appreciate me lighting up in his office. "And I'm pretty flexible. I mean, I've got other classes, and I've gotta get my brothers home from school and make them dinner and stuff, but, ya know, otherwise."

What might be sympathy flashes through his eyes and then is gone. "Why don't you give me your schedule, and we'll figure something out."

I do, and we make an appointment to meet back in his office on Friday. I used to reserve Fridays for sleeping off hangovers, but I have a feeling I won't be going to any more Sigma Psi parties anytime soon.

I'm just about to walk out when Connor calls my name and I turn around. "Where are they? Your brothers, I mean."

"Hotel. Well, motel. Looking for a place." I smile sweetly. "Are you offering to let us move in with you?"

"I have a friend who's been trying to sublet a two bedroom for a while now. I've been there; it's decent. If you want his number—"

"*Yes*," I say, far more eagerly than I intend. The thought of potentially not having to go on an actual house hunt is just about the most tempting thing I've heard in forfuckingever. "I mean, sure. Please. That'd be great."

There's a hint of a smile on Connor's lips as he pulls out his cell phone to look up a number, then jots it down for me, along with a name—Alan. "Here you go." He hands me the note, and I tuck it into my purse. "Hope everything works out for you."

"I hope so too. I'll see you Friday."

"Thursday," says Connor.

"Didn't we say Friday?"

"We did, but you have class tomorrow. Step one to picking your grades up is actually starting to show up. Regularly," he adds.

A million snide retorts creep up my tongue but I swallow them down. He's tutoring me, and he might have found me an apartment; the least I can do is show up to his stupid class when he tells me to. "See you tomorrow, then," I amend.

He nods, and turns back to the papers on his desk, effectively dismissing me. Whatever. I got what I came for. Now I just need to see a guy about getting an apartment.

• • •

"And this is the bathroom." Connor's friend steps aside to gesture into a decent-size space in desperate need of a cleaning and a non-erotic shower curtain. As if I didn't feel dirty enough from the way he keeps checking out my tits. Next to me, Cait shudders.

"Who even *makes* nude Wonder Woman bath accessories?" she murmurs into my ear.

"I'm guessing the same company that makes the inflatable doll that was poking out from under his bed," I whisper back as I watch him glance at Cait's ass. I'm relieved the boys are at school right now, getting tours and introductions and missing out on this fantastic display of male role-model-dom. "Ignoring that, what do you think?"

"I think your TA has shady friends."

It *is* impossible to imagine that this guy and uptight, fussy Connor Lawson have ever shared airspace. I'm dying to know how they met, but given Connor's love for personal conversation, I suspect I won't be learning that anytime soon. "About the apartment. Do you think my brothers will like it?"

Cait shrugs. "What do boys that age even care about?"

I try to size up the apartment from my brothers' perspectives, but Cait has a point—there's room for a TV and a couch, and plenty enough floor space for Max's toys. The kitchen's outdated, but it'll certainly hold chicken nuggets, hot dogs, and pizza. Having only two bedrooms is a definite downside, but we're on a strict budget right now while we wait for life insurance to kick in. Plus, it's a ground-floor garden apartment, and I suspect all of us will appreciate the little patio that's just through the sliding doors in the living room.

Speaking of…. "Okay if I smoke on your patio?"

He shrugs. "Sure. Need a light?"

"I'm good." I walk outside with Cait and pointedly close the door firmly behind us. "God, he is gross. But I think I'm gonna take it." I light up, then blow out a stream of smoke, away from Cait. She's convinced my secondhand smoke is going to destroy her lacrosse skills or something. "They want to send the social worker out as soon as possible, and this place still beats a motel."

"I still can't believe you're really moving out," she says glumly, leaning against the brick exterior. "I thought we were gonna be roomies all four years."

"I did too, but I'm pretty sure we've established that you guys don't want my brothers as roommates," I remind her.

"At least Tyler's more subtle about checking out my ass than this guy."

"This guy's not living here." I roll my eyes and take another puff. "It's a sublet."

"He's keeping a key, though, right?" She wrinkles her nose as I exhale. "What if he randomly stops by and lets himself in?"

"That's not gonna happen." I glance back through the glass doors. Alan's leering at us. We both shudder and turn back. "Is it?"

Cait shrugs.

I inhale once more and grind my cigarette into the flagstone, then push the door open and walk back inside. "I'll take it," I announce to Alan. "*If* you give Connor your set of keys."

"But—"

"Only way I'm making the deal," I say flatly. "I'll even let you keep your shower curtain."

He grumbles for a bit but goes to get the paperwork while I try to hide my repulsion and pull out my phone.

Thanks again for the apartment tip, I text Connor. *I'm taking it. Though it could use some major de-perving.*

If Connor's at all amused or even comprehends my message, it doesn't show in his response. *Glad it worked out.*

Rolling my eyes, I tuck my phone back into my jeans pocket.

I wonder how he'll feel about having to babysit the keys.

• • •

"Elizabeta! Povtoritye, pazhaluysta!"

I blink. The Russian words are so familiar, but my sleep-deprived brain is having trouble processing them. I was up moving stuff from the motel and dorm into the apartment until 3:00 a.m., and then had to force myself up only four hours later to get the boys fed and over to school.

Four hours of sleep does not allow for ideal Russian comprehension conditions.

I'm about to ask her to please repeat when I finally realize that's exactly what Professor Ivanova was commanding *me* to do. Unfortunately, now that I understand her actual words, I have no idea what it is I'm supposed to repeat.

And then, because I was dumb enough to think this

was the worst it could get, my phone starts ringing.

Fucking Cait, I think immediately, but of course, it's not Cait; it's Ty's school, because *obviously*.

"Elizabeta!"

"*Izvenitye!*" I blurt, dashing outside the classroom even as I excuse myself. I pick up the call with a smooth "*Privyet, eta Elizabeta*," because of course *now* my Russian comes back to me. "Sorry, hi, this is Lizzie. Is Ty okay?"

"I'm afraid I'm going to need you to come in," a cool, female voice that grates on me instantly declares. "Tyler's been suspended for the rest of the day."

Oh. Come. *On*.

"Miss Brandt, there's no need for yelling."

Oh, shit. I hadn't realized I'd said that out loud. "Sorry," I mumble like a scolded teenager, which, oh right, I am. "I'm in the middle of class. Can't you just keep him in detention or something?"

"We don't have detention at this school," she says, impatience creeping into her voice. "And we have a zero-tolerance policy for fighting."

"Tyler was *fighting*?"

"Yes, with another boy."

"You suspended two boys?"

She's quiet for a moment, and then says, "Miss Brandt, please come pick up your brother. He'll be waiting for you in the principal's office." Then she hangs up.

"Oh, for…." I shove my phone in my pocket and storm back into my classroom to gather my things. "*Izvinitye*," I say again, because I don't even know what else to say. "*Eto moy braht.*"

Thankfully, my teacher, Irina, nods with understanding when I tell her "it's my brother"—she's been informed of my situation—and I bolt out with nothing more than a bunch of whispers and stares in my direction.

Ty's school is a seven-minute drive from my new apartment. I get there in four.

"Lizzie." I can tell Ty's not sure whether to be panicked or relieved at the sight of me. Honestly, I'm not sure which one he should be either.

"What happened here, Tyler?" When I get closer, I can see some dried blood under his nose. His cheekbone's not looking great either. "Where's the other kid?"

"In class," Tyler says with a sniff. "Are we going home?"

"Not yet." I push past him and see an icy blonde sitting behind the desk. "Are you the one who called me?"

"You are…?" She gives me a onceover, taking in my ripped jeans, faded Foo Fighters T-shirt, and, judging by the way she wrinkles her nose, the smoke undoubtedly clinging to every inch of me after my manic post-call chain smoking. I'm guessing my brown

43

skin isn't winning any points with her, either, especially since Ty and I are totally mismatched in that department; there's no telling we're siblings by looking at us.

"Lizzie Brandt—Tyler Brandt's sister and guardian," I say firmly. "I'm going to talk to the principal now."

"You can't—"

"Oh, please, of course I can." I storm into the office, but there's no one inside. I return to the blond bitch's desk, slamming the door behind me. "Where is he?"

"If you would have some patience—"

"No. I have literally none," I inform her in a voice of steel. "I am *eighteen*, acting like a single parent while in school, and you have the nerve to pull me out of class to have me pick up my brother when the kid he got into a fight with isn't even in trouble? What happened to your zero tolerance policy? Or is it just zero tolerance for the kids who don't have parents to fight their battles?"

She turns a full shade whiter, and I don't give her a chance to respond before grabbing Tyler by his arm and yanking him out of the school. "What the hell happened today?" I demand as I hustle him toward my car; I've got Byzantine History in half an hour and after yesterday, it's pretty clear I can't be late.

Ty is stone silent as he shoves himself in the front

seat.

Ugh, fuck it. I don't have the time or patience for this shit right now. I get into the driver's seat and start the car, just as Ty says, "It smells like an ashtray in here."

"Yeah, you're welcome for picking you up," I snap, inhaling deeply because I know my parents would kill me if I smoked in front of Tyler. Hell, they would've killed me if they knew I smoked at all. Lord knows it isn't a habit I picked up in Pomona.

It isn't until we're stopped a red light two minutes later that Tyler speaks up. "It wasn't my fault," he mutters.

"I'm not assuming it is. I just wanna know what happened. It's not like you to fight."

"Alex was being a dick."

"Tyler! Language."

He snorts. "Oh please. You said 'fuck' like a thousand times during the move."

"We're not the same age," I say with a sigh, but the truth is, I don't give a shit. Trying to be my mother is exhausting. The light turns green and I press down on the accelerator. "Okay, whatever, just not in front of Max. Now tell me what happened."

"He was making fun of me that I didn't have a parent to sign my permission slip for our class trip next week, so I punched him."

"He *what*?" I slam on the brakes so hard that the

cacophony of horns in response is deafening. And then, the inevitable.

Crunch.

And that's it. I've hit my limit. As the driver of the car that just crashed into my bumper stomps over to yell at me, I just barely manage to make sure Tyler's okay before dropping my head into my hands and screaming loud enough to wake the dead.

chapter five

"You look like shit," Cait declares as I settle into our favorite booth at the campus coffee shop, one day, a whole insurance mess, a permission slip signature, and yet another pathetic e-mail to Connor later. "And what is that godawful smell?"

"Well, you're either referring to the nicotine gum I'm chewing, which is absolutely disgusting, or the fact that I haven't showered in two days, because I can barely find time to breathe in between dealing with my car insurance and Tyler's principal." I snap the gum a couple of times before spitting it into a napkin. It really is gross, but I need something to settle my nerves—they've been shot ever since the fender bender. Turns out, getting into a car accident less than two weeks after your parents died in one will do that to you. "Where's Frankie?"

"Flirting with some guy with a guitar over by the

teas. And speaking of the tease...." Frankie bounds over just then, drops a kiss on my cheek, wrinkles her nose, and then slides into the booth next to Cait.

"You smell gross, Lizzie B."

"So I've been told."

"How's your car?"

"Looks as shitty as I do. They gave me a rental in the meantime, so if you see a snazzy Chevy Malibu outside, you're looking at its temporary owner."

"Sucks, Boo," Cait says with a sympathetic tilt of her blond head.

I open my mouth to respond when a burst of laughter from the entrance attracts all three of our attention. At the sight of Sophie Springer, standing there with two of her bitchy Epsilon Rho sisters, blatantly pointing at me as they whisper, my appetite for a grilled cheese and fries dissipates completely.

"Guess she's not so thrilled with me about the whole Trevor thing," I mumble, reaching for the salt and pepper and pushing them around each other. "Did they do a whole messy public breakup thing after the cops took me away?"

Cait and Frankie exchange a glance. "What?" I demand.

Cait sighs. "They didn't actually break up."

"Seriously?" I bang the shakers against each other, enjoying the little crash of sound. "How stupid is she?"

"He said you were just some random guest hiding

in his room at the party, that he didn't even know you were there." Frankie glances at Cait again, and Cait shrugs.

I narrow my eyes. "*What* is with the looks? If you guys hide anything more from me, I'll kill you." There's another burst of laughter from Sophie, and I cringe at the sheer volume.

"He's telling people you're mentally unstable, and the only reason he's not reporting you to the cops for trespassing is because he feels bad for you about your parents. Word's...kinda spreading around campus." Frankie's voice drops to a whisper as she says this last bit. As if I'm more concerned about my worsening reputation than that the guy I've been hooking up with since last spring wishes he could've had me arrested.

Cait squeezes my hand. "He's a fucking asshole."

"Yeah, I wasn't really wavering on that fact," I bite out.

"Do you want to go somewhere else?" Frankie asks.

"Definitely not." I yank a menu from behind the napkin dispenser with as much defiance as one can muster for such an act and smack it loudly on the table, even though I haven't looked at a menu here since probably my first semester. "If some naive sorority bimbo wants to invade my space, that's her problem."

Cait drops her head into her hands with a groan at the volume of my voice. Not that she cares what those bitches think any more than I do, but Caitlin Johannssen is not one for conflict. Or "stupid girly shit"—her words, not mine. When most of your life revolves around charging other girls on a field while using a stick to throw a ball into a net, I guess who banged whom at a party isn't all that interesting.

"I don't think a restraining order is too severe either." Undoubtedly in response to mine, Sophie's voice rises and carries across the coffee shop. "I mean, I understand that sometimes, people do *crazy* things in reaction to trauma"—the emphasis on "crazy" is so strong, it's like she's trying to teach its meaning to a non-native speaker—"but there's a desperation limit, you know? Like, you have to keep yourself safe when you're around someone *so delusional*."

"Let's just get out of here," Cait says quietly.

"No," I reply firmly, just as our waitress shows up, a sulky goth chick who looks like she'd rather be dead than serving fellow Radleigh students. "Hi there!" I greet her.

The death glare she gives me in response could grill my cheese any day.

I ignore it. "I'll have the steak and eggs, please. And an espresso." Caffeine and protein—battle fuel of champions.

"Maybe you should get a salad," Sophie suggests, sidling up to the table, minions in tow. "You really don't need all that with your figure already what it is, do you?" She clucks her tongue with what I'm sure is very genuine concern for my health and well-being.

"And can you get this girl something with a laxative effect?" I add to the waitress, refusing to spare Sophie a glance as I slide my menu back into place. "My treat. I just can't stand to see someone so full of shit, you know? Especially when her boyfriend keeps feeding her more of it."

"Lordy," mutters Cait.

"You don't know a damn thing about my boyfriend, you nutcase," Sophie snaps.

"Oh, right, I forgot," I say coolly, pushing my glasses further up on my nose. "He and I had never met before that night. He definitely wasn't fucking me six ways from Sunday last spring during your mixer when he pretended to get sick and left early. And it was probably someone else moaning that I give 'the world's fucking greatest head' in the backseat of a black BMW, license plate SigPsi69."

"Lizzie," Cait groans, but I ignore her, because I can't stop, couldn't if I wanted to. Every memory with the guy I was literally having sex with when the cops came and fucked up my world is fighting its way to the surface, forcing itself to be heard as if to combat how completely he's ignored me since I entered that police car.

And Sophie's eyes, shooting sparks, are only spurring me on.

"That couldn't have been your boyfriend who sent two frat boy underlings to build your furniture a month ago instead of doing it himself, so he could go for another round with me in my dorm room. And how could I confuse Trevor for someone who might've said, 'Christ, I wish Sophie had tits like yours'? I mean, how does that even make sense? Who the fuck is—ohhh, shit. This is so awkward."

"Lizzie, *stop*!" Cait hisses. Frankie's trying to smother her laughter behind her hands. The waitress looks the most delighted I've seen her all afternoon.

Sophie...not so much.

I know Cait's right, and I've gone too far already, but I need to tap a nail in this. I'm already the pathetic girl who lost her parents; I can't have Trevor's rumor about my mental health pervading the campus too.

I stand up, bracing my hands on the table, and return her murderous glare with one of my own. "Freckle near his right nipple, dick hangs slightly to the left—which isn't as unpleasant as it sounds—and he screams 'Bonzai!' when he comes extra hard. Tell me *who the fuck* is delusional now."

Frankie applauds. Cait shakes her head. I'm pretty sure the waitress just came in her uniform.

I expect Sophie to storm out, but she doesn't. Instead, she narrows her eyes into slits, though I can see her entire body is shaking, and spits, "Your parents deserved to die for raising a slut like you."

52

And just like that, even as she stalks out of the café, she wins.

Because all she's lost is someone she never really had.

And I've lost everything.

• • •

I stay for lunch with Cait and Frankie, but I can barely eat after that encounter with Sophie. They suggest going to a movie, but I decide to cut them a break from baby-sitting the crazy orphan and tell them I have to go to the library.

Now that I know what Trevor and Sophie have been saying about me, I'm conscious of the stares and whispers everywhere I go. I'd noticed some sympathetic ones every now and again since my return, but I'd assumed it was because I'd lost my parents. Now I don't know if it's that, or fear because they think I'm an insane stalker.

Awesome.

I suck in a deep sigh of early-autumn air and keep my head down as I walk through campus, dead leaves crunching under my riding boots. There seems to be no limit to the amount of trouble I can get into these days.

It's weird to think about the day I came to Radleigh. I was such a completely different person then. I didn't *look* all that different—same black hair my parents were sure I'd dye pink; same complexion no one makes a foundation to match (what my old friend Ellen Hsu and I used to call "the Biracial Girl's Lament")—but I was so...bright-eyed. Bushy-tailed. I was Kendall High's valedictorian, its great hope, and I was going to kick some ass.

That lasted all of three seconds, and all it took was my first B, followed by my first panic attack, followed by my freshman year roommate suggesting I tag along with her to a frat party to take my mind off things. Turns out, it *is* easy to ignore how much you're tanking after a few drinks. Even easier when a random hot guy who happens to have a single helps you forget your own name.

The trick to not letting your high expectations of your own success bury you when you fail to meet them?

Lower them to practically nothing.

I pause in my walk to duck behind a tree and pull out a cigarette, though the sight of it between my fingers makes me pause for a moment before I can lift my lighter to it. I didn't smoke back when I started here, either. Never had. My mother hated cigarettes. She would've sent me to a convent in Manila if she'd seen me with them.

It was a habit I picked up from Frankie, though she promptly stopped after a month, the same way she does with all of her phases. I kept it up, partly because I enjoy it and partly because Trevor found it to be the world's biggest turn-on.

Trevor. What a stupid fucking mistake. That first night we hooked up, I believed him that Sophie was just some clingy ex who couldn't let go. The second time, too. It wouldn't have been hard to find out he was lying, but truth be told, I wanted to let ignorance be bliss. I'd never had a real boyfriend, and I was flailing at school, and this guy who was actually doing life right wanted *me*. I guess I thought it'd rub off, or something. By the time it became clear he was just a lying, cheating bastard, I was too spoiled to quit—by the power of the distraction, the access to parties, the insider info he had on teachers and classes…. God, just thinking about it now, I could drown in a vat of self-loathing.

I drop the cigarette in the trash without having lit it and pull out of a piece of that noxious gum instead.

When I resume walking, I realize I don't really have anywhere to go. Normally on a Friday afternoon, I'd either be sleeping off a hangover from the night before, or taking a post-lunch nap in order to prepare for whatever party I'd be going to that night. Since I'd spent the night before watching a Pixar movie with the boys on TV and then doing the reading for my English class, and my plans for tonight look pretty much the same, I'm not exactly drowning in my usual Friday haze.

Really, the only place to go is exactly where I'd

told Cait and Frankie I was going. It'd been a long time since I'd been inside the Radleigh library—not since first semester freshman year, when I had myself a charming little panic attack in the stacks. I snap my gum and crunch loudly through the leaves as I head in the library's direction. At least I'm no longer the same fucking idiot who had to wheeze into a paper bag when she got her first B.

Now a B would be pretty damn awesome.

The sad thing about all my freakouts over the fact that I couldn't keep up with college is that my parents wouldn't have given a shit. Well, they would've cared that I was upset, but not that I wasn't bringing home A's or whatever. They were really damn good parents that way. They probably would've been proud of anything I'd decided I wanted to do. Anyone I'd become.

Except for the pathetic asshole I am now.

It's a fucking miracle I finished last year with the 3.5 I needed to keep my scholarship, and I'm woman enough to grudgingly admit that for all the ways he sucks, Trevor—and his frat's access to old tests—played no small part in why I'm still here. Which is embarrassing on so many levels.

The huge brick library looms large across the street, and it takes a few deep breaths before I can force myself to enter. Once I do, though, I'm not even sure where to go. I don't really want to wander aimlessly through the stacks, so I just walk straight ahead in the table-filled study room.

I spot a cluster of familiar faces almost immediately, a study group from my Russian class I didn't even know existed. I don't know all of their names, certainly not their real ones—I know the redhead goes by Dasha in class, the blond guy by Boris, the black guy by Misha—but I walk over anyway. "*Privyet*," I say, wincing inwardly at how shy I sound. "Can I study with you guys?"

They look at me blankly. The little brunette I think goes by Xana looks almost afraid of me. Dasha just looks pissed. I know they know who I am; even though my attendance record hasn't always been awesome, I skip Russian the least, because I actually like it. Plus, after the little scene I got stuck creating because of Ty's school, there's no way anyone missed me.

So why isn't anyone saying anything? Have the rumors about my insanity actually spread this far, this fast?

"Let me try that again," I say, because I can't turn around now. It would just be too pathetic. I've had enough pathetic for one day. "*Mozhno zanimatsya c vami?*" *Can I study with you?*

It's not perfect, I'm sure—instrumental case still trips me up—but it's enough to make Misha smile. "*Konechno*," he says, pulling his backpack off the chair next to him. The familiar "Of course" lifts a weight off my chest, and I see that everyone else looks a little more chilled out too.

Apparently they just assumed I wouldn't know how to say shit in Russian.

Can't say I blame them, after this week's brilliant display of ineptitude.

As I take a seat and dive into the homework with the rest of them, I inwardly pat myself on the back. I know I still have a long way to go, but I have my first session with Connor in the morning and the entire weekend to work on my English paper. For the first time in a long time, I actually hope my parents are watching.

chapter six

Connor's door is open when I arrive at his office for our first session, but I resist waltzing in and instead rap lightly on the door. He looks up from whatever he'd been attacking with a blood-red pen and gestures to the seat across the desk.

"Good morning to you too," I greet him as I drop into the chair just gracefully enough to avoid spilling my coffee everywhere. "Whose work are you ripping apart?"

"Yours," he says bluntly, turning the paper around and sliding it across the table so I can see the massacre. "Constantine VI is best known for being the son of Constantine V? Really?"

"'Best' is subjective," I offer, taking a sip.

"Facts aren't. They weren't even father and son."

"Oh."

"Not even part of the same dynasty."

"Whoops."

"Yeah, whoops. Elizabeth—"

"Lizzie."

"If I'm going to spend hours tutoring you, I need to know that you're going to put in more effort than this."

"I will," I say immediately.

He raises his eyebrows.

"I wouldn't have come to you otherwise." This part is actually true. "Please, Mr. Lawson."

"Mr. Lawson? When have you ever called me that?"

"Professor Ozgur calls you that."

"Connor is fine," he says on a sigh. "But—"

His phone rings just then, cutting him off. "Sorry, I'll—oh, I actually need to take this. Excuse me."

I shrug. "Go right ahead."

He does. "*Bonjour, Maman.*" What follows is string after string of fluent French that makes my mouth drop. It's…unexpected, given that he doesn't have so much as an accent as far as I can tell. It's also weirdly sexy. He catches me gaping, and the corners of his lips lift in a rare tiny smile. He points at something on the wall behind me, without breaking in conversation, and I turn to see a Canadian flag mounted above a bookshelf.

I walk over, leaving Connor to his conversation with his mother, and examine the picture frames on his shelves. In one, Connor and a pretty brunette are smiling at the camera, a hockey game in the background. They're both wearing jerseys. It looks like a cute date, which surprises me, since I can't quite imagine Connor out with a girl. Then I look at the other picture—same brunette, plus an older woman—and realized all three share a marked resemblance.

Of course she's his sister. Connor Lawson with his arm around an actual woman is just too hilarious to contemplate. I can't even imagine what kissing him must be like. Boring, probably. Prosaic, somehow. Soft-looking hair and gorgeous eyes can't cure that personality.

"See anything interesting?"

His voice makes me jump ten feet in the air. I'd forgotten he was even in the room, his French conversation drifting away like background music. "Your sister's pretty," I blurt, because the only other thing in my brain is the image of him kissing, and that doesn't seem like a wise subject to broach.

"She gets that a lot."

"Are you from Quebec? Is that where your mom and sister are?"

"I am from Quebec, and my mom's still there, but Sarah isn't." He waves a hand at what I now see are a bunch of postcards on the wall behind him. "She's kind of...all over. Has been for a while. She's a travel blogger."

"What does she blog about?"

He shrugs. "Which hotels only have thread-count in the double digits? I have no idea."

"You don't read it?"

"I've read a few. I read her post on Istanbul. Speaking of which…." He pats the desk.

I take a seat, but I'm not done with my questions. "What about your dad?"

"What about him?" Connor asks coolly.

"That close, huh?"

"Even Canada has assholes."

I snort with laughter, and Connor purses his lips, obviously not pleased with himself for having said that out loud. Which is a shame. It made him so much more human for a minute.

Almost like someone I could actually enjoy hanging out with sometime.

"We should get started," he says, more firmly this time, and I know we're done with questions for the afternoon. "Did you do the reading on Symeon's invasion of Byzantium?"

I stare back blankly. Reading probably would've been a good thing to do before this session. I'm not really sure why that didn't occur to me, but I feel like an ass right now. So much for the high of being on top of my work.

He sighs. "Do you have your book here, at least?"

"Yes!" I say far too excitedly, considering it's not even the bare minimum of what I should've done in preparation. I pull it out of my bag, hoping Connor doesn't notice how absurdly new and untouched it looks, outside of the water rings (which are more likely beer) on the cover.

He notices. Even though I'm pretty sure I wasn't supposed to see that eye roll.

"Page 194," he says. "Read it. Out loud."

I raise my eyebrows. "You want me to read out loud? Like, first-grade style?"

He raises one right back, the meaning clear. *Do you really think you're above that level right now?*

Touché.

I do as he says, and though I feel like an idiot doing it, he's actually pretty nice and helpful when he periodically stops me to go over what I've just read. Plus, hearing the words out loud seems to make them stick in my brain. By the time I finish the reading, I feel for the first time like I actually have a clue what's going on. Or at least as much as I'm going to, given it's maybe the third or fourth reading I've done all semester.

"Sounds to me like you're getting it," Connor observes as I close the book. His tone is somewhere between curious and suspicious, and he obviously wants to say something else, but he's keeping his mouth shut.

"What?"

"What what?"

"What aren't you saying?"

He presses his lips in a firm line while he ponders his word choice. "I just don't understand why you insist on not doing the work when you're obviously a very capable student."

The words are like a punch in the gut. If only he knew how many times I'd asked myself the same thing. I don't have any more of an answer now than I did a year ago. "I'm sorry I came unprepared," I say firmly as I get up and put the book away. "I'll do the reading in advance next time."

"Elizabeth, I wasn't—"

"Lizzie."

"Lizzie, I wasn't scolding you. I'm genuinely curious."

"And I'm genuinely late for a study date with my friend, so, thanks a lot for this, and I'll see you in class on Tuesday." I'm actually an hour early to meet Cait—she's a secret math nerd and agreed to help me with my Statistics homework an exchange for the use of my car this weekend—but Connor certainly doesn't need to know that.

I push out of the room without another word, even though I can feel his eyes burning into my back as I go.

• • •

I decide to make a little less of a liar out of myself and head back to my old suite, where I'm meeting Cait.

I still have keys—housing wouldn't issue a partial refund since it's too late in the year to find a replacement roommate—and the standard-issue bed and desk are still mine until winter break.

When I let myself in, I'm surprised to see Matina standing at the fridge, probably looking for an apple. I'd never known anyone to take the "apple a day" maxim as seriously as my pre-med former roommate. She greets me with a brief wave, as if seeing me walk in is an everyday occurrence; I wonder if she even knows I've moved out. I don't bother starting up a conversation, but just let myself into my old room and hop up onto my old, naked mattress.

It's not my first time back in the room since I moved out my things for good, but the other visit was quick, just stopping in for Cait to grab a sweater. It's weird to be here now, seeing the walls stripped bare of my old posters, and the one picture of my family that's now on my new fridge. You'd think the room would look neater without my crap all over the floor, but instead, Cait's just taking up double the space.

Still, even though I only lived here for a month, it feels far more familiar than my new apartment does. It's amazing how many places I don't live in that I'd sooner call home than the one place I do.

Not that my parents' house is really home anymore. Sooner or later, I'll have to deal with selling it. It doesn't make any sense to hold on to it. But I'm not ready to let it go just yet.

The sound of the door slamming behind Matina is enough to drag me out of my morbid thoughts, and I get to work spreading out the contents of my bag. Much as I enjoy pissing off Connor, I have no desire to sit through another session of Lizzie Learns to Read. I have an entire syllabus of readings I completely ignored this semester, so I pick up a highlighter, start from the beginning, and keep going until I hear the front door to the suite open, heralding Cait's arrival.

I hop off the bed and am about to open up the door when I hear her laugh and say, "*Just* a drink. I have someone coming over."

"Could I take this someone in a fight?" a masculine voice I don't recognize responds.

"Probably, since she's about five-foot-six, but I'd rather you didn't," Cait teases back. I suppose I have to appreciate that at least she doesn't want me to get my ass kicked, even if she's the only person on campus who doesn't. Still, whoever this guy is, he needs to GTFO; I've got Stats to study for and I need to pick up Max in an hour.

"Ohhh," I hear the guy's voice come knowingly through the door. "You live with that psycho bitch, right? The one who was banging Matlin? He's been going ape-shit since she told his girlfriend. Tryin' to hunt her down an' shit."

My stomach seizes up and I wait quietly for Cait's response. She doesn't disappoint. "My friend is not a psycho bitch, and Trevor Matlin's a dick. When you leave here, *now*, you can tell him that if he's looking for her, it better be to apologize."

His muttered reply is drowned out by the sound of her slamming the door shut behind him. Then I hear a long, deep sigh, and brace myself.

"Oh, shit," are her first words when she opens the door and sees me sitting on my old bed.

"Sorry for the accidental cockblock." I don't really know what else to say.

She closes the door behind her and hops up next to me on the bed. I instantly drop my head onto her shoulder, and she strokes my hair. "I'm sorry you heard that asshole. He's just a stupid prick, and he's obviously not getting laid by me today or any other day."

"I don't want to be fucking up your social life. It's not your fault you got saddled with me as a crappy roommate."

"Oh hush. Though I *did* warn you pulling that crap with Sophie was going to bite you on the ass."

"Yes, master. Can we save the 'I told you so's until after Stats? I have to pick up Max in an hour. And *yes*, I'll fill my car with gas on my way home so it's in tip-top shape before you borrow it tomorrow."

"Deal." She pulls her hair up into a ponytail while she waits for me to put away my history stuff and find my Stats homework. "But seriously, what are you gonna do about Trevor? He's not gonna let this go. Neither's Sophie."

"Trevor and Sophie can suck it," I say flatly, even though I know she's right. "I have more important stuff on my mind right now. If I lose my scholarship and can't afford Radleigh anymore, they won't even be an issue."

She sighs. "Guess I can't argue with that." I can tell it's still bothering her—Cait's hatred of drama extends to her absolutely despising it going without resolution—but thankfully, she doesn't say a word, and instead focuses on helping me understand the mess of numbers and formulas my brain cannot compute on its own.

Before I know it, the time is up, and my homework's only half done, but I've gotta go. I thank Cait profusely, peck her on the cheek before hopping off the bed, and tell her what time I'll drop off the car tomorrow. And then I'm off, forcing myself to move, and leaving my old room behind yet again when all I want to do is bury myself under the covers that are no longer there and pretend life outside isn't happening.

chapter seven

Without my car, and parties, and friends, my weekend is obscenely productive, especially since I've pretty much locked myself in my room to give the boys free access to the TV in order to make up for the fact that I can't take them anywhere. Every now and again I have to go outside to feed them, mediate arguments, or beg them to get at least a few minutes of fresh air by doing their homework on the patio, but inside, armed with nothing but textbooks, my laptop, and my own thoughts, I'm actually putting a dent in my work.

I'd spoken to Professor Ivanova about doing some extra credit to make up for handing assignments in late earlier in the semester, and she'd been more than happy to heap on the work. The same had been true for my English teacher. My Stats professor wasn't budging, but fortunately, my mini-session with Cait had been helpful enough for me to at least catch up on the newest assignment, if not make up for earlier sins.

I save Byzantine History for last, waiting until the pizza delivery is devoured and the table's cleaned off before I tackle it. After how smoothly it went with Connor in his office—relatively, anyway—I expect it'll go quickly. But after ten minutes of wading through the muck of dates and names and locations and battles, I start having flashbacks to my first few weeks at Radleigh, and the panic attacks that followed.

I slam the textbook shut.

In high school, I was pretty decent at history. It wasn't my best subject—that was Spanish, helped massively by the fact that my mother was fluent—but I never struggled with it the way I do here. Probably because my parents loved helping me study for it, quizzing me on names and dates, making a game out of hanging up information on Post-It notes around the house. Plus my mother could talk about Spanish Colonialism forever, and was more than happy to do so as she brushed my hair or let me practice my nail-polishing skills on her.

I should've studied with her via webcam. I should've taken Tagalog or something. I should've done *anything* that would've pushed me to spend more time with her while she was there and I was here.

Why do I *always* fucking realize these things when it's too late?

I grab my phone from my desk before I can allow sanity to settle back in my brain and stab the keys in an angry text message: *Your class sucks.*

Connor's nothing if not quick with his replies, always. *I hope that means you're doing the homework, at least.*

Ugh, how is he always so…unruffled? What a pain in my ass. Couldn't he just cry, or something? *I'm trying. How is anyone supposed to remember all this crap?*

This time, he takes a minute to respond. Then, *Check your email.*

I do, wondering if this is some sort of trap. There's a new message from Connor, labeled "Study Aids." Inside is a whole bunch of files, from a color-coded map to an illustrated family tree, and even some cutesy poems tying certain rules to certain events. They look like study materials for seventh graders, and already I know they're going to be exactly what I need. *Why do you have these??*

Are they helpful?

If I can ignore that they make me feel like I'm in junior high, probably.

Good, I'm glad.

Stupid Connor. I just wanted someone to be a bitch to for a few minutes. Why did he have to go do a nice guy thing? Well, a sort of nice guy thing. Does he think I'm stupid? Is that why he's plying me with graphics for little kids? He'd mentioned thinking I was a capable student at our last session. Was he just being patronizing then? Because I'm pretty sure he's being patronizing now.

It's Saturday night. My fingers fly across my phone in a digital rage. *Why are you even available to answer my text messages?*

I'm at a frat party, he types back. *I'm just an excellent multitasker.*

The very imagine of Connor at a frat party...well, there is no image. It does not compute. *Seriously?*

No, Elizabeth, not seriously. Goodnight.

Okay, fine, Connor won that round. And I'll probably check out the stuff he sent, just in case.

But he's still an asshole.

• • •

He isn't the biggest asshole on Radleigh's campus, though. That honor belongs to Trevor Matlin, hands down. I still haven't seen him since that night in his room—I've been avoiding Greek Row like the plague, and as a Business major, he takes all of his classes in a different part of campus than I do—but it hasn't stopped him from taking his revenge out on me for telling Sophie all our dirty little secrets.

"I'm so, so sorry," Cait says for the million-billionth time.

"Cait. Chill. It's not your fault." It really isn't, but it's getting harder and harder to reassure her when all I want to do is punch my fist through every window of my car. No, not my car—my *rental* car, because my real car is in the shop. I don't even know how Trevor's frat brothers knew the Malibu was mine, but I doubt it was Cait's being behind the wheel that led them to spray paint "Crazy Slut" on the exterior.

"You lent me your car for one day—"

"Yeah, I did, and you didn't pop a tire or dent a fender or drive it off a bridge. So this is not your fault." I sigh. "Unfortunately, I still need to get this taken care of. I can't drive my brothers to school in this. Do you know anyone *else* who has a borrowable car?"

"Can I be blunt?"

"Always."

Cait crosses her arms. "How many people at Radleigh do you really think would lend you a car right now?"

Ouch. It might be less painful if it weren't so completely and utterly true. Lord knows I'd burned any bridges I might've had with the Sigma Psis—if I ever really had any—and Frankie's preferred method of transportation is a stupid bubble-gum pink Vespa. "Think anyone in my Russian class would be open to lending?"

"Do you have a phone number for anyone in your Russian class?"

"I have email addresses," I say lamely, knowing I won't use them. No one in the class even trusts me with a phone number; who's gonna trust me with a car?

"Maybe I can paint over it? I'm sure Frankie get can get me stuff from the art department."

"Unless you're gonna paint the entire car, I'd rather not embarrass the crap out of my brothers. I'm pretty sure they have it hard enough with the whole 'me being the responsible adult in their lives' thing."

At that, Cait smiles. "You're a sweet big sis, Queen B."

"I'm a lousy big sis," I grumble. "I can't even guarantee my brothers a ride to school in a car that doesn't say 'Crazy Slut' in neon orange."

"Maybe someone can pick them up?"

I raise an eyebrow. "You think I've made friends with neighborhood soccer moms? Let me tell you who I *definitely* don't have a phone number for." I drop my head into my hands. "Ugh, I do *not* want to explain to them why I have to take them to school in a cab tomorrow. *And* I'll need to drive to the shop in that stupid car, *and* I'll need to take a cab home to pick me up. I do not have the cash to be this fucking stupid."

As if triggered by the word "stupid," the worst idea in the world comes to mind, and I groan just thinking about it. "What?" Cait demands.

"I have someone I'm pretty sure will do it, but I would kind of rather die than ask."

"Would you rather drive your brothers in the Slutmobile than ask?"

"Possibly. Especially if it requires me to explain *why* my car is indisposed." As if Connor didn't already think as little of me as humanly possible. I'm not sure I could even look him in the eye again after this.

Cait glances at her watch. "I'm so sorry, Boo, but I really have to run to lacrosse practice. I'll drive the Slutmobile to the shop to get painted. Are you gonna call for that ride?"

"Yeah," I grumble, because I have to at least try. And I know in my gut he'll say yes.

"Good." She kisses me forehead. "Again, I'm so, so—"

"Cait?"

"Yeah?"

"Get out."

• • •

I'm not a morning person, but I've been up for about an hour longer than necessary today, watching the parking lot through the living room window. It's a fucking miracle that he agreed to this, though he refused to flat-out lend me his car, insisting on picking us up instead. I refuse to be even a minute late, knowing this is probably the last favor I'll get to ask of him.

A car pulls in, and when I squint I can see it's an old gray Altima, just what he said to keep an eye out for. "Boys, get out here! Time to go!"

"Why is some random guy driving us to school again?" Tyler whines as he tromps out of their room. "You realize if I had my bike, I could take myself."

"Well, we didn't bring your bike up here, so you can't take yourself, now can you?" I point out, though I know it was my own stupid fault we didn't; I had no idea how to put a bike rack on my car, and therefore no way to drive it up. Once upon a time my rather handy father would've gladly done it. Now it's just another thing on the list of shit I need to learn, fast, so I can stop being the world's crappiest guardian. "I'll get you a new one," I promise hastily, though I have no idea how much one costs. "Please just help me get Max outside and we can go this weekend, okay?"

"Really?"

"Really."

Thankfully, the bribery works, and Connor's wait is no more than three minutes before we pile into the car. The boys go into the backseat immediately but I hesitate, unsure whether it's weird for me to climb in next to Connor. Then I think it's probably weirder to make him ride alone upfront like the Brandt family chauffeur, and I jump into the passenger seat before I can change my mind.

"Boys, this is Con—um, Mr. Lawson. He's doing us a *big* favor by driving us this morning, so buckle up and be good, okay?"

"What's wrong with the car again?" asks Max. "I thought we got a new one."

Goddammit. "That's Max," I say, trying not to grit my teeth. "And the bigger guy is Tyler. He's first. Barrington Junior High. I can direct you."

"Are you my sister's boyfriend?" asks Tyler. "She says you're not, but she wouldn't tell us if you were."

"Tyler, Jesus Christ. I already told you, *no*." I knew this was a mistake. Seriously, the Slutmobile would've been better than this.

"Why not?"

"Max!"

"If you're not her boyfriend, why would you be driving us to school?" Tyler demands.

"Because he's nice," I snap back, "unlike certain brothers who are being jerks right now when I told them to be good."

"I'm *being* good!" Max cries. "And I'm buckled!"

"I'm buckled too," says Tyler, as if that makes up for anything.

"Your turn," says Connor, and I realize they're the first words he's said since we got in the car. I glance up to see a tiny smile playing on his lips. He's enjoying my misery. Why am I not surprised?

"My turn for what?"

77

"To buckle up," says Connor. "Everyone else is ready to go."

"Oh for the love of…." I snap my seat belt in place and narrow my eyes at Connor. "Ready?"

"I will be when you tell me where to go."

Tyler snorts, and if I wasn't regretting everything about this decision before, I am now. "Left out of the parking lot," I all but growl.

"Yes, ma'am," says Connor with a perfectly straight, even smile, and I turn and glare out my window as he hits the gas.

• • •

They continue to be utterly annoying—all three of them—right through dropping Tyler off, though mercifully it's more of the "talking about sports and other shit I don't care about" variety. I had no idea my brothers were into hockey, or that Connor was into football, but apparently they all have far more in common with each other than I do with any of them.

"All right, Max," says Connor. "Your turn. You gonna tell me how to go?"

Max laughs. "I don't drive."

"You don't? Well, you should! Come on up here. Let's switch places."

"Really?"

I sigh. "He's kidding, Max. You can drive when you're thirty." I whack Connor on the arm. "For the love of God, please do not get his hopes up like that."

I expect some sort of know-it-all grin in response, but when Connor apologizes, he sounds genuinely contrite, and suddenly I wish I hadn't said anything at all. After that, the ride is awkwardly quiet but for the sounds of me directing him to Sweetwater Elementary, and then saying goodbye to Max as he scoots out of the car.

"Are you gonna come pick me up, too?" he asks Connor.

"He can't," I tell Max, and watch his face fall, as if Connor's already become his new best friend. "But I'll come get you in a cab, okay? You'll get to ride in a taxi, like that time you did in New York City, remember?"

Just like that, his face lights up again. "Cool. Bye!" He runs off, the picture of little-kid resilience.

Connor grins. "I can see why you've got your hands full."

"Right?" I roll my eyes. It's sort of nice to have someone else experience my new morning normal with me; Cait and Frankie doesn't understand why getting them out each day isn't a matter of letting them throw some waffles in the toaster oven and then shoving them out the door.

"I'm sorry if I—"

"Don't," I cut him off. "I'm sorry. It's fine. The kid is seven. If he doesn't know you're kidding about driving, he's already beyond hope."

He laughs. "You've got a point there."

"Listen, thanks so much for doing this. I know I've been asking a ton of you, and—"

"Hey, is that Lauren Samoset?"

I turn to follow his eyeline, and I have no idea why, since I've never even heard that name before. "No idea."

"I think it is! Come on. I'll introduce you."

"What? Connor—"

"Come on, Elizabeth. Just do what I say for three seconds, will you?"

I swallow my snappy response—he did drive me, after all—and follow him out of the car and over to a tall bronze-skinned woman with face-framing curls who looks *way* too good for morning. I feel distinctly troll-like in my jeans and sweater, even though it's probably the dressiest I've been before noon since starting at Radleigh.

"Connor Lawson? Is that you?" She comes dashing over and greets Connor with a kiss to both cheeks I find borderline repulsive. "What are you doing here?"

"Just doing a favor for a friend," he says dismissively, and the word "friend" flops around in my stomach. "Lauren Samoset, this is Lizzie Brandt." I open my mouth to correct him out of sheer habit, then realize he's actually gotten my name right for once. "Lizzie's with me at Radleigh, and her brother Max just started here. She's serving as guardian for him and their other brother, and she needed a hand."

"Oh, wow," says Lauren, and I can see newfound respect filling her eyes that sort of makes me want to puke. Why is Connor subjecting me to this awkward conversation? "If there's anything I can do to help...." She fumbles through her purse and digs up a business card, which she hands over. "I'm sure we can work out some sort of carpool situation."

Oh, that's why.

"That'd be great," I say feebly, feeling like an ass for not realizing this would be an attempt to help me. I tuck the card into the back pocket of my jeans, wishing I had my own to give over. "I'll, um, text you my number."

"Great." She smiles warmly, then puts a hand on Connor's arm. "And we should catch up, Connor. It's been way too long."

"For sure." He seems to mean it, because of course he wants to hang out with the pretty lady who has her shit together, but it's weird to see him act all...friendly. They don't exchange numbers though, and I wonder if that means they already have each other's. Either way, it doesn't come up, and we get back into the car and head out of the parking lot.

"So, um, as I was saying, thank you," I say sheepishly. "Again, I guess. You're sort of a nonstop favor machine, aren't you?"

"It's a right at the light, right?"

"Right." I wait for him to acknowledge the thank-you, but it doesn't come. Maybe he didn't hear me? "Tha—"

"Are you ever going to tell me *why* your car is out of commission all of a sudden, days after you *actually* told me you got into an accident and so couldn't come to class?"

"Oh fuck," I mutter without thinking. How had I completely forgotten that Connor knew about car number one being out of commission?

"I'll take that as a no," he says, his voice tinged with anger.

The idea of telling him about the Slutmobile makes my gut roil, but somehow, the idea of him thinking I lied to him feels even worse. "It's not what you think. That was real. This was my loaner car."

"You got in a second accident?"

"Not exactly."

"Oh. It's all clear now." He makes a left without checking to make sure it's the right way to go. It is, but I almost wish it weren't, just because it'd be nice to see him screw up for once.

"Can you just trust me?"

"You tell me. Can I?"

"Christ, Connor, why did you even agree to drive us this morning if you thought I was lying?"

He glances at me for a second before returning his eyes to the road. "Honestly, because I was too shocked you asked to say no. But I did hope that you'd volunteer the truth at some point."

"Well the truth is embarrassing, okay?"

He snorts. "Oh, come on. How bad can it be?"

"Bad enough to call my TA for help," I reply pointedly.

"And you really thought I wasn't going to ask?"

I press my lips together, stare out the window.

"Elizabeth."

Dammit. I can feel my eyes stinging now, but there is not a chance in hell I am going to cry in front of Connor Lawson.

He sighs and pulls up to a red light, and I can feel him looking at me, but he doesn't push. "Fine," he says, a little flatly, but I can tell he's trying to sound kind; it just doesn't come all that naturally. "I believe you. And you're welcome."

I nod, a little afraid of what'll come out of my mouth if I actually speak, and we drive back to my apartment in silence.

chapter eight

"They painted 'Crazy Slut' on my rental car," I say the instant I walk in to Connor's office the next day, before I even sit down, before I even close the door behind me. He deserves to know the truth, after everything he's done for me, or at least to feel like I'm capable of being honest with him. That's the decision I've come to over a sleepless night, anyway.

"I'm sorry, what? And who's 'they'?"

I close the door and take my usual seat across from Connor at his desk. "Trevor Matlin's frat boy underlings, I assume. Or Sophie Springer's. Either way—'Crazy Slut,' spray painted on my car. I didn't want my brothers to see it, so my friend Cait took it in to get repainted and I called you. There, now you know everything."

He shakes his head slowly. "No, Elizabeth, now I know even less. Why the— and why would—" He exhales slowly. "Do I want to know?"

"That I was screwing Trevor the night the cops came to tell me about my parents, and now the entire campus knows, and multiple people are out for my blood? Probably not. Oh, but Trevor's telling people he had no idea who I was and I was just a random stranger hiding under his bed, so, that's where the 'Crazy' is coming from. Well, either that or my very publicly informing Sophie that her boyfriend is a lying piece of shit. It's hard to say."

Connor opens his mouth. Closes it. Tries again. Same result. "I wish you'd told me sooner," he says finally.

I snort. "Why on earth would I want you to know any of that?"

"If your property is getting vandalized—"

"It's a one-time thing," I say dismissively. "Probably. Hopefully. I think we're even now, right?"

He raises an eyebrow.

"I knew I shouldn't have told you."

"I didn't even say anything."

"You're judging me. You think I'm a crazy slut."

"First of all," he says with a sigh, "no, I don't. Second of all, any judgmental thoughts I *would* have are about the fact that it sounds like you unapologetically cheated with this girl's boyfriend and

85

then publicly humiliated her about it. But of course, I'm not having any of those thoughts."

His words make my stomach turn with their...non-inaccuracy. "She's a bitch," I offer in the most pathetic defense ever. "She said my parents deserved to die for birthing me."

Connor sucks in a breath through his teeth. "Did she really?" He mutters something I can't make out. "What is *wrong* with people?"

"See? She sucks."

He gives me a pointed look.

"Fine, it's possible I suck a little bit too."

"I'm not saying a word."

"You engage in the loudest silence ever, Connor Lawson."

His lips quirk up a bit at that. "Yes, well. I can't be blamed for what your conscience whispers in your ear."

"Ugh. This is why I didn't want to tell you anything. My conscience sounds way too much like you these days. Have you ever even done anything wrong? Like, ever? Other than crimes against fashion?"

"I can't tell if that was the tightest combination of compliment and insult in history, or if that was just entirely mocking." He narrowed his eyes. "And what crimes against fashion?"

"Oh no." I hold up my hands. "I'm so not falling into that trap."

"You're the one who mentioned it!"

"I take it back. You dress impeccably. Cary Grant should rise from the dead and learn from you. Can we study Byzantine History now?"

Connor's eyebrows shoot up. "Wow, talk about six words I never thought I'd hear you say."

I smile sweetly. "See how studious I am?"

He rolls his eyes. "Yes. Completely fooled. But, given that you have the right idea, I'm going to ignore the fact that you're weaseling out of your fashion comment. Did you do the reading about Choniates' account of the Fourth Crusade?"

"I did, thank you very much."

I can't tell whether he believes me, but he says, "Good, then let's jump right in to the homework questions. How does he describe the common people of the capital?"

I'm relieved to know the answer, even though this isn't a usual tutoring day, and the next hour flies by as we zoom through the questions. Connor even gives me a little pop quiz on dates and a map, which I pass with flying colors. When the time is up, he's clearly both surprised and impressed, and it makes me embarrassingly joyful to see it. "Guess it's possible your study materials for dummies worked," I admit sheepishly as I start packing away my stuff.

"They're not for dummies," says Connor. "Some people just learn more visually, like I suspect you do. A lot of the visual learning we get accustomed to in elementary school and even high school tends to disappear in college; studying strictly from textbooks and slides isn't for everyone, but it's how a lot of college classes work. It's not how *I* learn best, though, so I created more visual materials. Same with the poems—that kind of thing has always helped me, and I figured it'd help others. It's a different way of learning. Doesn't mean it's a stupid way."

Well, I feel like an asshole. Again. So of course I choose that moment to say, "It's the pleat-front pants, Connor."

"What's wrong with pleat-front pants?" he asks, far more defensive-sounding than he was about the study materials.

"Nothing. Except for everything."

"Subtle," he says with a snort. "And what, in your esteemed opinion, should I be wearing instead?"

"Flat-fronts. Duh."

"Are you trying to turn me into a hipster?"

"I said flat-fronts, Connor, not skinny jeans and a fedora. I'm trying to turn you into a non-hopeless dresser."

"Which I would be if I wore flat-front pants," he says dryly.

I shrug. "It's a start. I figure it's the least I can do as thanks for the study materials."

"Thank you so much for those words of wisdom, Elizabeth. Now we've *both* learned a lot today."

"If you're going to be sarcastic, Connor, I won't share any more fashion tips with you."

He mimes a lip-zipping motion, and the fact that he actually cares what I think seems to open the fashion-advice floodgates. "More slim-fitted shirts wouldn't hurt you either," I add. "And maybe get them without those skinny stripes."

"Do I want to know what's wrong with the stripes?"

"They're…ugly?"

He looks down at his shirt. "This is ugly?"

"You don't really think I'm going to answer that, do you?"

The corners of his lips curve up. "Oh, come on. Suddenly you're gonna hold back?"

"My grades are bad enough without telling my teacher I think his shirts are ugly and corduroy pants are a travesty."

"That's some excellent restraint you're showing."

"Thanks, I thought so," I say sweetly. Then I notice the time out of the corner of my eye, and realize I've way overstayed—now I'm gonna be late for the Russian study group that already thinks I'm a delinquent. "Crap, I'm sorry, I gotta go." Wait, why am I apologizing? Of course I should go—we weren't even supposed to have a session today, and I've been here for over an hour. "I mean, not…sorry. We're, um, done, and I've got Russian group."

"All right then," he says, completely unruffled despite the fact that for some reason I suddenly have more words in me than my entire Byzantine textbook. "I'll see you in class."

"Yup." I want to say more, but he's already focused his attention on a paper in front of him, as if I'm already gone. Almost as if I were never even there, really. He might not think I'm a crazy slut, but I'm still just one of his lousy students coming to him for tutoring. It's weird that for a minute, I actually sort of forgot that.

It's a good thing I don't care what Connor Lawson thinks, or that might actually sting.

• • •

Whether it's the idea of Connor thinking of me as just another dumb student that spurs me to have an insanely productive afternoon, I'm not sure, but by the time I go to sleep at almost 3:00 a.m., I'm completely caught up. I actually blinked a few times at my computer screen as I typed the conclusion on my English paper.

The best part is, I can sleep in. I'd spoken to Connor's friend Lauren as soon as I got back to my apartment from study group, and she offered to drive Max. I'd taken Tyler to get a bike as soon as I got the loaner car back with its expensive new paint job—and made a mental note to stick the bill to Trevor's door with a fucking dagger—and he'd be taking himself to school, at least until it got too cold. That means seven blissful hours until my first class, and I intend to enjoy all of them.

It all sounds like a lovely, perfect plan, which comes to a screeching halt—literally—at 4:18 a.m.

I don't even recognize the sound as human at first, and my instinct is to bury myself under my covers. But then I realize the sound is all too man-made, or rather boy-made.

It's the sound of a seven-year-old having a horrible nightmare.

I race out of my room and nearly smack into Tyler coming to get me. We both dash back to Max, who's screaming "Mommy!" over and over at the top of his lungs. Shushing him doesn't quiet him in the slightest, and when I drop onto the bed next to him and wrap my arms around his shoulders, the only change is the feeling of dampness on my legs and seeping into my sleep shorts.

He's peed the bed.

"Shit," I mutter, jumping up. I don't know how I missed the smell, but I can tell from the way Tyler's wrinkling his nose that he didn't. He doesn't say anything, though. Just rocks back and forth on his feet, chewing the hell out of his thumbnail, looking every bit as at a loss for words as I am. I'm desperate to jump in the shower, but I know the neighbors are going to come knocking on the door any second if I can't get Max to stop screaming. "Max, please, you have to calm down. Please, talk to me and tell me what happened."

He doesn't calm down, and the knocking happens right on cue. I have to beg Ty to get the door while I continue to try soothing Max; I can only imagine what a neighbor's reaction would be to seeing—and smelling—me soaked in pee. Tyler goes reluctantly, and even from the bedroom and with Max continuing to scream, I can hear that our neighbor—probably one of the pre-meds who heavily populate the complex and have to be up in less than an hour—is at least sympathetic.

It takes another ten minutes until Max is too hoarse to go on, and another fifteen before I can force his whimpering form out of bed and into the bathroom. He won't let me bathe him, though—that task falls to Tyler, who looks so exhausted and terrified that it breaks my heart to leave the two of them alone. I have no choice but to keep moving, though. The sheets need to come off the bed, and I have no idea how to even begin dealing with the mattress.

I want to call my mother so badly it hurts. If I had the luxury of being able to cry right now, I would've fallen apart at the seams. But I don't, so I call Nancy.

She answers sleepily on the third ring, and I apologize profusely for waking her up, but she's every bit as nice about it as I knew she would be. She talks me through the cleanup and promises we'll speak more tomorrow…including about setting both boys up with therapists. I know she wants to suggest that I see one too, but we both know that I won't, and she doesn't push it.

Instead, I trudge to the laundry room with the sheets, text Lauren that the boys are sick and won't be needing a ride after all, and try to remember the feeling of that one hour and eighteen minutes when I had everything under control.

• • •

Eventually, both boys fall back asleep—Ty in his own bed, and a newly bathed and re-pajama-ed Max in mine. Meanwhile, I lug my laptop into the living room and try to figure out the mental health coverage situation on my brothers' insurance plan, and how soon I can get Max to see someone.

The health center opens at nine, and I do laundry, clean the rest of the living space, and read my Byzantine course packet until then. Then I call to get Max an appointment, wake him up, get him dressed, and leave Ty some cash and a note instructing him to go to the coffee shop on campus for breakfast and text me when he gets there.

Like getting Ty a bike, I know signing the boys up for therapy is something I should've done the second I brought them back here, and for the millionth time since That Night, I can't help wondering if I really am the best choice to be their guardian. It's clear I have no idea what the fuck I'm doing. Even the fact that Max looks like a perfectly happy kid walking next to me right now is due only to the fact that I bribed him with the promise of a doughnut to get him to campus.

"Is the lady gonna be nice?" he asks as we hit the edge of the main campus.

"I don't know if it's gonna be a lady," I tell him, "but I'm sure he or she will be very nice, yes."

"The man who drove us to school Monday was nice," he says matter-of-factly.

I wince at the mention of Connor, glad Max is too distracted by his surroundings to notice. He certainly had been nice, and I'm not sure I would've gotten through the past month without him. But I'm not his responsibility, and I'm not his friend, and I'm not sure how or when I forgot those things, but I need to start remembering them, stat. He's my TA—not my chauffeur, not my broker, and not my confidant. I still can't believe I told him about the Slutmobile.

"Yeah," I mumble when I realize I still haven't answered Max. Thankfully, it's a short-lived subject, and for the rest of the walk, Max peppers me with questions that are easy enough to answer—what this building is and that, what various signs say, and why so many boys and girls walk around wearing funny-looking pictures (i.e. Greek letters) on their chests.

Then there are the slightly harder ones, like, "Why is that boy's hand in her skirt?" Asked extremely loudly, of course, about a couple fondling each other on a bench bordering the quad.

A twinge of loneliness both unfamiliar and unwelcome worms its way into my system at the sight of the happy, snuggling couple. I yank him in the other direction, for both our sakes. "He's keeping his hands warm," I say hastily as we take a slightly alternate route to the health center.

I'm so busy keeping an eye out for other situations I don't want to explain that only Max's tugging hand keeps me from bumping into a couple standing just outside Nijkamp Hall, the biggest of the grad student dorms. "Crap, sorry." Apparently it's my destiny to have couples shoved in my face today. I step around them, squeezing Max's hand tighter, but then the guy speaks.

"Lizzie? Max?"

Against my better judgment, and because there's a witness, I turn at the sound of the familiar voice. It's Connor, of course.

And he's wearing flat-front pants.

I want to both laugh and cry at the sight. He looks really, really fucking good, and I look like a teen mom on one hour of sleep who doesn't own a single article of unwrinkled clothing and couldn't be bothered with so much as a hairbrush this morning, let alone lip gloss.

Meanwhile, the blonde he's with looks like she got dressed by cartoon birds.

"Good morning," I say, pasting on a smile. "Max, say hi to Mr. Lawson."

"Mr. Lawson, huh?" the blonde teases. "And here I've been letting the kids call me Jessica. Clearly I need to take a more authoritative approach."

The kids. Fuck you, Jessica. I do not like you.

"The bigger kids get to call me Connor," he says with a smile and a wink in my direction that makes me want to hate him but instead does a weird flip thing to my stomach I'd prefer to pretend isn't happening. "Jess, this is Lizzie, and this is her little brother, Max."

"Jess" crouches down and holds out a hand for Max to shake. "It's nice to meet you, Max." He shakes her hand with a toothy smile and I decide that maybe she's not a megabitch. Maybe. At least until she straightens up and says, "I have to run to class, but I'll see you tonight," to Connor before squeezing his forearm.

We exchange "Nice to meet you"s before she walks off, but my brain's still working to process the past few minutes. Connor has taken my fashion advice. Connor has also, apparently, taken a lover. Or already had one.

And I care, apparently.

Which means I need to get laid.

"So, took my fashion tips, huh?" I can't help teasing when Jessica's out of earshot. "Guess the girlfriend approves?"

He smiles. It's not something he does much, and if he did—if I'd ever noticed that dimple before, or how perfect his teeth are minus the tiniest of chips in front—I'd probably have paid a lot closer attention in class. "You tried my study materials; the least I could do was take your advice in return. And she's not my girlfriend, but she *did* ask me out in the hallway this morning," he says with a wave in the direction of Nijkamp Hall, "which I'm guessing means she approves."

Connor Lawson is going to get laid tonight. I officially live in a world where Connor Lawson has more sex than I do. I don't even know what to do with that information. I didn't even know he was capable of a flirty interaction with a woman until just now.

"Well, if that doesn't get me an A, I suppose nothing will."

He opens his mouth to respond, then glances at Max and shuts it. "So where are you two off to this morning? No school today?"

I rack my brain to think of a lie, but Max renders it unnecessary. "I'm going to speak to a lady about my mommy and daddy," he declares. "Or maybe a man. And then I get a doughnut."

"That's great, Max," Connor says softly, but I can feel his eyes on me even though I won't meet his gaze.

I know they're filled with a desire to help somehow, and I need to stick to my resolve to stop taking advantage of the fact that Connor's a sucker for a student in distress.

"Yeah, so, we should go. I'm hoping to get him an emergency session that aligns with my ten o'clock Stats class."

"Isn't your class over an hour?" Connor asks.

"Yeah, why?"

"Appointments at the mental health center are only forty-five minutes."

"Oh, sh—darn," I mutter softly. "I should've thought of that. They better let Tyler come pick him up. I have a quiz."

"I don't think they're going to release him to a minor," Connor says. "Look, I'm just running to the library to photocopy a few things and then I don't have a class until noon. You can authorize me to pick him up, and he can play video games in my apartment or something until you get him after your quiz."

"Connor, that's ridiculous. It's fine—I'll figure it out. You don't have to babysit."

"You have video games?" Max asks with wide eyes. I have to admit, I'm just as surprised.

"That I do," Connor says with a grin. Then he glances back at me. "It's no big deal, Lizzie. Seriously. It's just a half hour."

It *is* a big deal, and he must know that, but it's also a pretty perfect solution for me, and one I know Max will be happy with. Once again, selfishness wins out over sanity. "That would be awesome, Connor. Thank you. I promise, I'll come straight from class."

"I'm just in room 326 in Nijkamp," he says, adjusting the strap of the messenger bag slung across his conspicuously non-striped shirt. "We'll be there when you're done with your quiz."

I nod. I'm pretty sure I've used up all words of gratitude on Connor already. "I'll see you then," I say, turning toward the health center with Max. Then I turn back around, despite everything in the rational part of my brain telling me not to. "And hey, Connor?"

"Yes?"

"Nice job on the outfit. You look good."

He smiles sheepishly, raises a hand in a wave, and takes off for the library, while I force myself not to watch him go.

• • •

I finish the quiz as quickly as possible to minimize the amount of time Connor's stuck babysitting, but when I get outside and turn my phone back on, I see a text from him. *Take your time. You looked like you could use a cup of coffee.*

Well, that's a semi-polite way of telling me I looked shitty this morning, as if I didn't know. But he's not wrong. I allow myself a stop at the coffee cart on the quad before heading to Nijkamp Hall. I grab one for Connor too—literally the least I could do—though I have no idea how he takes it and can only guess he likes it bland and boring.

I've never been in the grad dorms before, but they look pretty ordinary. Still, it's weird to be there, and I feel like I need to be extra quiet in the beige hallways for some reason. I have no free hands to knock on his door, so I nudge it with my sneaker a few times, but no one hears me over the sound of the video game. I kick harder, and wince when it leaves a light scuff. *Goddammit.*

"What the—" Connor swings the door open, still dressed in business casual despite the fact that he's sitting around in his apartment with a seven-year-old. I can't even imagine what he wears to football games. "Lizzie!"

"No free hands," I say apologetically, handing him the plain black coffee. "Sorry." I don't mention the scuff. Hopefully, he won't notice. More realistically, he will, and he'll paint over the entire door as soon as I leave. "It was for a good cause."

"Much appreciated, thank you." He smiles and takes it. "How'd you know I take it black?"

I stifle a snort. "Lucky guess."

Like the coffee, his apartment's pretty bland and flavorless. Shelves overflowing with books, old maps on the wall, a navy-blue futon doubling as a couch…the closest thing to personal style he possesses is a bizarre throw pillow with "Istanbul (not Constantinople)" stitched on it.

I try not to imagine "Jess" lying on said throw pillow later tonight, but apparently my brain is trying to drive me to drink this morning.

"Not terribly impressive digs, I know," he says, and I realize he's been watching me scope out the place. He takes a sip of coffee. "I spend most of my time in either the library or my office, so, didn't seem like much point in putting a lot into it."

"It's lovely," I lie badly, and he laughs. "Hey, Max, are you gonna say hi to me or what?"

"I'm about to beat the guy!" Max whines, and I just roll my eyes and follow Connor to sit on the futon with our coffees.

"How'd it go?" I ask, keeping my voice low.

He shrugs. "Great. Max seemed to like her. He wanted to know when he was getting his doughnut." I can tell he wants to say more, but he hesitates.

"What?"

"It's just—not to question your, uh, guardian-ing or anything, but why was this an emergency appointment?"

I glance back at Max; he's fully involved in the video game and definitely not paying attention to the old people on the couch behind him. "He had a really,

really bad nightmare, and I freaked out," I admit in a whisper. "I thought if he talked to someone today, it'd lessen the chance of him having another one."

"How bad is really bad?"

"Let's just say the fact that I don't smell like pee right now is a miracle of modern hygiene."

"Yikes."

"Yeah." I take a sip from my cup. "I suck. I should've taken him sooner. Both of them. I know that now."

"And you? Have you been going?"

Did he seriously just ask if I go to *therapy*? "Nice as it is to know you think I'm fucking nuts, no, Connor, I do not see a shrink."

He rolls his eyes. "Must you *always* put words in my mouth? I don't think you're nuts any more than I think you're a crazy slut. I think you're an eighteen-year-old girl in an extremely sad and difficult situation and talking to somebody would be a good thing for you."

For some reason, it's the "eighteen-year-old girl" part that stings. I can handle him thinking I'm a slut, maybe—he wouldn't be alone—but not that I'm a little kid. "I'm fine," I bite out, "but thanks for your concern."

"So it's something you *obviously* should've done for your brothers, but not for yourself?"

My mouth drops open. "Where do you get off—"

"It helps, okay?" he snaps. "That's all I'm saying. And you obviously know that or you wouldn't have taken Max today. It's okay to look out for yourself too, you know."

I turn his words over in my head, and realize the fact that he knew Max's appointment would be only forty-five minutes was a dead giveaway. "You've gone," I say slowly.

"I have. I don't anymore, but I did for years, and yeah, it helped."

"Why'd you go?"

"Why do you think?"

In a flash, our conversation from his office comes back into my head. "Daddy issues."

"Daddy issues," he confirms.

I look down into my coffee; it's cold by now, but I take a little sip anyway. "What's the story there, anyway?"

Connor shrugs. "He just didn't want kids. He stuck it out for Sarah for a few years, but either he *really* didn't want a boy, or he just didn't want two, or...who knows. Maybe he saw the sign of Satan on my forehead at birth or something." He takes a swig of his own undoubtedly cold coffee. "He took off before my mom even got home from the hospital."

An unexpected flame of white-hot rage flickers inside my chest at the thought of his father abandoning their entire family like that. What a complete fucking asshole.

"Pretty much," says Connor with a sigh, and I realize I've said the last few words out loud. I glance over at Max, but he's still blissfully lost in his video game. "And you can imagine how much my mom appreciated that I 'ran him off.' As if I was somehow responsible for my own conception."

I chew my lip. "Yeah, I see how that could get...therapy-requiring. How long's your sister been gone?"

"Since the second she graduated high school, pretty much. Sarah's always been plagued by wanderlust, and there wasn't a whole lot keeping her at home. I at least played hockey, did Model UN—enough to keep myself busy. Sarah just counted the minutes until she could get out, and then ran."

"So it was just you and your mom for a while?"

He smiles wryly. "Those were the heaviest therapy years. And I didn't get quite as far away as Sarah did afterward, either. But I moved across the border as soon as I graduated McGill, and never looked back."

I start to ask what his mom is like, but I'm cut off by the sound of a text message beeping from my phone. It's Tyler. *I'm here. You coming?*

"It's Ty," I explain apologetically, surprised to feel myself a little sorry to be cutting this conversation short. "I promised him lunch at the coffee house, and I still owe Max that doughnut."

At the sound of the word "doughnut," Max perks up. "Is it time?"

"It is," I say. I turn back to Connor, who looks a little drained, despite the fact that he's still sipping the coffee. After ruining his day with all this depressing talk of topics he'd clearly prefer to leave buried, I can't just leave him sitting here, all sad in his new pants. "You wanna join us?"

He glances at Max before returning his gaze to me. "Nah, I shouldn't. I've got…stuff to do."

"Right," I say, shoving down what I hope are just hunger pangs disguising themselves as disappointment. "And you've got your date later, so."

"Yeah, right. That." He smiles faintly but I can't begin to read it. "I'll see you in class tomorrow." He turns to Max. "And I'll see you around, buddy."

"Max, say thank you to Connor for watching you today, and for the video games," I prod.

He does, and after he makes Connor promise that he'll have him back to play some other game, we head out of Nijkamp Hall without a backward glance.

chapter nine

When I walk into class the next day, it's staring me in the face that on top of everything else, my TA has a really nice ass. He's wearing flat-front pants—again—as he walks up the aisle, handing out what I really hope isn't a pop quiz. I try to deduce from his step, his posture, his…anything whether he had a good date last night, and whether it was still happening this morning. Then I realize I'm pathetic, and I trudge up the aisle just as Connor turns.

"Elizabeth."

He sounds surprised to see me, which irks me. As if I haven't been making perfect attendance, minus the family emergencies. He just saw me yesterday; he knew I'd be here. "Lizzie," I say coolly, holding out a hand for what's actually just a new map—Constantinople in 1205, the year after it was sacked the first time.

"Of course," he says wryly before continuing down to his front-row seat, leaving me standing there with the flimsy map dangling from my fingers like a white flag. I take the closest seat and stare at the sheet in front of me.

Pathetic, really, how thoroughly the Byzantines had their asses kicked. But then, they did manage to rise again.

And it only took them fifty-some-odd years.

The sound of someone else's ringing cell phone reminds me to turn off mine, but when I pull it out of my bag, I see I have an e-mail from Max's school. I take a quick glance, and groan. It's a reminder for parent-teacher conferences this Friday. Possibly the last thing in the world I want to do, plus sessions are in alphabetical order, which means mine will overlap with my Byzantine tutoring.

When class ends, I make my way up to the front of the room, to where Connor is gathering up his things. It takes him a moment to see me, and when he does, he greets me with a brief, tight smile I'm not sure how to take.

I take a deep breath. "Hey, so, I'm really sorry, but I can't make it to your office on Friday. I have to go to a parent-teacher conference at Max's school. Is there any chance we can reschedule?"

"Sure," he says with a shrug. "When did you have in mind?"

"Whenever. Not like I have loads of plans lately. Unless you count making mac 'n cheese with bacon bits for dinner tonight. According to my brothers, those are pretty much the most important plans in the universe."

"Totally understandable. That was always one of my favorites too." His fond grin makes his eyes crinkle in the corners, and I really, really hate that I ever noticed what a beautiful blue they were, because now I can't stop seeing it. "Man, it's been a while."

"Do you wanna come?" I offer, a second before I realize how weird that invitation is. Ugh, hanging around Connor has made me fucking awkward. Of course he doesn't want to come to dinner with me and my little brothers. Even Cait wouldn't want to come to dinner with me and my little brothers.

"You sure your brothers wouldn't mind sharing?"

"Huh?" It takes me a few seconds to process that he actually said yes, and then another couple to realize I'm way too excited about that fact. "I mean, no, of course not. I make a ton, and I owe you *something* for all your efforts." This all, at least, is true.

He smiles again, and I do not appreciate the way my body reacts to it at *all*. Clearly, the sexual deprivation of the past few weeks is getting to me. "You don't," he says with an un-Connor-like dose of warmth, "but I'll take you up on it anyway, if it's a real invitation. Haven't had home-cooked food in a while."

That makes me strangely sad, even though I rarely did either, before my brothers moved in with me. I mean, I had it at home, when my mom was making it, but obviously, those days are over. "It's a real invitation," I assure him, hoping my face doesn't look as hot as it feels. Because it sorta feels like I just asked my very proper TA on a date. With my brothers. Because I am insane. And now I need to make an awkward joke, because it's all that will keep me from sinking into the floor. "Wear a suit. My brothers and I are very formal."

"Then I can't wait to see what you'll be wearing," he jokes back, which only makes my face burn hotter. At least this time, his flames too. "I...did not mean that the way it sounded."

I can't help laughing. At least I'm not the only ragingly awkward one. "I should hope not. That's a pretty terrible pick-up line." Only, maybe it isn't, because suddenly what I'll be wearing is all I can think about. Which is crazy, because this is *not* a date. And this is Connor Lawson. He's probably saving his virginity for the third rise of Constantinople.

Not that I'm thinking about sleeping with him, obviously. That would be certifiable.

Am I certifiable?

"Lizzie, are you okay?"

Crap. "Sorry," I mumble. "Just got a little distracted thinking about salad. You know, want to make sure everyone's getting their vegetables."

You, Lizzie Brandt, are a fucking idiot.

"How very responsible," says Connor, and he actually sounds impressed. "How about I take care of the salad? You can just worry about slipping in some extra bacon bits."

He's bringing a salad. It's official: I want to fuck Connor Lawson.

Fuck.

"Deal," I reply in a voice that sounds remarkably helium-filled. "Six o'clock. It's—well, you know where I live. Hell, you can let yourself in."

He laughs. "I promise to knock. I'll see you at six."

I make what I hope is a noise of agreement but probably sounds more like the mating call of the African buffalo, and flee from the room.

• • •

I'm actually nervous when the clock hits six that night. Like, palms sweating, can't-focus-on-what-I'm-doing nervous. Which is so stupid. It's just dinner, after which he's going to tutor me. Because he's my *TA.* This isn't a date. I don't even *want* it to be a date. Why would I? He's not even single! Hell, after his date last night, he's probably marrying Jess. What's there even to think about?

A knock sounds at the door, and I glance at the clock on the microwave. Still six o'clock on the dot. It'd be easier not to be into him if he weren't so fucking dependable. Not that I ever gave a crap about "dependable" before, but I sure as shit do now. When you're on your own with two kids, dependable is everything.

I glance down at my outfit as I walk to the door. I spent more time choosing it than I wanna think about. Which of course means that after deciding everything looked like I was trying too hard, I ended up in jeans and a blouse-y thing that I'd klepto'd from Frankie a billion years ago.

The first thing I notice when I open the door is that Connor looks every bit as unsettled as I do. Okay, no, the first thing I notice is that it's the first time I've ever seen him in jeans, and they look really, really good. But the second thing I notice is that his hands are jammed into his pockets, his lips are pressed together, and he's radiating "I've made a terrible mistake."

Good start.

"Hey, come on in," I say as cheerfully as possible, pretending I don't see what I know I do. I step aside to let him in, and bite my lip when I realize the jeans look even better from behind. "Not too different from the last time you were here, probably. I'm a shitty decorator."

"I like that you kept the Christmas lights," he says with a smile, gesturing at the twinkling dots of color wrapped around the curtain rod over the patio doors.

"I thought it added a touch of class. I kept the shower curtain too."

"Seriously?"

"No. I'm not a fucking idiot."

He laughs.

"So, I'd offer you a beer, but…." I gesture toward the boys' room, where I've all but locked them inside to do homework on the threat of withholding bacon from the mac 'n cheese, a parenting tactic my dad would have approved of for sure.

Connor raises an eyebrow. "Water's fine, thank you, and I'm pretty sure I'd have to say no to a beer offered to me by an eighteen-year-old."

"*Touché.*" I lead him into the kitchen, where I pour him a glass. He leans against the counter to take a sip, and I busy myself with checking on dinner so I don't watch him.

"*Câlique*, that smells good," he says, inhaling deeply as I open the oven.

I immediately close the door and whirl around. "I'm sorry, what was that?"

He furrows a brow. "I said it smells good. The mac 'n cheese. And the bacon. Mmm." The "mmm" sends a very unwelcome bolt of lust-lightning southward as I contemplate just how much I would like to get him to make that sound again. "Oh!" He holds up the bag at his side. "I brought salad. Well, I brought vegetables; I got held up at the library, and figured I'd just make it here. Can I borrow a cutting board?"

I pluck the wooden board from a cabinet and gesture to the knife block I keep on the counter, out of Max's reach. "All yours, if you explain your little burst into French right there."

To my genuine shock, Connor blushes. "Sorry about that. I have sort of a dirty French-Canadian tongue."

Aaaand that one's going right into the spank bank. "Sorry?"

"High school habit I've never been able to break, despite being in the states for seven years." I'm oddly drawn to his Adam's apple as he takes another sip, and then he puts the glass down and starts pulling vegetables out of the bag. "I'm no you, but I do swear occasionally. We have different profanity in Quebec, though. Catholic holdover. They're all holy words."

"That's…bizarre. So what'd you say?"

"*Câlique.* It's like a…milder version of *Câlice*, which literally means chalice."

"And figuratively?"

"Closer to 'fuck.'" He presses his lips together as soon as it comes out of his mouth, then focuses extra hard on the head of romaine lettuce in his hand. "Okay, this is definitely not the right kind of tutoring."

*Probably not, but I really want to hear you say it again. In French, in English—whatever. Preferably with you on top—*I shake my head to get the image out of my brain. I am so twisted. "It's interesting. Kinda cool, in a weird, puritanical way."

"That's me," Connor deadpans. "Puritanical to a fault."

Are you? I'm dying to know, but then the door to the boys' room pops open, and Tyler whines, "Is dinner ready yet?"

I open my mouth to snap at him to be patient, but Connor cuts me off. "Hey, Tyler. Two minutes, okay? Almost done with the salad."

Max's dark head pops out. "Hi, Mr. Lawson! What are you doing here?"

Connor grins. "Hey, Max. I'm gonna eat with you guys and then help Lizzie with her homework. Is that okay?"

Max scrunches up his nose. "Mrs. Yang never came over for dinner. You're a weird teacher."

I know locking kids in the bathroom is probably illegal, but I would kill to do it to Max at that moment, especially when I see Connor's jaw twitch and I wonder just how much he's regretting walking into my apartment tonight.

Thankfully, for once, Tyler saves the day. "Connor's cool," he assures Max. "Mrs. Yang was *not* cool."

Connor's shoulders relax. "Wow, I don't think I've ever been called cool before. Thanks, Tyler. Max, wanna help?"

"Okay!" Max bounces over and sets him up with a carrot and a peeler.

"You know how to use one of these?" he asks as he holds out the latter.

"Mmhmm. I used to help my mom when she was alive," Max says proudly. He sets to work on the carrot, and Connor glances at me.

I wave a dismissive hand and busy myself with fussing over the table I already set an hour ago. Connor doesn't need to know that every mention of my mom or dad from one of the boys still feels like someone tweezing out every one of my body hairs. Nothing like refolding the napkins to distract myself, ensuring the tears pricking my eyes will dry up rather than spill over. Then, behind me, I hear, "Maybe let's do this over the garbage, buddy. The floor isn't the best place for carrot peels."

And somehow, that little bit of instruction combined with gentle discipline, perfectly stated and coming from someone Max has met exactly twice before, makes me want to cry hardest of all.

I mumble about needing to grab something from my room, and close the door behind me. I am fucked up. Why else would I invite someone so deep into my life who in no way sees me as anything other than a lost cause of a student to be rescued? And *why* the hell would I let myself...feel things for said person, apparently?

Ugh, Connor. *Connor.* How the fuck did I end up liking Connor?

I never should've told him about flat-front pants.

• • •

At least I was the only one who sat through dinner utterly miserable; no one else even noticed. Tyler and Max were too busy hanging on every word of Connor's stories of traveling to hockey games across Canada, and then Max ran off to play with his toys while Connor filled Tyler in on good bike routes near Radleigh. Except for a couple of emphatic compliments on the food, I was essentially invisible. Finally, I excuse myself onto the patio, grabbing a lollipop from the candy bowl as I go.

Connor joins me a couple of minutes later. "Tyler's doing his homework." Then he notices the lollipop stick. "That's not a cigarette, is it?" he asks as he slides the door closed behind him.

"What if it was?" I ask, though I have to pull it out of my mouth to do it, which kinda ruins any sort of defiance in the gesture.

"Then I'd say you should quit smoking."

"And I'd probably say it isn't any of your business. Good thing this entire conversation is irrelevant." I pop it back into my mouth.

I expect some sort of admonishment, but all he says is, "Can't really argue with that, I guess."

We're both quiet for a moment, looking out at nothing, and then he says, "So do you want to study?"

"Not really," I admit. "Do you?"

He laughs. "Not really." But he doesn't move to go, so I gesture to one of the cheap lounge chairs I picked up at Target and take a seat in the other one. "I do have to admit, a beer would be pretty perfect right now. But that mac 'n cheese was pretty damn good. Thanks for having me."

I pluck the candy back out of my mouth. "Thanks for the salad, and turning into my brothers' new hero," I say with a hint of sourness I wish wasn't there and know he won't miss.

He turns to me. "They love you, you know. Like crazy."

I shrug. "They don't really have a choice. They're stuck with me, no matter how much I suck at this whole parenting thing."

"They're happy," he argues. "You make this place home for them. You take great care of them. Please tell me you see that."

"I see them surviving," I say. "All of us—it's all we're doing. Tyler hasn't found a new best friend or

girlfriend or band. Max doesn't have play dates. I'm…"
Pining after you. "Whatever."

Connor braces his elbows on his knees and peers up at me. "Whatever?"

"I don't want to talk about me anymore," I say, swirling my tongue around the grape-flavored candy. I don't even mean anything sexual by it, but a quick glance at Connor reveals he's watching me do it. Which makes me do it again. "How was your date last night?"

"What?" He blinks, looks away from my mouth. "Oh, with Jess? Yeah, it wasn't. I had work to do."

I raise an eyebrow. "Work? You bailed on a date for work?"

"It's not a big deal," he says defensively.

"That *is* a big deal, Connor," I shoot back. And yes, maybe it's because I've been tearing my hair out at the mental picture of them together for nothing, but it still makes me angry, however irrational and unfair that may be. "That girl likes you, and you just…bailed. And you're not a guy who bails. At least not when it comes to poor loser students who can't get through life without having their hands held."

"You're not a 'poor loser student,' Elizabeth, and I'm happy to help you when I can."

"God, even when you're saying I'm not pathetic, I feel pathetic," I mutter.

"Somehow, I don't think that's my fault."

"I didn't say it was."

He narrows his eyes. "You're seriously angry because I blew off a date with a girl? How is that even any of your business?" he demands, rising slowly out of his chair.

It's not. It's so, so not. "I'm sorry. You're right. It's not. Just forget it."

"I don't want to forget it. I want to know what your problem is."

"You!" I snap, jumping up to face him before I can stop myself. "You making me your charity case. You being there every single time I need you. I know it's my fault for constantly fucking up, but I turned to you too damn much and you let me, and now it's fucking with my head."

"So let me get this straight," he says slowly. "You're angry because I've been too reliable when you needed help."

"Well, when you put it *that* way, it sounds stupid."

"And how should I put it?"

I open my mouth to answer, and shut it. I can't answer that. Because the problem isn't that he's been too nice. It's that his being nice has made me like him. A *lot*. And I'm not stupid enough to believe that a guy who blows off dates with girls like Jess for work, who knows the entire campus thinks I'm a crazy slut, who takes being a TA way too seriously, is ever going to reciprocate that.

So I don't say a word.

Connor exhales an exasperated breath. "Only you could make someone feel like shit for helping you."

I wince at the fact that he's being both cruel and correct. "I don't mean to do that. I just...you don't need to. I'm fine. I'm sorry I took advantage of the fact that you expressed a willingness to help, and of your guilt over not believing me at first, but you don't owe me anything for it."

"Has it ever occurred to you that I don't do these things out of pity, or because I'm just a sucker?" he asks, shaking his head. "Like maybe I *actually* like spending time with you? Maybe I even *like* seeing you outside of class?"

My stomach tightens into a ball of lead and the autumn air suddenly grows far too cold. I know he's not saying what I think he's saying. Which just means I've gone way too far past the point of delusion. Christ, maybe Sophie was right after all.

"No," I say honestly, my voice thin and weak. I so badly want that to be true, but I haven't exactly been given a lot of reason in the past year to believe a guy like Connor could genuinely *want* anything to do with a girl like me.

And yet his words are turning around in my brain and no matter how many different ways I try to explain them away, I can't.

He steps toward me, and though he's only about half a foot taller than my five-six, it feels like he's towering over me. "For fuck's sake, Elizabeth. Ask me the real reason I didn't go on that stupid date."

But I don't have to ask. I see it now. His eyes are blazing with lust and I finally fucking see it. I'm not crazy, and I'm not alone in this, and I want him to touch me so badly I feel it in every bone in my body. "Kiss me," I whisper, and it sounds like thunder in my ears.

He crushes his mouth to mine with a breathless groan I swallow whole. It's the first real human contact I've had since That Night, and I drink it—him—in as if I've finally been offered a canteen after weeks in Death Valley. I cannot pull him close enough, taste him deeply enough.

Both our hearts are pounding, pulses racing, and we are so fucking full of life, I could weep. Or scream. Or both. Instead I push Connor up against the brick exterior of the building and press up against him instead, settling into the cradle he makes for me of his legs.

"*Sacrement*, Lizzie...." He wraps his arms around my waist and pulls me so close I can feel him branding my thigh. I'm thinking the unholiest of thoughts right now, until he drops his head to suck at my throat and I cease to think at all.

"Don't stop," I whisper, even though he shows no signs of letting up. His hands slide up the back of my sweater, impossibly warm, keeping me balanced while he samples every visible inch of my skin. I didn't even know how much I'd missed the feeling of another person's warmth until just this moment, and I want it everywhere. "Don't let me disappear."

His fingers had been inching up toward my breasts, but now they freeze on my rib cage and he pulls back, leaving both of us panting for breath. *Why* did I say that? I hadn't even known I'd been thinking it. "I'm sorry," I mumble, stepping back and yanking my sweater down. "I'm fucked-up."

But he just shakes his head. "No, you're not. That was…" He exhales sharply, rakes a hand through his air. "I should go."

Fuck. Fuck fuck fuck. The thought of Connor walking out right now brings tears to my eyes, which means he's definitely right. I *am* fucked-up, but I can't lose him. "Connor, please, don't. We don't have to—I mean, we can just pretend that never happened. Or something."

His eyebrows shoot up. "You can pretend *that* kiss never happened?"

No, I definitely can't. My entire body is still thrumming with it. I shake my head, not trusting myself to speak.

"We're in trouble," he murmurs.

At that, I can't help smiling a little. Being in trouble's a concept I'm familiar with. For once, Connor's the untrained newbie. Just the thought is enough to make me rise onto my toes and kiss him again, but just as he relaxes back into it, the sound of Max calling my name makes us jump apart again.

"Okay, now I really need to go," says Connor. He straightens out his shirt, then glances down at his bulging fly. "In a minute," he adds sheepishly.

I bite my lip, knowing he's right to walk out of here, but wishing he didn't want to. But I can't stop him, and I can't beg, so I just nod. "I'll see you tomorrow," I say quietly. "Just...are we okay?"

He laughs ruefully. "With each other? Yeah. In the grand scheme of Radleigh? No, definitely not."

"This may shock you," I say, "but I care a lot more about the first one." I rise up on my toes and give him one last peck, and then I disappear inside to help Max.

chapter ten

The next morning, I wake up burning with the need for some estrogen. As soon as I drop off Lauren's kids and Max, I text Cait and Frankie and tell them their presence is required at lunch.

Understandably, Cait's a little hesitant to return to our usual coffee shop, so instead we meet for pizza at a hole-in-the-wall place Sophie Springer wouldn't be caught dead entering. I'm all of two bites in to my barbecue chicken slice when I crack. "So, I sort of made out with someone last night. A little."

Cait drops her slice onto her greasy paper plate. "For the love of all that is holy, please tell me it was not Trevor."

"Cait! Are you kidding me? No, of course it wasn't. I haven't even seen him since...everything."

"It wasn't that hot black guy in your Russian group, was it?" asks Frankie. "The one I talked to for a minute when I came to return that book last week?"

"That is so random, Frank, and no, not him either."

"Good. I think I'm gonna hook up with him."

"I'm pretty sure he's gay."

She shrugs and pops a slice of pepperoni into her mouth. "So? Didn't stop that guy from the art gallery."

Cait and I roll our eyes at each other. Frankie's convinced everyone on earth is pansexual and just doesn't realize it yet.

"It's no one you know," I say, which is sort of true. "Just a guy from one of my classes." Even more true! Not that I want to lie to my friends; if I thought I could've trusted them to keep it quiet, I would have.

"And how was it?" Cait asks.

I swallow, hard, remembering the feeling of Connor's lips on mine, the warmth of his body and firmness of his grip. "Good. Really, really good." I take a swig from my water bottle, wishing it were something harder. "Top Five, I think."

"Oooh," they both gush, which is justified, since the Top Five has always been sacred among us. "Who does mystery man knock off?" asks Frankie.

I contemplate the answer as I chew thoughtfully on my crust. Danny Perotta in the church parking lot had been holding steady at number five for some time, but there was no question kissing Connor last night had blown that out of the water. For that matter, it'd beaten number four—Casey Farhadi, my partner in last year's

New Year's Eve singledom—by a mile.

No chance I was thinking beyond that.

Cait whistles. "Wow, this sounds big! Where did this guy come from? I had no idea you were even flirting with anyone."

"I wasn't. Or maybe I was. I don't know," I mutter. "Anyway, I don't think anything's gonna happen with it. It was just a good night."

"Oh, come on," says Frankie. "Look at you. You're practically dripping on the seat just thinking about it. I haven't seen you like this in forfuckingever."

"Gross, Frank." Cait flicks a mushroom at her.

"Whatever, I make no apologies. And you are *not* giving up on this boy."

Man, actually.

"I'm with Frankie," says Cait, picking at the cheese on her second slice. "If this guy's really Top Five, I don't understand why you're not all over it."

I knew talking about this would be a mistake. "It's just…logistics," I say lamely.

Frankie snorts. "Like that stopped you with Trevor."

"Not my finest hour," I remind her sourly. "Or months. Can we just pretend that never happened?"

"Depends," says Cait with a grin. "How's your car?"

"Don't make me throw food at you." I take another swig of water. "So, okay, if it were you guys, and you hooked up with a guy you were interested in who needed a little convincing...."

"You're kidding, right?" Frankie shakes her head. "Guys aren't complicated, Lizzie B. You know this. Hot lingerie. Trench coat. Done."

Cait raises an eyebrow. "Does that seriously work for you?"

"Every damn time," Frankie says with a wolfish smile. "Seriously, I'll lend you the trench coat. Just promise me you'll give it a shot."

I try to imagine Connor's expression at the sight, and even just a couple of days ago, it would've been impossible to envision. But now, I feel his hands on the small of my back and his tongue stroking mine as clearly as if it were still happening, and a slow smile creeps over my lips. He'd been hard as a rock when we were kissing last night—nothing complicated about that.

I grin back at Frankie and pick up my second slice. "How soon can you get me that coat?"

$$\bullet \ \bullet \ \bullet$$

I chicken out of the lingerie thing—it's autumn in upstate New York, after all—but I'm still determined to see Connor, alone, to continue whatever we started at my apartment. It's possible this is the stupidest thing I've ever done, but I'm amped on adrenaline and the memory of his warm mouth on mine the night before and before I know it, I'm at his door.

Taking a deep breath, I picture him sitting inside as I knock, bent over a paper, the glasses he occasionally wears sliding down his nose. How can someone so bookish be so cute? Or kiss so well?

"Come in," he calls, sounding tired. I bite back a smile as I turn the knob. I'm pretty sure he's about to wake up with a vengeance.

"I've decided that you work way too hard," I say slowly as I close the door behind me. He is, indeed, bent over a paper, though he's wearing contacts today; no glasses in sight. He stands up, obviously surprised to see me, though whether or not he's pleased remains to be seen. "Figured I'd come say hi and help you take the edge off."

Before I can lose my nerve, I walk right up to him and press my mouth to his. But I don't even get my arms around his neck before he's jumping back, a wild, horrified look on his face. "*Tabarnac*, Elizabeth...I...no. I'm your teacher. I can't—"

No. *No.* I can't have read this wrong. I didn't. I *know* I didn't. This is such complete and total bullshit. "Seriously, Connor? Fuck you for pulling this shit after last night." I step back, folding my arms protectively over my chest, as if I had in fact shown up in the black lace ensemble I'd considered. "You think calling me Elizabeth is fooling anyone? Is fooling *me*?" He winces at each word out of my mouth, and it only propels me forward, in his face, until I'm so close I could actually kiss him again. "I'm not a little kid. I *mother* two of those now. So don't talk to me like I'm some high school cheerleader who just made a pass at you behind the bleachers."

He opens his mouth to respond, then closes it on a slow exhale. It's like I'm exhausting him just by being in his presence. I don't know what the hell happened to the adorable, smart, sexy nerd who could barely detach himself from my lips to breathe last night, but he's not in this office.

Apparently, he doesn't exist at all.

"I should've known," I mutter, buttoning my coat with fingers that feel three sizes too big to function. "Of course it would be too good to be true. Idiot Lizzie."

"Eliz—"

"Stop fucking calling me Elizabeth!" I shout so loudly they can probably hear me down the hall. Who even cares anymore? I'm sick of just surviving, and of course when I finally think my life could be more than that, it turns out Sophie was right—I *am* delusional.

Still, I lower my voice to continue, edging it in steel instead of volume. "I was there too last night, Connor. I didn't force your tongue down my throat. I didn't suck my own neck. And it's certainly not the imprint of *my* rock-hard dick I was feeling against my thigh. So enough of this bullshit. You're not interested anymore. Fine. You just got horny in the moment. Fine.

Be a man about it."

"I'm *trying* to be a man about it," he whispers back fiercely. "I'm trying to do the right thing! I can't sleep with a student. You can't sleep with a teacher. You're skating on thin enough ice as it is."

"Funny, I've been doing just fine in *your* class lately."

"I'll find someone else to tutor you," he promises, squeezing the bridge of his nose.

Sighing, I shake my head. "Forget it, Connor. There's no point. I'm not staying in your class."

"What do you mean, you're not staying?"

If I don't pick up my grades in *all* my classes, that scholarship is toast. And I'm pretty sure I'm done being able to focus with Connor sitting in the front row. I'd rather beg and plead my way into another class a month late and pay an actual tutor than flail like this. "Just that," I say, hoisting my purse higher on my shoulder. "You can just ignore my last paper. Save yourself some grading time. I'm withdrawing."

I let myself out, unable to even muster a goodbye, but when the door closes behind me, I'm too worked up to take another step. I can't believe I even have any tears left, but there they are, working their way down my cheeks, just to add insult to injury.

Tipping my head to rest it against the door to his office, I take deep, cleansing breaths until the tears stop. I'm about to step away when I hear Connor's voice through the wood, sounding utterly defeated, say, "I already graded it. You got an A."

It's more than I can take. I rush out of the building as if I'm on fire and jog back to my apartment to make dinner for the boys, praying it'll be the one thing today, this month, this year, I don't royally screw up.

• • •

"And then Tracy gave me a doughnut and said not to tell," Max informs me proudly that night, over lasagna with broccoli thrown in to stave off child services. Somehow, the kid's made more friends in his month at Radleigh than I have in over a year. Apparently Tracy's the reason I can barely get Max to eat two bites.

Not that I'm doing much better. Fighting with Connor and my decision to drop his class have sapped both my appetite and my will to do more than nod as Max happily babbles about his day.

"How was your day, Ty? Any free baked goods for you?"

He just shrugs. He's still pretty moody about the move—or maybe it's about Mom and Dad—but he won't talk to me about anything. He's barely talked all night.

"How's the lasagna?"

Another shrug. It makes me want to shake him, but I can't; I hated when my parents pried. It was like even in my own head, I couldn't get any privacy.

Sort of what hanging out with Connor's like.

Sighing, I put down my fork and start clearing the table. It's obvious no one's really up for dinner.

"What's for dessert?" Max asks, oblivious to the general air of depression.

"Sounds like you already had dessert today, Mister." I ruffle his hair and try to smile. "Need help with your homework?"

"Nah, I got it." He takes a long drink of his milk and runs off to his room.

"What about you, Ty?"

"Nope."

"You sure?"

He shrugs again.

I put the dishes down in the sink and take a seat next to him. "Okay, how about this. I'd like to help you with your homework, because I had a crappy day, and I could use the distraction. Please."

The trace of a smile is so faint on his lips that I never would've noticed it if I hadn't been praying for it. "Yeah, okay. How's your memory of sophomore English?"

"Awesome," I lie. "*Scarlet Letter*?"

"*Song of Solomon.*"

"You're studying the Bible?"

Ty rolls his eyes. "It's by Toni Morrison. God, no wonder your grades suck."

"My grades do not suck! I'll have you know, I got an A on my latest history paper," I declare proudly as he grabs his stuff, ignoring the twinge in my gut I feel at the memory of learning that particular piece of information. We settle onto the couch, and Ty fills me in as best he can, though admittedly I'm not the most mature in reaction to learning how Milkman, the main character, got his nickname. (I'm sorry, but the guy breastfed until he was *four*. That's beyond being "old enough to ask for it" and practically into being "old enough to make your own breakfast.")

I'm pretty sure Tyler's relieved when a knock sounds on the door, forcing me to leave him alone to go answer it. Admittedly, I'm a little relieved too, at least until I see who's on the other side.

"Connor."

He holds up what I recognize as my paper on the Byzantine empresses Zoe and Theodora, though this is the first I've actually seen it with its new bright-red A at the top. "I thought you should have this. It's a great paper."

"You're making TA house calls now?" I raise an eyebrow and cross my arms as I lean against the doorpost, barring entry he hasn't even asked for.

He glances behind him in both directions. "Can we please talk?" His voice is so low I have to strain to hear it. "I can't stand out here."

Reluctantly, I step inside and let him in, then close

the door behind him. "Ty, can you finish up in your room?"

"Wha?" Tyler looks up. "Oh, hey, Connor. I hope you're here to tutor her in English."

"Smartass."

He sticks out his tongue at me as he slides off the couch and disappears into the boys' bedroom.

I wait until I hear the door firmly close behind him before turning back to Connor. "I'd offer you a drink, but I don't want to." My mother is definitely frowning down at me for my lack of Filipino hospitality right about now. "So what brings you to my doorstep, teacher?"

He shoves a hand through his hair so hard I'm afraid he'll yank it all out by his roots. "I can't do this with you, Lizzie."

"You said that already this afternoon. Message received."

"Did you mean what you said?" he asks. "About dropping?"

"I'm not sure yet." No point in lying, especially to the one person who's actually been helping me organize my thoughts. It's not like I *know* I can get into another class this late, but I do know the idea of sitting in one with him is torture. And the truth is, it's not just his class I've been thinking about leaving. The more of Tyler's moodiness I observe, the more I wonder if Radleigh itself just isn't the right place for us right now.

"You can't make me the difference between staying and going," he says tightly, bracing a hand on the back of kitchen chair. He doesn't meet my eyes, but instead watches his own knuckles go white from his grip. "That's not fair."

I snort. "First of all, you're talking to someone who lost her parents in an instant and became an eighteen-year-old mother of two, so if you want to compete about 'fair,' you've brought a fucking watergun to the Second Crusade."

"That's not—"

"Second of all, this isn't a 'boo hoo, the boy I like doesn't like me back so I'm uprooting my life' situation, okay? I need an A in *all* my classes this semester in order to keep my scholarship, which I need to stay here. Now my transcript is shot to hell. Honestly, it'd probably be better for both me and the boys if I stopped wasting money on my tuition altogether and got a full-time job instead. Maybe then I could actually afford to get the boys' their own damn bedrooms."

"But you're getting an A in the class…."

"Maybe for now, but you think that's gonna hold up without you tutoring me?" I all but growl, taking care to make sure the boys can't hear me through the door. "You think I'm gonna be able to focus in class every day? Watching you hand out papers and remembering how those hands feel on my skin? I'm supposed to listen to you lecture and not think about how you said my name like I was a glass of water and you were dying of thirst?"

"Lizzie, stop." His knuckles are so white now I swear I can see bone through the skin. But I don't care. I'm not done.

"I can't be around you. I'm sorry if that sounds crazy to you or whatever. But I *need* to focus, and I don't see myself doing that when all I can think about when I see you is finishing what we started."

Connor swallows hard. "Even now?"

"I threw myself at you earlier *today*, Connor. Just because your feelings go away with the snap of your fingers doesn't mean mine do." The humiliation of my admission burns in my face, and I gather up the remaining dishes with a clatter and stalk past him to drop them in the sink. When I turn back around, he's standing in my face, so close I can feel body heat radiating from every inch of him.

"You don't really think that's what happened, do you?"

"I don't know how else to explain it," I counter, but all the fight's gone out of my voice. He's just too close. The heady scent of his aftershave is scrambling my brain cells.

"I told you—because I'm your TA. And everything you just said is exactly why they forbid us from getting involved."

"Then why are you here?" I rasp.

"Because I can't not be." He takes the last step needed to close the space between us and slides his hands into my hair, pulling me into a starving, searching kiss. His tongue sweeps my mouth as if he doesn't want to miss a spot, and pressed up against him as I am now, there's no doubt he wants me every bit as much as he did last night, if not more. Even when he pulls away, panting.

"*Tabarnac.* Lizzie. I'm sorry."

"Oh God. Not again with this—" I break off, certain I'm going to scream.

"It's not okay! You know it's not okay. You listed *exactly* why it's not okay."

"I listed why I wouldn't be able to concentrate if I didn't have you," I point out, hooking a finger into a belt loop on his jeans. "If I had you, that wouldn't be an issue."

At least that makes him smile. Sort of. "You don't honestly believe that, do you?"

"I don't know what I believe." I swing the loop from side to side for a second before sliding my finger out and bringing my hands up to rub my temples; I can feel yet another headache coming on. "I don't have the energy to argue with you. I barely have the energy to get my ass to class. Both my sanity and my scholarships are hanging on by a thread, and if I can't get my shit together, I'm gonna lose my brothers to foster care."

I step back and drop my hands, feeling utterly defeated. "So I won't fight you on this. I can't. I just don't have it in me. I am too. Fucking. Tired."

Connor bites the inside of his lip, the first real nervous, contrite gesture I've ever seen from him. "I'm sorry," he says hoarsely. "I didn't mean for this to happen."

The words sting more than I expect. "No one ever does," I snap. "I'm just that incidental that somehow comes along with the ride. Well don't worry—Trevor shook me easily, and so will you."

"That's not—"

"Save it, Connor. I was being selfish. You made me happy when I didn't think anything could, and I've had a hard time letting that go. I'm supposed to be trying to turn myself around and obviously I'm still just the same idiot I was a month ago. My brothers deserve better, and so do both of us."

He shakes his head slowly as he walks to the door. "It's fucked up that all I want to do right now is kiss that sad look off your face and then curl up in bed with you for the rest of the night, right?"

It feels as if he's reached right through my chest cavity to squeeze my heart, but I won't allow myself to respond to it. "Very." I press my lips into a firm line, because if I don't, I'll rise on my toes and kiss him, and that'll be the end of this otherwise clean, decisive break.

"In another life, maybe."

The squeeze settles into a far more permanent-feeling dull ache as I concede, "Maybe," and close the door quietly in his face.

• • •

An hour later I have cleaned up from dinner, put Max to bed, and finished my mercifully short Russian homework, but I haven't managed to banish Connor from my mind at all. My eyes keep drifting to my phone, as if there's a snowball's chance in hell he'd call me. As if even if he did, there'd be anything to talk about.

I need some fresh air. I grab my phone and keys, tell Ty I'm going for a walk, and let myself out into the crisp autumn night. I've forgotten how chilly it gets in upstate New York in November, and in no time at all I'm regretting that all I've got on is my leather jacket over a thin dress. Still, I don't feel like heading back to the apartment just yet, so I wrap my arms around myself and walk around the complex.

It takes a couple of minutes to realize that what's missing from this picture is a cigarette. Within a few months at Radleigh, I wouldn't have walked five feet in the cold without one. But between Connor's disdain for them and my natural inclination to keep them away from Ty and Max, plus that nasty-ass gum, I seem to have somehow kicked the habit.

The realization is enough to make me want one.

Unfortunately, I'm not carrying any, I didn't grab my wallet, and a quick check of my pockets reveals I'm not carrying around any cash. Of course. That'd be way too neat. But no wonder I'm all high-strung. I haven't smoked in weeks, haven't had a drink in almost that long, haven't had sex in…. Christ.

Haven't had sex since the night my parents died. Since the night I was with Trevor, in his room, at the party. Since the night the cops came knocking on his door.

It's not like I haven't thought about that night a million times before, but the realization of just how many things have changed since then brings me to my knees right there in the grass surrounding the parking lot, hidden only by a couple of trees. It's dark out, a beautiful, starry night interrupted by the faint sounds of TVs coming from the apartments above me and the crickets around me. And I have to go ahead and fuck up the near-silence with the sound of my crying.

Once it starts, I can't stop. I'm in a sitting fetal position, my arms grasping my knees to my chest, my face buried in my knees, and I'm soaking my skin and probably making a racket but I can't shut it off. I can't make it stop. I can't. Undo. Anything.

And then, "Elizabeth?"

Oh, shit. I swipe at my eyes, my nose, everything. Push back and look up, bracing myself on my palms in the grass. "What are you doing back here, Connor?"

He settles next to me on the grass and pushes tear-soaked hair out of my eyes. "I never went anywhere," he says quietly, handing me a tissue.

"You've just been sitting in your fucking car?"

He shrugs. "It's a nice night."

"It was," I say bitterly. "Go home, Mr. Lawson."

His hands leave my face, dig into the grass, pull at the blades at his sides. "Don't you think if I could have, I would have?"

My eyelids flutter closed, and I take one last halfhearted swipe at my nose with the tissue. "I told you, I can't play this game with you. What do you want from me?"

"I don't know."

"Well then I *definitely* can't help you."

He huffs out a sigh, and I open my eyes. He might be annoyed, and as tired as I am, but he's settled back against the trees now, and he's obviously not going anywhere. "What do you want from *me*, Lizzie? Because I'm pretty sure what you need is more than I can give."

"Pretty sure, huh?" I don't mean to sound flirty, but the thing is, even tired, and angry, and infuriating, Connor Lawson, in his stupid professorly attire, is still the sexiest thing I've ever seen. Especially in the moonlight. Especially when he's sitting in the moonlight, next to me, because he actually gives a shit about who I am and what I need.

His lips curve up in a smile despite himself and he shakes his head. "You are so…you."

My fingers find the soft, smooth back of his hand, trace it with their tips, slide into his in perfect interlocking formation. He doesn't pull away. "Who else would I be?"

For the first time since he got out of his car and found me in the grass, Connor looks up at me, into my eyes, and I can't help wondering what it is he sees. "You're incredible, you know that?"

It's a rare compliment from him, and I'm not great at those. "I'm an asshole, Connor. You just came to check on me because I was crying over my dead parents and I'm sort of hitting on you."

He smiles softly, squeezes my fingers. "There's no right way to grieve, Lizzie. You are who you are, and you feel how you feel. As long as you're getting through the day, that's all that matters."

"What if I'm not?"

"You are," he says firmly. "You're here. Your brothers are fed. They're in your apartment. They're safe. Your parents couldn't have asked for better care."

"I'm not talking about my brothers right now."

"I know," he says. "But if I talk about you I am going to say some things I really shouldn't say."

"I can't tell if that's promising or threatening. Like?"

He laughs wearily. "*Sacrament.* You're going to be the end of me, Elizabeth Brandt."

"That sounds closer to promising." And then, because he's making me smile, because he's making me forget, because his holy French-Canadian swear words are so cute, because he's making me feel things that aren't pain and death and despair and failure, I kiss him. His lips are soft and warm and yield to mine like they've been waiting all night for exactly this.

Strong hands cup my face, gently cradling as tentative touches of tongues slowly become bolder in their explorations. And then I'm straddling him there in the grass, up against the trees, my dress pooling around my waist as his hands stroke my thighs, gently at first and then firmly, like the kiss, like my hands on his chest, like the erection rapidly hardening beneath me, so close to the right spot, yet so far away.

I shift just an inch until I'm perfectly situated for an iota of relief, and Connor hisses in a breath as I do. "*Criss,* Lizzie." I roll my hips again, and again, desperate for relief, desperate for *some* of this tension sapping all my strength to leave my body. Connor slips my jacket down my arms and bites my shoulder to keep from crying out. The tiny bit of pain is so perfect, it brings me right to the edge.

"We need to stop," he whispers, even as he continues to thrust upward, fucking me through way too many layers of clothing.

"You asked what I want from you," I remind him, keeping my voice low, dropping my hands down to his belt. "This is what I want."

He grabs my hand, traps it in a vise. "No, Lizzie, we actually need to stop. I don't have…protection."

The magic words. Just like that, I release his belt and let myself fall off his thighs and onto my back on the grass. "Of course you don't." I shake my head, and laughter bubbles out of me. Connor looks down at me as if I've gone a little crazy. Which I might have. "Fuck. Of course you don't."

Connor sighs. "Lizzie?"

I stop laughing. "Yeah?"

He rolls over, straddling my knees. "Shut up." And then before I can get out a single indignant word, he leans in and presses his mouth to mine, swallowing my moan of surprise as he slides a hand down my beyond-soaked panties.

My hands grip his hair, keeping his lips on mine to cover the sounds threatening to emerge as he gently caresses me for a few moments before slipping a finger, then two, inside. My entire body feels like it's on fire, made worse by my inability to cry out, but then he focuses on kissing me, not just keeping me quiet, and the feeling of his tongue and fingers keeping the same pace makes my entire body tremble in the cool air.

I'm so close I can feel it, just out of reach, but then, without warning, he pulls back. And takes my underwear down with him. Then he lowers himself down between my legs and takes a long, firm stroke with his tongue, ending with a swirl around my clit that radiates out of every nerve ending in my body.

"*Fuck!* Connor—"

"Another time." His voice is slightly muffled, given that his mouth is very, very busy. "Just relax."

I give up and let my head drop back against the tree, my eyelids fluttering closed as I give myself over to the sensation of Connor's mouth licking and sucking and nipping. Only as I feel myself building back up to a crescendo do I realize I'm a fool to be missing out on the sight of him. I open my eyes to see that he's watching me too, his dark-blue eyes downright predatory.

A moan escapes my lips, and I quickly shove my hand in my mouth to muffle the sound. There's protection behind the trees for sure, but we're still outside, still in public, and "Oh, *fuck*." He's returned his fingers, and it's getting impossible to stifle my reactions, to stop my body from writhing against his lips and tongue. I can *feel* Connor smile smugly against my clit right before he sucks it into his mouth, curls his fingers, and makes me explode.

He's relentless with his dual erogenous assault, and waves of bliss rack my body in what feels like a never-ending ocean of orgasm. Weeks and weeks of stress and tension and misery come floating out of every extremity, fading into the night air on the chirps of crickets. When I finally can't take it anymore, I manage no more than a whimper to declare as such, but it's enough, and Connor pulls back.

We're both silent and still for a minute, just watching each other as we catch our breath, when a cool breeze swirls in and reminds me that I'm lying half-naked in half public. I push the skirt of my dress back down and ball up my underwear. I'm about to shove it in my pocket when in a burst of evil inspiration, I ask Connor, "Want 'em?"

He snorts. "I'm horny, not depraved."

Same old Connor. I can't help smiling as I shove them in my pocket. "Did you mean it?"

"Mean what?" he asks, subtly wiping off his mouth on his sleeve.

"When you said we'd fuck another time." I know I'm smirking, but I'm on such a high right now, I feel like I can say or do anything. "Because I'd like to make an appointment."

"You're incorrigible," Connor informs me, sitting back on his heels. Judging by the size of the hard-on threatening to bust through his khakis, he's not particularly mad.

"Use words like that and I might not return the favor," I say with a nod toward his groin.

He rolls his eyes and untucks his shirt to cover it. "You're not returning any 'favors' tonight, Elizabeth. I should go, and so should you."

I sigh. "We're back to 'Elizabeth' now?"

"I *like* the name Elizabeth," Connor informs me. "Multiple queens. Elizabeth Bennet. It's a good name."

"I hate Jane Austen."

"Of course you do." He says it as if I'm utterly absurd but then kisses me, deeply enough that I can taste myself on his tongue. "We'll talk about this later, okay?"

"You're really going to leave now?"

"Don't you have to get back to your brothers?"

I glance at my watch. "Holy shit." I had no idea how much time had passed. "Yes, I definitely do." I scramble to my feet, and Connor does the same. "And what are you in a rush for?"

He nods downward. "I've got business to take care of." He kisses me one more time, briefly, then walks to his car with what looks like a limp.

It takes all my self-control not to laugh as he seats himself in the car with a grimace and then waves briefly before pulling out of the lot and heading back to his apartment.

chapter eleven

It's amazing, the difference an earthshattering orgasm can make.

My English paper? Done. Stats homework? Ditto. Groceries? Replenished. Laundry? Spotless and put away, both mine and the boys'. I even got a pedicure over the weekend. A little sexual satisfaction and suddenly I'm Suzie Sophomore.

By the time I see Connor again in lecture on Tuesday, I actually feel like I can handle it. Granted, I do a lot of staring at the back of his head, and I obviously redress him—no man who can give head like that should be wearing a sweater vest—but I also listen during class. I take notes. I feel dates and events imprinting themselves on my brain.

I feel good.

"Remember, your papers on a topic relating to either of the first two Crusades is due a week from

Thursday. Please sign up for office hours with Mr. Lawson in order to discuss and confirm your paper topics."

With those final words, Professor Ozgur snaps his briefcase shut and moves out, and everyone else begins the shuffling process of gathering their books together and getting on line for the sign-up sheet. I take my time getting up there, because admittedly, I like checking him out when he's otherwise engaged, and I've got nowhere else to be just then.

I wait until the last guy on line files out, and then I take the signup sheet in hand. Slim pickins. I deliberately avoid conversation or even eye contact with Connor, because I'm so content right now, I don't want to give him an opportunity to ruin it. Instead, I stare at the sheet as if it'll tell me whether I prefer first thing on a Thursday morning or last thing next Thursday.

Connor sighs, walking up behind me and bracing a hand on the desk. "This is why it's a mistake for TAs to fool around with students," he says under his breath.

"I'm supposed to be here," I remind him, taking the Thursday morning slot; Max would wake me up by then anyway.

"Not because you're here. Because I just spent an hour-long lecture in a class I'm *supposed* to lead a discussion about tomorrow morning thinking about how gorgeous you look when you come."

149

Holy shit. "Jesus, Connor. Warn a girl before you completely soak her panties, would you?"

"Lizzie," he growls. It's not an intentionally sexy growl. He actually sounds pretty pissed. I'm tempted to bend over Professor Ozgur's desk to ask for punishment.

"Connor."

"I shouldn't have done that Friday night."

The bitter regret in his voice stings like nail polish remover in an open wound. "I'm so sorry you debased yourself in that fashion, Mr. Lawson. I feel terrible about the way I shoved your head between my thighs. Oh, wait."

"I didn't say you forced me," he says through gritted teeth. "I said I shouldn't have done it."

"Then why *did* you?" I demand, whirling around to face him.

"Because you needed it," he shoots back.

"Oh, great, so it was, like, a sympathy tongue-fuck? Awesome. I feel so much better now."

He winces, whether because of my crude word choice or spot-on accuracy, I don't know. Either way, I hope he feels half as shitty as I do right now. "Elizabeth—"

"Once again, Connor, fuck you." I hoist my messenger bag onto my shoulder. "I'll see you Thurdsay morning, bright and early. And if I show up looking like I just rolled out of somebody else's bed, I probably did."

I storm out of the classroom.

He doesn't call after me.

• • •

Of course, out of nowhere, the first thing Tyler asks me at dinner that night is, "So why'd Connor come by last week?"

"He wanted to drop off a paper." It's the truth. Sort of.

"Doesn't he hand those back in class?"

Ugh, when did my little brother stop being an idiot? "He was also...checking on the apartment," I improvise. "For Alan."

Tyler grins; there's pizza sauce on his teeth. "You are such a shitty liar."

"Ty!"

"Tyler said 'shitty,'" Max singsongs.

"Maxwell Christopher Brandt, don't even think about introducing that word into your vocabulary."

"He totally likes you," Ty continues, either unaware he's walking a thin line or spurred on by that knowledge. "Has he nailed you yet?"

"Ty!"

"Lizzie, what does 'nailed' mean?" Max's eyebrows scrunch up.

"Tyler, what the fuck is wrong with you?"

Max gasps. "You said 'fuck'!" he declares in a reverential whisper.

I stand up, bracing myself on the table, eyes narrowed. "Tyler, go to your room. Now. Seriously."

"You're the one who said 'fuck' in front of Max!"

"Go to your room *right now* or I'll call—"

I freeze. We all do. There isn't anyone to call. There isn't anyone on the other end of my parents' old phone numbers. I'm the highest authority right now, and I have no idea what I'm doing. I sink into my chair and drop my head in my hands. Whatever steam I had, I've lost it.

If a seven-year-old says "fuck" and he has no parents alive to hear it, does it really even matter?

We resume eating in silence, but nobody seems particularly hungry anymore. Finally, the boys trudge off to their room, leaving me to clean up the mess.

• • •

I'm not feeling any better about anything by the time I knock on Connor's office door first thing Thursday morning. On the bright side, I'm actually pretty well prepared for this paper, assuming my topic gets approved, but whatever calming effect that had disappears as soon as Connor's voice calls, "Come in."

I drop noisily into one of the chairs across from his desk and say, "I want to write about Byzantine influences on Russia. Can I go now?"

152

He flinches backward as if I've spat the words in his face. Maybe I did. I'm not really paying attention. I just want to get out of this tiny room, scene of my failed seduction. I can tell his recovery isn't as quick as he'd like, but he's quiet as he writes down my topic. "Do you need help figuring out where to begin with research?"

"This isn't my first paper," I bite out. "If you'll recall, I got an A on my last one. I think I'll be fine."

"You can stop hating me anytime now, Lizzie."

For some reason, this one time, I wish he'd called me Elizabeth. "Whatever, Connor. I had a really shitty past couple of days and I want to go back to bed."

His expression softens. "I really hope you understand I'm not trying to hurt you."

The stupid attempt at tenderness makes me snap, and I jump up from the chair. "This isn't about you! Not every fucking thing is about you! My parents are *dead*. It's possible I might give a little more of a shit about that than whether some game-playing asshole in an argyle sweater wants to fuck me that day."

I can physically see my rant knock all the wind out of him, wipe all the color from his face. Just like that, all my self-righteousness gives way to self-loathing, and I collapse back in the chair. "I'm sorry," I manage quietly. "That was an awful thing to say."

"Yeah, it really was."

We sit in silence, the last vestiges of my rage radiating off me in waves. Finally, he asks, "Do you want to talk about it?"

"No. I mean, yes, but not with you. I'm having coffee with Cait and Frankie later."

He nods, and the room goes quiet again. I can't stand it, so I force myself to give a little. "Just having a little trouble keeping my family under control."

"Do you need help?"

I laugh shortly. "You need to stop that, Connor. You can't be in my life just for the white knight moments."

"So I'm just supposed to let you drown in all this?"

"Yes, if the alternative is stepping in and giving mixed messages to everyone in sight," I say firmly. "You know what Ty and I fought about the other night? You."

"Me?"

"He asked if you were nailing me yet."

He massages his temples. "*Crisse*. Did I talk like that when I was thirteen?"

"You probably had no idea what sex was when you were thirteen, history nerd."

He drops his hands back into his lap and his lips curve up at the corners. I can't help mirroring his tiny smile. "I think you underestimate how closely I studied the life of Anne Boleyn. Don't be fooled by my Byzantine-loving exterior."

"You mean, you weren't always the diehard Alexios Komnenos devotee you are now?"

"Shocking but true. Byzantine history was a passion I mostly developed in college, in fact."

"So you're saying I could be you in five years?"

"If you're lucky."

We both smile again, and I know it's time to go; get a move on while things are calm and pleasant without being sexually fraught. I stand up. "So my topic's okay?"

"Your topic is fine."

"Great." I smile briefly. "Then I'll see you in class tomorrow."

I watch him hesitate, but then he nods. "Yes, Elizabeth. I'll see you then."

• • •

I'm early to meet Cait and Frankie, but I have reading to do anyway, so I get my caramel macchiato and grab a table in the corner. Not that I can focus on a single thing I'm reading. My eyes keep blurring the words. What *happens* when Connor goes home at night? Why are we kissing one night, then fighting the next day? Practically screwing one night and more fighting the next day? Where does all that progress *go*?

I'm still contemplating this when Frankie and Cait come bounding through the door, Frankie in the brightest peacock-esque scarf-and-jacket combo humanly possible, and Cait in her typical all-black. They look made to contrast, to be seen together at all times. Meanwhile, I'm still wearing the yoga pants and zip-up I'd worn to meet Connor. Next to them, I feel like a troll.

Never one to ignore such things, Cait immediately asks, "Did you go to the gym today?"

"Early meeting with my TA," I grumble, wrapping my hands around the cooling mug of macchiato. "Who the hell has office hours at 8:00 a.m.?"

"Hot TA?" asks Frankie, shedding her coat.

I wonder if Frankie would get mad if I punched her in the face.

"How's tutoring going, anyway?" Cait asks as she unwraps her scarf and sets it aside. "Is it helping?"

"Doesn't compare to your assistance with Stats," I reply, knowing it'll successfully change the subject.

Cait does not disappoint. "Well, obviously. No one compares to me. Did I tell you guys I'm starting next game? You better be in the front row, bitches."

"Ooh, will Nora be there? I'm totally in if she is."

"Frankie. No. I already told you my teammates are off limits."

"Come on! Isn't she, like, second string? What difference does it make?"

As they go back and forth about lacrosse and Frankie's next target, my mind drifts back to Connor. He'd said he wasn't trying to hurt me, and I knew in my heart that was true, but it didn't stop it from happening, over and over again. But maybe he wasn't the problem. Maybe I was. After all, Connor had almost been entirely been responding to my sadness, my neediness—I was the one constantly asking him favors, letting him see me cry, generally falling to pieces in front of him. Maybe what I thought was a mutual attraction actually *was* a series of sympathy gestures.

Holy shit, it *was.* How had I not seen that before? Was I so clouded by grief and lust that I didn't realize I was throwing myself at someone who only spent time with me out of some misguided sense of responsibility?

"*Hey.* Brandt. Where the hell are you?"

I blink. And wonder how long Cait's been snapping in my face. "Sorry," I murmur, grabbing a menu to hide my face. "Just...spacing. I need my coffee."

"No kidding," says Frankie with a snort. "Jesus, I thought you were in a fucking k-hole or something."

"Please, I've barely even had a drink since my brothers moved in with me," I remind her.

"Well that's just unacceptable. Caitlin, I think it's time we take this young lady to a party."

Cait rolls her eyes. "I don't think Lizzie's really up for partying these days, Frank."

"Ouch." Not that I've really had any time for parties lately, and attending them definitely goes against the whole plan to clean up my act for my brothers, but somehow, the comment stings. "You don't think I'm fun anymore?"

"I didn't say you're not fun," Cait says carefully. "I just...didn't think you had any interest in going to parties anymore."

I don't, I know I should say, but the thing is, right now, I do. I'd kill for a night of drinking with my friends again, though my friends are definitely fewer in number these days. The idea of a casual, no-strings-attached hook-up with a guy who has nothing but sex on his mind and absolutely no requirements under the Radleigh University moral code to abstain from me suddenly sounds glorious.

Why had I ever gotten involved with Connor in the first place? It wasn't as if my life needed *more* complications. He was just a guy who was nice to me, who'd helped me, and now I had an apartment, and my car, and my brothers were in school and in therapy, and I was caught up on my classes. He'd served his purpose, and he'd made pretty clear he wasn't interested in serving any others.

Frankly, a party sounded like the perfect way to celebrate all the things that were finally going right and forget the one thing that had gone temporarily off course.

"Actually, I think a party sounds great," I say confidently. "Ty can babysit. What's happening this weekend?"

Cait and Frankie exchange a glance, and I know what Frankie's going to say an instant before the words come out of her mouth. "There's a Sigma Psi party on Friday, but—"

"Perfect," I say, because it has to be. Because I need to get a little of the old me back. Because Trevor and I are even, and in the massive sea of people that always floods their house at parties, what are the odds he'd even notice me? "I'll meet you guys at the suite and we can all go together."

I know they want to make an excuse to get out of being seen with me there, but they're good friends, so they don't. And I'm a lousy friend, so I don't offer an out.

I'm going to this party, and I'm coming back the Lizzie Brandt I used to be before my life fell apart.

chapter twelve

It's been so long since I've been to the Sigma Psi house—or a party—that the first step inside is a physically painful assault on my senses. The music, which is always a mix of hip hop, electronica, and whatever the guys think will get them laid the fastest, used to fade into the background for me almost immediately. Now it makes my ears hurt and my heart pound uncomfortably in time with the bass.

"I need a drink," I announce, clutching Cait's forearm. A drink or three should take me back to normal. Nobody's noticed me yet, but eventually, someone will, and it probably won't be pretty. I can't be *this* off my game when it happens.

"Ditto," Cait mutters, and I follow her eyeline to a vaguely familiar looking guy. I don't remember ever seeing him with Cait, but in a flash I realize he's probably the guy she kicked out of the suite for calling me a bitch. I squeeze her arm.

Thankfully, Frankie springs into action, twirling over to Doug Leach, the Sigma Psi Recruitment Chair she makes out with occasionally. He's sort of obsessed with her, but isn't stupid enough to think she has any interest beyond keeping him in her makeout harem. Still, we all know he'll do anything she asks, and sure enough, one hand on his arm and glimpse down her shirt and he's off toward the keg.

"You are terrible to that boy," Cait says when Frankie triumphantly returns to us with three red Solo cups of beer in hand.

"Oh, I am not. I let him touch my boobs when we make out now. Trust me, he's a happy camper." She flips her long chestnut curls over her shoulder, the blue and purple stripes of her hair chalk catching the light. "So, do you want—"

"Lizzie Brandt. No shit."

The three of us whirl around to see Jason Pollard, Trevor's vice president, grinning like a fox. Trevor hates him—something I know from those stupid confidences you share in the afterglow of sex, whether you like your partner or not—and I wonder now if it's mutual, because Jason seems awfully happy to see me.

Or maybe it's malicious glee curling his lips. It all looks the same to me, really. Tough call. "In the flesh," I say breezily.

"You look good." His eyes rake me up and down, and you'd think I was wearing Saran wrap rather than jeans and a tank top. "Really good."

"Doesn't she?" Frankie fawns, throwing an arm around my neck, her bangles jangling. "I'd kill for those tits."

I roll my eyes, but in my mind, I'm making out with Frankie right now. That girl is the best confidence booster ever.

"They are great tits," Jason agrees, his eyes glued to them as he takes a long swallow of beer.

For no good reason, I try to imagine Connor saying something that crude, and snort. *Whoops*. Jason raises an eyebrow and Cait and Frankie turn to look at me. "Nice line," I say wryly, banishing Connor from my brain, and take a drink of my own.

Doug joins us then, wrapping an arm around Frankie's waist and whispering something in her ear that makes her laugh. Cait and I exchange a "Doug's getting more than boob tonight" eye roll, and then Frank flutterwaves goodbye before letting Doug lead her away.

"I'm gonna go say hi to Tessa," says Cait with a sigh, and then she's gone, which just makes Jason leer harder.

"So, Lizzie." He slides an arm around my waist, slips his hand in my back pocket, gives my ass a squeeze. The gesture makes me want to knee him in the balls, but I don't. Because this is what partying was like before That Night, and before Connor, and I used to enjoy this, and all I want is to get that back. "You wanna—"

"My sloppy seconds, Pollard? Really?"

Trevor's voice cuts through the room. If people didn't notice me there before, they sure do now. Fuck. Coming here was such a stupid idea.

I pull away from Jason, but I have no intention of backing down from Trevor. I haven't seen his face since That Night, but looking at it now I see everything that is sad and hateful in my life. He is apathy and loss and death and I am…I don't know what.

But I do know that I'm all out of people to answer to, and maybe that's what makes me fearless now.

"So I'm your sloppy seconds now, am I?" I step away from Jason, closer to Trevor, and make no effort to keep my voice down. "That's funny, because I could swear I heard we'd never hooked up, never even met before that night."

"Yeah, well, apparently you had a bigger mouth than I realized. You'd think it'd help you give better head."

There are snickers and "burn!"s and "ohhhh"s all throughout the room, but I just roll my eyes. If ever there were an arena where I don't doubt my skills…. "Please. Like I'd take oral advice from a guy who wouldn't go down if it were a graduation requirement.

Not that I believe for a fucking second you had any complaints. Jesus, Trev, doesn't lying get exhausting? Or are you just so naturally hardwired to be a complete and total piece of shit that it's effortless at this point?"

Trevor's eyes blaze with fury; it's obvious he didn't expect me to stick up for myself, and he's fresh out of eighth-grade insults. "What the fuck is wrong with you?" he growls. "What the fuck are you even doing in my house? No one invited you here. No one wants you here."

Behind me, Jason is conspicuously silent. Guess my tits aren't that great.

Another voice, however, calls out, "I invited her, actually." We all turn to look. Doug shrugs, and I know in a second he's gonna get laid for this bit of chivalry. I silently pray for Frankie to get multiple orgasms in thanks. "Sorry. Didn't realize it was a thing."

Frankie yanks his head down to hers and shoves her tongue down his throat. Everyone laughs and catcalls, and Doug gives a thumbs-up as she mauls him. Even I have to smile at that.

"Just get out," Trevor orders me wearily. "Get out, and don't come back here. We used to fuck, and now we're done, and unless you're looking for one last hurrah…."

"Never in a million years."

"Good," he says coldly, as if he isn't fucking dying for it. "Then you're fresh out of business here."

He's got me there; there's really no point in my being at the house now. I'm not going to dance. I'm not going to hook up. I'm done drinking. I don't even *want* to be here with these people.

I want to be with Connor.

But Connor doesn't want to be with me. I'm no more to him than I am to Trevor. He might not treat me like a piece of gum stuck to his shoe, but the fact remains the same—I'm alone. And that's not changing anytime soon.

I shrug. "When you're right, you're right."

And then I turn to leave.

There's some jeering behind me as I go, but as I think about spending another night alone in my bed while Trevor parties here like some kind of hero before bringing some bimbo back to his room, the injustice of it all hits me like a double shot of tequila, and I whirl back around.

"No, you know what? I do have one last piece of business here," I spit at Trevor. "Even if I *were* a stranger who'd just shown up in your room that night, I'd deserve better. But I wasn't. We'd been fooling around for *months*, and you were *right* next to me when the cops came to tell me my parents had been killed. How the fuck do you not call, not care, not *anything*?"

He pales but doesn't respond, and I know that at least I'm not completely insane. He should've cared.

He should've called. Not because I was his fuck-buddy but because I'm a fucking *person*.

But other than Cait and Frankie, only one other person on campus has been treating me like one. Or at least he had until recently. Now I was just some sort of disposable problem to him too. How and when had that even happened? And *why*?

For the millionth time that week, I wonder what the hell happens when Connor goes home at night, to turn him from the guy who couldn't keep his hands off me at my apartment to the guy who hid from me in his office. From the guy who came back to my home, who went down on me by the parking lot, to the guy who said Never Again.

There are no answers to be had to my question for Trevor, but it doesn't really matter; we're out of each other's lives now, for good.

But I'm going to get at least one answer tonight. And I'm going to get it now.

• • •

"Open the door, Connor," I call, wincing at the sound of my voice echoing loudly in the hallway. "I know you're in there." I bang on the door again.

Finally, I hear a fumbling on the other side, and then there he is, in a Montreal Canadiens T-shirt and flannel pajama pants, his expression warring between panic and rage. "What are you doing here, Elizabeth?"

he whispers fiercely, yanking me inside and shoving the door closed behind me.

"What happens at night?" I demand. "What happens that makes you forget that you actually enjoy hanging out with me? How is it that I left that first kiss thinking, 'Man, I can't wait to take this further with Connor tomorrow,' and you left it thinking, 'This is a terrible thing that can never happen again'? What happens at night that erases everything that happened that day?"

"Elizabeth—"

"*Tell* me, Connor. I can't deal with any other men on this campus screwing with me. If this is all in my head, you need to be man enough to tell me that. If you're coming back here to somebody else, you need to be man enough to tell me that. Now answer the fucking question."

"What happens at night?" he repeats, and I nod. He exhales sharply, raking a hand through dark-brown hair that's grown just this side of unruly before scrubbing it over his scruffy jaw. "What happens is that I come back here, and I'm lonely, and then, inevitably, I think of you. What you probably think of the outfit I wore that day. How genuinely Max makes you laugh. The glimmer of excitement you get in your eyes when an idea clicks. The way you nibble on the earpiece of your glasses when you're writing. It makes me feel like I see what the old you must've looked like."

My stomach clenches at his words, but before I can say anything, he marches onward, an edge of steel creeping into his tone.

"Then I think of that very first kiss, and how you tasted like grape lollipop. How soft the skin is on your lower back. I think of the way you sigh when I suck your neck in just the right place. The infuriatingly sexy whimper-moan thing you make when I bite your lip. That was bad enough. Now, thanks to my incredible stupidity last week, I jerk off while thinking about how sweet you taste. Every. Fucking. Night."

I all but collapse against his doorpost as I try to take it all in, this awful night suddenly doing a complete one-eighty. "Holy crap, Connor. You…really like me." There are a million hummingbirds in my insides right now, doing some sort of awkward mating dance.

He raises an eyebrow, his face a neon "Are you an idiot?" sign. "You say that like you had no idea. I've been telling you that every day."

"No, you haven't." I'm sure of this fact. I burn with certainty. Because it's what I've been dying to know, and if he'd given me even an inch, I would've leapt on it like a jungle cat. "All you ever say is 'we can't do this.'"

He laughs. It's mirthless. "Why do you think it matters so much to me that we stop? You think I'm just scared of getting caught? At the risk of sounding like a dick, trust me when I say that if all I wanted was for us to fuck each other's brains out for a night, I would've brought you back here the second you kissed me in my office, and we would've gotten away with it. I don't push you away because I'm afraid of getting caught one night."

He sounds so utterly unlike himself, caustic and coarse, and for the first time, my own tipsy brain processes that I'm not the only one who's had more than one drink tonight.

"The problem is, I don't want just one night. And I don't think you do either. Do you?"

I want anything you're willing to give, I think but don't say. *I want you inside me. Tonight. Every night.* The thought makes me shudder, and I don't know if it's just because I'm full of emotion or, as I suspect, because I like that Connor wants more than a night with me. And he's right that I want more than one with him. "If I say yes, can we go to bed?"

To my utter shock, he cracks an actual smile. Not showing teeth, of course, but it's not a stern "Lizzie" or even "Elizabeth." It's almost like he has a sense of humor. Almost.

"Is that a yes?" My eyebrows shoot skyward. I'd been bluffing, but if Connor's suddenly down to get down....

He rolls his eyes, but snorts a laugh. "No, it's not a yes. I just...*maudit*, you're good at making me smile."

169

He shakes his head, and his expression goes serious, his dark-blue eyes fixing on mine. "I like you very much, Lizzie Brandt," he says soberly. "I'm sorry if I haven't said it that way, or made it feel that way. And I'm sorry it doesn't matter that I feel that way."

I've experienced a lot of pain in the past few months—hell, just tonight alone. Excruciating, unbearable pain. And while nothing will ever compare to losing my parents, his words make me ache in places I didn't even know could feel.

"What happens at night?" I ask again, softly this time. "When you've done your fantasizing, and gotten off, and all of that's behind you and you can think. What happens?"

He sighs, raking a hand through his already rumpled hair. "I feel like a fucking pervert, if you want to know the truth."

"Connor—"

"You are *eighteen*—"

"For another six weeks!"

"And I'm twenty-five. And your teacher. I'm supposed to be someone you can trust."

"Okay, in case you haven't noticed, there isn't anyone I trust *more* than you in the entire world. Don't you get that? Don't you realize how supremely screwed up I would be without you? You listen to me. You've helped my grades. You found me an apartment—"

"And I shouldn't have done that. I overstepped my boundaries as your teaching assistant. I was only supposed to tutor you. That's *all*."

I can't believe I'm hearing this now; I thought we were past all *that* shit, at least. "Christ, Connor, do you have to be such a fucking martyr? You did those things before you even liked me!"

Another brief, mirthless laugh. Another disbelieving, self-loathing-riddled shake of his head. "No, I didn't."

"Yes—"

"Lizzie, I'm telling you. No, I didn't."

I'm stunned into silence, but only for a few moments. My desperation to know the truth wins out. "When? Why?"

"The first day. You wore a miniskirt, and you have fantastic legs. And your glasses. You look so fucking sexy in those glasses. You were kind of hard to miss."

"Thinking I'm hot isn't—"

"You sat down and made some joke that made everyone around you crack up. Then Hudson Roberts made a sleazy comment about you being exotic and you told him to go fuck himself gently with a chainsaw." He takes a deep breath, and then a faint, fond smile quirks his lips. "You kept pretending not to give a shit, but you were sneaking glances from your phone to the blackboard, not the other way around. I know what it looks like when someone loves to learn, and no matter how much you try to hide it, you do, Elizabeth. So yeah, you were on my radar from day one."

"Connor...." I don't even know what to say. The hummingbirds are frantic now, beating against my heart, my lungs, my spleen.

"Do you know how much it kills me that after years and years of dating 'appropriate' girls—family friends, and fellow grad students, and girls I've met at the library—I've fallen for an eighteen-year-old student who chain smokes?"

"I've stopped that," I point out meekly.

"I noticed. For me?"

"For a few reasons. You might be one of them."

He scratches at his chest, and I wonder if he feels the same ache there that I do. His gaze wanders off to some point in the distance, and I know in my gut that we're not done with the pain-inflicting portion of the evening yet. "Then there are the nights I convince myself the age difference isn't so bad, and I won't be your TA anymore in a month anyway, and I know in my gut I've never given you a grade you didn't deserve."

"So...in a month, then?" That seems to be what he's saying, and if so, I can handle that. I know I can, if I know we'll be together at the end of it. But his face isn't saying "in a month." Not his sad eyes, or his firmly pressed lips.

He can't even meet my gaze when he responds, sounding utterly gutted. "In a month, you'll still be a guardian to two kids, and no matter what else we can get past, I'm not sure I'm ready…for that."

"Oh." All the hummingbirds bite it at the same time. Just like that, I'm a leaky balloon, all my air sapping into the ether. I have nothing more to say; that part isn't changing anytime soon.

"I know I'm an asshole," he mumbles, and in that instant, I can't help feeling how stupid it is that age gap has ever been an issue. Because in this, Connor can be a child. I have no choice but to be an adult. "But…*osti de tabarnac de calice*. I'm not even mature enough to stop myself from fooling around with one of my students. And it's not like I've had a great role model when it comes to fatherhood. How can I—"

"Yeah," I interrupt, suddenly finding it hard to breathe in his tiny apartment. "I get it. I gotta go."

"Lizzie—"

"There's nothing left to say. Just stop." There's nothing to grab, nothing to do but whirl around and run from Connor's apartment, back to my own, back to the two boys who depend on me to be their everything.

chapter thirteen

I barely sleep at all that night, and in the morning, Tyler and Max refuse to do me the small courtesy of getting themselves ready. Instead, it's a bitchfest of "Why is there no bacon or waffles?" when I hand them boxes of cereal, and "Where's my blue shirt?" to remind me I haven't done the laundry in over a week.

It's almost as if they're trying to prove Connor's point. "Of course he doesn't wanna deal with us" is the obvious subtext of Tyler's complaining his cereal bowl is sticky. "What twenty-five-year-old guy would sign up for this?" is implicit in Max's refusal to wear a raincoat even though it's already pouring outside.

By the time I get the boys to school, I'm too exhausted to go back to sleep. Instead, I nurse a mug of coffee through a crappy morning talk show I can barely hear over the pounding rain. Then I start on a second cup to do my reading for English lit. It's amazing how many more hours there are in the day for the boring stuff, now that I'm not sleeping off hangovers or wasting another morning in Trevor's bed while he pokes me—no hands!—for another round.

The mere thought of Trevor's familiar morning wood makes me squirm on the couch. Not because Trev was so great in bed—he was okay at best; he staunchly refused to go down, then had a hissyfit because I countered by refusing the same—but because frankly, I need to get laid.

Connor's Magic Orgasm wore out right around when he did.

I pull out my phone and text Cait. *We're going out tonight. Off campus.*

It takes her an hour to text me back—at least one of us got to sleep in—but when she does, it's with emphatic agreement.

I'm a woman on a mission, and tonight, failure is not an option.

• • •

"Yowza!" Cait and Frankie whistle at me when I meet them in the parking lot, painstakingly made up and dressed to kill. "You are going to destroy tonight," says Frankie.

"That's the plan." I smile smugly, settling into the backseat of her Prius. My outfit is a never-fail. It's just a plain black sheath, really—one that hugs my curves and stops at mid-thigh. But it's the glasses that make it work. And the stiletto Mary Janes.

Some guys love toned, athletic, Amazonian blondes; Cait eats them for breakfast. Some guys like the freaky artist type, figuring she'll be great in bed; from what I hear, Frankie never disappoints.

But if you're one of those guys with a sexy librarian fetish? I am your walking wet dream. And the fact that I know Connor's one of those guys gives me a flash of vengeful satisfaction I can barely tamp down.

Delta is a stupid bar with a stupid name, but they're tough on fake IDs and after that last disaster of a party, I know I don't want to see anyone else from Radleigh tonight. Cait, Frank, and I all have real IDs— they're just not ours. They were pricey, but worth every penny for a night like this when you just wanna disappear.

Tonight's bouncer is a Frankie boy, and he only half-ass glances at our IDs because he's too busy trying to see if she's wearing a bra underneath her filmy tunic. (She isn't.)

Inside, it's surprisingly busy, or maybe I just haven't done this on a Friday night in a while. Either way, we have to do a whole lot of pushing and squeezing to get to the bar, but at least the male population doesn't seem to mind.

"Three lemon drops," Cait orders on our behalf, because she has no shame about being a walking cliché.

I've actually always liked about Delta that they have a pretty extensive scotch menu; it reminds me of my dad, and how he used to sneak me sips. If Cait and Frankie weren't here, I'd probably order Glenfidditch—his favorite—but they are, so we "cheers" with our sweet-and-sour drinks and I laugh like I'm not at all thinking about how my dad will never see me turn legal.

"All right, Brandt," Cait declares after we've all taken a couple of sips. "What's your pleasure tonight?"

"Hmm...." I think of Connor, with his desperately-in-need-of-a-tan skin and those twilight-sky eyes. "I'm thinking dark. Dark and maybe tattooed. Definitely no one from the university." I cock my head to size up the guy who just served us our drinks. I've never hooked up with a guy with a shaved head before. "What do you think of the bartender?"

"Jamie's fucked him," Frankie says with a shrug. She takes another sip. "She said he was okay. Bald everywhere, if ya know what I mean."

"No, Frank, please crack that code."

"Hey, be nice or I'm not helping," she says petulantly, but she grins. "Okay. Dark. Either tatted or dirty, at four o'clock. No, wait, eight o'clock." She stops, frowns, looks down at her chunky plastic watch. "Make that five—no, wait.... Oh, shit, he just started grinding on some chick."

I toss back the rest of my drink and call the bartender back for a second round. This time, it's a cosmo for Cait, Manhattan for Frankie—she likes the color—and Long Island iced tea for me. I'm just taking my first sip, hoping the copious amounts of alcohol will dull my brain, when Frankie says, "Hey, isn't that your TA?"

I straight-up choke on my drink. "Which TA?" I manage around coughs, even though I know full well I only have one Frankie would recognize. Why the hell does he have to be here, tonight of all nights?

Then again, maybe he needs to drink away last night's encounter as much as I do.

"Hottie Historian. Over there." She gestures eagerly with her glass down the bar, her enamel bracelets making a racket as they clink against each other. Connor's deep in conversation with a guy who looks vaguely familiar from campus. He's actually kind of hot, in a preppy, Cape Cod-esque kind of way that's totally not my style.

Which gives me a terribly wicked idea.

"Hey!" I flag down the bartender. "Can you send a drink to a guy for me?" I ignore Cait and Frankie's whistles and catcalling and press on. "See the guy down there in the white shirt, with the blond crew cut? Send him a…what's the dirtiest, most blunt drink name you have?"

"We've got the One-Night Stand, and the Fuckbuddy."

"Send him a Fuckbuddy," Cait declares

authoritatively.

"From me," I add pointedly to the bartender. "This isn't an offer for a fourgy."

The bartender grins. "You got it." I watch in nervous anticipation as he mixes Campari with gin and vodka, turning it all a lusty red. Then he knots two cherries together for garnish.

Cute.

My eyes are locked on the scene of the bartender presenting the prepster with the drink. Connor's friend tilts his head to get a better look, then lifts the Fuckbuddy with what he unquestionably thinks is an irresistible smile. I lift my iced tea in response and offer my own smile, and then wait patiently for Connor to turn around and see who's sent his friend a drink.

The glass-melting fury in his eyes when he spots me with my drink in the air and a smirk on my face is worth every penny of the drink just added to my tab.

I know this is where I wait for the prepster to join us, but I'm just not that patient. Instead, I slide off my stool, sucking my straw between pursed lips, and make my way over. "Hi there," I greet him, letting the words roll off my tongue like honey while I ignore Connor completely. My voice seems to have taken on a southern accent, and I go with it. "I'm Scarlett."

"Perfect name for a southern belle," he says, lifting my free hand to his lips. Connor snorts, and we both pretend not to hear. "I'm Brandon."

"Perfect name for a Yankee gentleman," I drawl, enjoying myself immensely. "How's the drink? It's been a while since I've had a good Fuckbuddy."

Now it's Connor who chokes on his drink, so loudly both Brandon and I instinctively turn to look.

"You all right over there, Lawson?" Brandon sounds genuinely concerned. It only makes me smirk harder.

"Fine," Connor croaks.

"Scarlett, this is Connor," Brandon says politely, indeed a Yankee gentleman. "He and I go way back."

"So nice to meet you," I say sweetly. Connor stares at my outstretched hand as if he wants to spit on it, though judging by the way his gaze roves down my entire body when he finally takes it and pumps it, just once, he's got other uses in mind for it too. He is pissed, but that's not strictly anger burning in his expression; I recognize that lust from the night we first kissed. For a moment, I regret this plan. I want Brandon to disappear so Connor can yank me into the men's room and throw me up against a wall.

Then his words from the night before sink back into my brain, and I decide to twist the knife a little further.

I turn to Brandon. "I was just about to head out back for a cigarette. Care to join me?"

"He doesn't smoke," Connor answers for him, his voice hard as nails.

"Doesn't mean I can't keep the lady company." Brandon pushes the drink I bought him in front of Connor's face and says, "Here. You need a good Fuckbuddy even more than I do." Then he hops up, pats Connor on the head, and wraps an arm around my waist to escort me out back.

With the heated rage emanating from Connor as we go, I'm not even sure I'll need my trusty lighter.

• • •

Brandon and I are outside for no more than five minutes when Connor storms outside, just as I'm showing off my skills with smoke rings. (And by skills I mean my ability to get guys staring at my mouth while thinking I'm both sexy and adorable for not being able to produce said rings, no matter how strongly I insist I can. They're so dumb.) "Okay, Lizzie," he snaps. "That's enough. You've had your fun."

"Oh, chill out, Connor." I blow a steady stream of smoke in his direction. "Your friend and I are getting to know each other."

"What happened to your accent? And who's Lizzie?" Poor Brandon.

Connor sighs. "She has no accent, and she shouldn't be here. Go home, Elizabeth. Take your underage friends with you."

"We're not in class, *Mr. Lawson*. You can't tell me what to do."

"Class?" Brandon looks terrified now, as if Connor teaches high school. "What the—"

"Go inside, Brandon," Connor says tightly. "I'll handle this."

Brandon could not have moved faster if I'd held my lighter to his ass.

"Put that out," Connor says tiredly as soon as Brandon's gone.

"Say please."

Connor's not amused. He storms over, snatches the cigarette from my hands, and extinguishes it against the stone wall of the back patio. "You need to go home."

"No, Connor, I don't. What I need is to get laid. And since you've made it very clear that you're not up for that task, I'm taking my ladyparts elsewhere."

"To Brandon."

"To I don't give a shit who," I snap. "Why should I? As you so thoughtfully reminded me last night, I probably won't have a boyfriend for the next eleven or so years. So I can turn into a nun, or I can meaningless-fuck my way through my brothers' minority years. Which one sounds like more fun to you?"

"I didn't say—"

"Yes, you did." I walk right up to him and smooth his collar; he flinches at my touch, and I smile. "You like me, Connor. You have for months. Unless you were lying when you told me that, which would just be incredibly stupid."

His jaw tightens as I trace my finger down the buttons of his shirt, along the metal of his belt buckle.

"And you want me," I continue, lowering my voice as I snake my finger along his waistband, around to his back, and up his spine before lightly tickling his nape. "I bet you're thinking of bending me over that wall, shoving up my skirt, and burying yourself inside me. Right. This. Second."

He doesn't say a word, doesn't move a muscle, but I can see his jaw clenching.

"All that," I murmur, sliding my hand up through his hair, sifting the soft brown strands through my fingers, "and you know I'm willing. You know how hot you make me. How incredibly wet. Hell, you've tasted it. Buried your fingers and tongue inside me and made me come so hard. Remember that?"

He's fighting an impossible battle with himself, and it's got him in a sweat, but he still doesn't break. His nostrils are flaring, his breathing unsteady, but the fists at his sides aren't unclenching to reach for me.

Not that I thought they would.

I inject my voice with as much acid as possible. "And even so, you still don't want to be with me. So who the fuck ever will?" I stalk past him, letting my shoulder ram into his arm as I do, and march back inside.

He catches up with me as soon as I get through the door and whirls me around. "Do you think this is easy for me?"

"I don't give a shit what's easy for you," I hiss back. "You're the one who has all the choices in life, and you made yours. Now I'm just making the few left that I can."

"Like which stranger to fuck in a bar?"

"Like which stranger to fuck in a bar."

"And you just naturally chose the one who would hurt me most?"

"What difference does it make?" I ask, crossing my arms.

"That you're trying to hurt me?"

"You *did* hurt me," I snap. "You do or do not; there is no try. And if the specifics of who I fuck bother you—"

"You fucking *anyone* else bothers me," he whispers back fiercely, far louder than he should. He knows it, too; immediately, he presses his lips together, blocking out whatever else he was gonna say.

"So I just shouldn't, then," I say coldly. "You don't want me, but you don't want anyone else to have me. That's perfect, Connor. Please, tell me—how goddamn lonely do I need to be to make you happy? Because I am at the rock bottom of solitude and you still don't seem too thrilled."

My voice breaks bitterly and I'm horrified to realize that tears are stinging my eyes. As if he has some sort of damsel-in-distress radar triggers by a woman's weeping, a bouncer suddenly sticks his head into the back vestibule. "Is everything okay, miss?" He looks at Connor suspiciously.

"Fine, thank you," I say with what I hope is a grateful smile. It's hard to see his reaction through blurred eyes.

"I'm gonna take her home," Connor adds.

The bouncer looks back at me. "That right, miss?"

I blink to clear my vision, then glance at Connor, who's wearing a completely neutral expression. I don't want to let him win, but I also don't want to be here anymore. Then, suddenly, I feel it—the slightest brush of warm fingertips on my palm—and I nod.

We both know I'm not going home with anyone else tonight.

• • •

The ride home is completely silent. We don't exchange a single word as we get out of the car, nor when we walk to my apartment, nor when he follows me inside, first through the front door and then into my bedroom.

It isn't until I've closed the door behind me and dropped onto my bed that he finally speaks.

"I never want you to be lonely," he says hoarsely, leaning back against the door. "I've spent so many years feeling that way, and it sucks. I never want that for you." He scratches a hand through his hair. "I was wrong. I'm sorry. I know I can't have things both ways."

He looks exhausted, and broken, and I feel like shit for everything I put him through tonight. It's not his fault he doesn't want to be with someone who comes with tween-boy baggage. Hell, I don't want to be somebody who *has* tween-boy baggage. Would I be doing this if my grandmother were lucid, or my aunt were sober, or Nancy didn't have infinite amounts of her own shit to deal with?

"You can't," I agree quietly. "I'm sorry too. But my life can't be quietly pining after you. There's too much pain inside me already."

They might be the most honest words I've ever said, and I hate how vulnerable they make me sound. He must too, because he pushes off from the door and comes to sit down next to me.

"I know," he says softly, so softly, as softly as he tucks one of my wild waves behind my ear. "I know."

I don't know who kisses whom—our bodies just melt together, lips joining to complete a circuit that lights up the room, the city, the world. It's not fast and furious like the first time. It's gentle but needy, as if someone had just dived underwater and affixed a regulator to my mouth at the exact right instant to save me from drowning.

It's everything.

I don't know how long we kiss for, or at what

point we lie down, or when we get under the covers, or how we commit to the fact that Connor is staying the night, but all of it happens, without us ever taking off a stitch of clothing or saying a word.

I'm halfway to dreamland, Connor's arm wrapped firmly around my waist, his warm chest pressed against my back, when he sleepily mumbles, "You look obscene in that outfit, by the way." I smile into my pillow as I drift off completely.

When I wake up, I'm alone, and I know he's made his choice.

chapter fourteen

A tiny part of me is relieved for my empty bed; I have no interest in or answers to any of Tyler's potential questions. And at least I feel well rested when Ty and Max bitch about another morning of cereal.

"Are we having cereal for Thanksgiving, too?" Ty grumbles.

"Dude, stop making it sound like Mom provided some sort of continental breakfast every morning. You ate plenty of cereal when she was the one feeding you." Then his words sink in. "Oh, sh-darn. Thanksgiving."

"You forgot?" Ty asks flatly. Max looks as if he's about to cry.

"Of course not," I lie. As if a holiday I have no desire to celebrate has penetrated my consciousness for even a second. Thanksgiving used to be my favorite, but that's when my mom made the turkey, my dad made the stuffing, and Nancy made sweet potato pie with perfectly browned marshmallows. "I just have to talk to Nancy."

"Are we going home?" Max asks.

This is home now, I think but don't say. "I don't know yet. Do you want to? Ty?"

"I don't know," Ty mumbles.

"I don't either," I admit. I scoop a handful of Cheerios from the box and crush one between my front teeth. "Max?"

"I wanna see Pete."

Pete is Nancy's beagle.

"I guess I wanna see Jake and Robbie," Ty says with a shrug. "And Amy. She texts me sometimes to say hi. She's cool."

Christ, I am selfish. I spend so much time thinking about how hard this is on me, and completely miss how hard it's been on them. Even though the thought of Thanksgiving without my parents—and at their house—guts me, I say, "Okay, then we'll go home."

"And you'll make turkey?" Max asks.

"And stuffing," I promise, though I have no idea when. Or how.

I'm not really sure what I'm getting myself into, but when Max smiles wide, and Ty says, "Okay, cool," I know I have to try.

• • •

I might've been unimpressively behind on the whole Thanksgiving thing, but it was pretty much the only topic of conversation come classes on Monday. Even Russian was devoted to the vocabulary of *Dyen Blogodoreya*, our assignments to write about our plans for the holiday and our favorite traditions. Not that I particularly wanted to dwell on any of those.

Even Cait and Frankie are psyched to go home, which for Cait is Burlington, Vermont, and for Frankie is some tiny town in Western Massachusetts, where she swears riding cows was a typical weekend activity when she was in high school. They try to assure me it'll be nice to go back to Pomona, but I can't imagine how.

I'm not in touch with any of my high school friends anymore, not even the few who came to my parents' funeral. I'm looking forward to seeing Nancy, but to being in my parents' house without them? Not so much.

The one perk of going home is that'll allow me to escape Connor for a while, a feat I've managed since I woke up alone on Saturday morning but am unable to do today, given that I've got class.

I don't so much as glance at Connor when I walk in, and I take a seat at the back that won't allow me to stare at the back of his head. He stays seated for the entire lecture, which keeps me from checking out his butt, and he doesn't speak.

Unfortunately, none of that stops me from spending the entire class remembering how soft his hair feels under my fingertips, how firm his butt is under my hands, or the raw, desperate way he said my name that first night.

He was right when he said we're in trouble.

It's just as well I've made the executive decision to skip classes tomorrow and drive the boys down to Pomona tonight. That way I can avoid excessive traffic, and also get over any potential mental breakdowns in time to do the cooking with Nancy. Any classes that are still happening will be a joke, anyway; it's only Tuesday and I can already tell from all the jiggling legs and watch-checking that no one's focusing on Professor Ozgur's words of wisdom on the barbarians of the West.

The second the bell rings, the entire class is up and rushing out the door, me included. Only a soft voice saying, "Miss Brandt, can I see you for a moment?" stops me in my tracks.

I halt at the door, but I don't retreat back to Connor until everyone else has filed out. When I finally do, the concern on his face makes me wish I'd just fled with everyone else. "What's up, Mr. Lawson?" I ask impatiently.

He winces and I pretend not to see it. "I just wanted to see if you were okay," he says quietly. "And to apologize. I should've done more than just disappear—"

"No, you shouldn't have," I say bluntly. "Message sent; message received. That was the point, wasn't it? I told you to make a decision, and you did. Right?"

His head jerks in a nod. "I'm sorry, but—"

"Stop. I don't need an explanation. Or rather, you've explained enough times. I got it. Teacher and student," I say, gesturing between us. "Nothing more. See? I have excellent learning comprehension skills."

He smiles sadly, and it breaks my heart in ways I wish it couldn't. "Have a happy Thanksgiving, Lizzie. I know you'll make it a good one for the boys."

I want to tell him to mind his own business, that he gave up any right to care about me and the boys. I want to tell him to go fuck himself, because it's tickling the tip of my tongue.

And I want to beg him to reconsider, every bit as much.

But if there's one thing I've learned in the past few months, it's that life isn't about what I want, so I mumble a "Thanks, you too," and hustle out the door.

• • •

It's a long drive home, and for every moment of excitement I feel at the sight of a familiar landmark, there's a stark jolt back to reality when I remember that no one's waiting for me, Ty, and Max at the end of this drive. The house isn't going to smell like rosemary and apples, and there won't be any crackling fire. The ride is so quiet once Max falls asleep, I can't help wondering if Tyler's having the same thoughts I am.

"So, what's the deal with Amy?" I ask him, trying to put both of our minds on a more pleasant track.

He grunts. "Nothing."

"Obviously something, if she's texting you."

"So I can't ask about you and Connor, but you can ask about me and Amy?"

Yikes. "Wow, okay, never mind." The silence returns to the car, heavy to the point of unbearable, and I switch on the radio, keeping it low so as not to wake Max.

After a minute, Tyler deigns to speak to me again. "This song sucks."

"So change it," I snap. I don't even know what song it is, what station we're on. All I can think about is the empty house and, now that Ty's brought him up, Connor.

"Jeez, you don't have to be such a bitch," Ty mutters as he reaches for the dial.

It takes all my self-control not to swerve off the road. "You've gotta be kidding me, Tyler. You can *not* talk to me like that."

"You're not Mom," he shoots back icily, and I know he's been storing that one up for a while.

"No, I'm not, and I'm not trying to be. It's not like I have anyone teaching me what to do here, Tyler. I'm doing the best I can."

"Well, your best sucks," he growls, changing stations.

My knuckles are white on the steering wheel, and I force myself to keep calm. *He's just acting out from grief,* I remind myself. It's something his shrink had warned me about, especially after the fight he got into at school. *It's not personal.*

Sure sounded fucking personal, but although tears prick at my eyes at his words, I refuse to give in. It's what he wants, which is shitty, and I won't do it. Instead, I get even shittier. "Good thing you're turning fourteen next month. Then you can tell a judge all about how much I'm torturing you, and see how much better you like foster care."

"I hate you."

"Well, that sucks for both of us, doesn't it."

"No wonder Connor doesn't like you."

The words are like a punch to the gut, and not for the reason Tyler thinks. I jerk to the side of the road, and slam to a stop in the shoulder before turning to my brother. "Actually, Tyler, *you're* why he doesn't like me. This might come as a shock to you, but playing parent to two boys *isn't* something every college or grad student dreams of doing. So next time you want to be an asshole, maybe choose a subject that's not *your fault.* Or, better yet, realize that you're not the only one who's had to make sacrifices, *or* who's lost Mom and Dad."

The second the vitriol has passed my lips, I regret every word, especially when Tyler juts out his jaw in a defiant gesture aimed to stop himself from crying, and fails.

And *especially* when Max's sad voice comes from the backseat, sleepy and sniffly. "Connor doesn't like me?"

Fuck. *Fuck.* I don't think I've ever hated myself so much in my entire life. "Of course he does, Max," I say quickly, stumbling over the thickness in my throat.

"No, he doesn't," Tyler says meanly, swiping his hand under his nose. "Connor doesn't, and neither does Lizzie."

"Of course I do," I say with far more fire than I intend. "I love you both, and I'm sorry. I should never have said any of that. This is hard for me too, and I'm not handling it well." Understatement of the century. "Connor...he likes you both, very much. He wouldn't have come for dinner if he didn't." That part, I realize, is actually true. "But you're probably not going to see him again. And it's not because of anything you did," I add hastily. "He just...has a lot going on."

Both boys are quiet, and I think I can actually hear my gut churning in the silence.

Finally, Ty says, "He's a dick."

195

I know I shouldn't encourage it, but I can't help laughing, which makes Max giggle too. "He's not," I insist, but then I laugh again, and eventually, even Ty does too. "Okay, a little bit," I concede, remembering waking up alone in bed that Sunday morning. "But he's a good guy. And he really does like you guys, a *lot*. And he's been a huge help to all of us. But we're all learning how to handle things now, and the three of us have to be in it together. That's what matters. Okay?"

The boys mumble their assent, and after we've found a song on the radio we can all agree on, I get back on the road for the last three hours of the drive home.

• • •

Even though I've been thinking about it non-stop, arriving at the house, only to see it dark, empty, and cold, is still a shock. The answering machine is full of messages from telemarketers unaware just how disinterested Edward and Manuella Brandt are in considering new car insurance options or cable plans. Just one more reminder of how many house-related things I have to take care of before we go back on Sunday.

It's well after Max's bedtime when we get there, and I put him straight into his old bed, which is still unmade from his last day here, after the funeral. Ty goes right to his room, too, presumably to get online and tell all his friends he's home. I debate going over to Nancy's, but it's late, and I know I'll see her first thing in the morning; no reason to bother her now.

Nothing to do but wallow and wait.

I didn't finish the scotch the day of the funeral, so I help myself to a couple more inches of it now and curl up on the couch in front of the TV.

One drink, a goodnight to Tyler, and a *House Hunters* mini-marathon later, I'm wide awake. And lonely as hell. My family was always perfectly comfortable—truly putting the middle in middle-class—but my house has never felt so huge. It doesn't help that I have no idea how to work the heater; Nancy will have to show me in the morning.

It's impossible not to think of Connor now, of that last night together, sleeping with him curled around me. How much warmer I would be now if he were here, his arm wrapped around my waist, his breath on my neck. It's a terribly dangerous road to travel down, but I'm cold and sad and just drunk enough to get myself off to visions of navy-blue eyes burning into mine while doing things I almost wish I didn't remember.

I drift off almost immediately after. When I wake up a few hours later, I'm nauseated as all hell, freezing despite the furry blanket—my mom's favorite—and the throw pillow is wet under my cheek, moisture I assume is drool until I rub my eyes. Crying in my sleep—a whole new low.

Wrapping the blanket around myself, I gather the empty highball and my cell phone and make my way upstairs. It's too cold to shower, but I chug a few glasses of water so I won't be a total waste of space when I see Nancy tomorrow. Then I take a deep breath and let myself into my parents' old room.

In here, the bed is made—just as they left it before going to visit my grandmother in her nursing home— and it's clear nothing has been touched. Nancy had gently suggested I go through it eventually, but there was too much to do then, and I can't stomach it now. All I want is a pair of my dad's warm sweats, and I find them easily. I hope that they'll smell like him, like his cologne or even his deodorant, but they just smell like a combination of detergent and stale drawer.

Still, they're warm, and wrapping myself in them is a comfort. I check on the boys, both of whom are sleeping soundly, and then I brush my teeth, slip into my room, and close the door. Once I'm back in bed, though, I find I'm wide awake again. Of course.

I take my cell phone from my nightstand and light it up to check the time. Only then do I see I have three texts.

From Connor.

Just wanted to make sure you guys made it home okay, reads the first one.

The second one says, *Sorry, I know I have no right to ask.*

And then, of course, the third: *But did you?*

I snort as I read through the messages. He has twisted ideas of what keeping his distance means, not that that's news to either one of us. But now my conversation with the boys in the car rears up slowly in my head. Connor *does* like them; I know he does. Hell, he volunteered to spend extra time with Max, and he certainly didn't need to. And coming to dinner? He knew he was in for more quality time with them. So why was he pretending he couldn't handle them being around?

The light fades out as I'm contemplating, and I realize I still haven't caught the time. I hit the button again. It's after three. It's late to text back, and I probably shouldn't either way. But then I think about how I would feel if he'd driven back to Montreal tonight and the texting situation was reversed, and I send a quick *Safe and sound.*

To my surprise, before I can even return the phone to my nightstand, I can see that he's typing back. Then he stops. Starts again. Stops. I keep watching my phone, but it goes dark, and stays that way.

For the best, I think, and slide back under the covers. My resolve lasts all of thirty seconds before I snatch my phone back.

I could see you responding, you know, I type. *Were you waiting up for me?*

There's a twinge in my stomach as I wait for his response. Just as I'm sure there's none forthcoming, my phone beeps. *Don't ask me that.*

Just like that, a flood of emotion sweeps through me, and I grasp the phone in a white-knuckled grip. I know it's just who Connor is, a guy who can't stop caring no matter how hard he wants to, but so help me God, it feels like more. It feels personal. It feels like….

I'm sorry, he texts. *Go to sleep.*

I can't. And then, because I can't stop myself any more than I can pretend I'm over whatever's happening between us, I call.

He picks up immediately, as if he was anticipating it, and I wonder if it was with hope or dread. It's not clear from the way his gruff voice says, "Go to sleep."

"Tell me a bedtime story," I reply, relaxing back onto my pillow. "Bonus points if said story is on the final."

"Counting on Byzantine History to put you to sleep, huh?"

"It always does," I say, though I can already feel myself growing sleepier, soothed by his voice.

He laughs, low and sexy, and it feels like the hug I've been needing all day. "Is that why you're skipping all your classes tomorrow?"

Only then does it hit me that I never told him I was driving home today. "Wait, how'd you—"

"I kinda figured you'd need some extra time to adjust to being back home," he says.

I sigh. "You live way too far inside my head, you know that?"

"I think we've established the reverse is true too," he says wryly.

From the way he utters the words, you'd think we were discussing some sort of misery, and I can't help a tiny laugh at the absurdity of it. "You really do know how to make the fact that we like each other sound like a fate worse than death, you know."

There's a long pause, and I wonder if I've somehow gone too far, though I don't see how. Finally, I swallow hard and change the subject, before I lose him for good and the night becomes quiet and cold again. "So when do you head home?"

"I don't," he says, and I'm relieved to hear his voice; I was almost afraid he'd hung up. "Canadian Thanksgiving was a month ago. I'm just taking advantage of some quiet on campus."

"That sounds…." Boring. Lonely. "Nice."

"Yeah. Should be. I'm counting on getting a nice amount of my dissertation done."

"Oh, come on. You're just gonna end up sitting around in your underwear and playing video games, aren't you?"

He laughs. "I cannot confirm or deny."

"Well, I'm sorry you're going to miss my first attempt at cooking an entire bird, because let me tell you, it's gonna be something special."

"Please tell me you're going to have ample amounts of supervision, and/or your version of cooking involves opening takeout boxes."

"Oh, no takeout boxes here. We Brandts are very serious about our turkey." I pause. "Or maybe we're not. I'm actually not that crazy about turkey. But my dad's stuffing recipe is amazing." I explain to him about Nancy, and our joint cooking plans, and our traditions, and he tells me all about Canadian Thanksgiving and what campus is like when it's completely deserted.

I have no idea at what point I drift off to sleep, but I could swear at some point I heard a soft laugh, followed by a "Goodnight, Lizzie," and there wasn't even a hint of chill in the November air.

chapter fifteen

Nancy shows up bright and early the next morning, bearing bagels, cream cheese, and bags of ingredients for making pie crust and stuffing. "Hi, sweetheart," she greets me after dropping everything on the table. She kisses me warmly on both cheeks. "Make yourself a bagel and let's get to work."

I can't help laughing—Nancy's the queen of getting down to business. She's pretty much the only reason we haven't fallen apart completely. Of course, at some point, I have to take over dealing with the finances and other crap that's become her problem by default, but for now, her German efficiency is a lifesaver.

Making us all bagels while Nancy puts up a pot of coffee, I call the boys downstairs for breakfast and to help unload the bags. Predictably, Max asks to see Nancy's dog before he can even swallow his first bite, and Tyler just shoves half the bagel into his mouth before asking if he can go see his friends.

"Aren't they at school?" I ask as I pour both me and Nancy mugs of coffee.

"Oh yeah," Ty mutters. "Just 'til noon today, though."

"How about you do your homework until then, so you can be free for the rest of vacation?" I suggest.

"That sounds like an excellent idea," says Nancy before Ty can object. "And maybe at some point today you three can go through some things."

Ty and I exchange a glance, but I nod, even though the thought of picking apart the stuff my parents left behind sort of makes me want to vomit. "Sure," I answer for all of us, because there's not much of a point putting it off any longer.

"How was the ride down?" Nancy asks, obviously trying to change topics to a more pleasant one than delving into my dead parents' things, not realizing she hit on a topic almost as bad.

"Fine," Ty says flatly, and Nancy glances at me.

"How are things here?" I ask, forcing a bright smile on my face.

She glances around the kitchen before responding with a "Fine" almost as a terse as Ty's, and it makes my chest ache. Much as I love and miss my parents, at least I'm up at Radleigh, where I'm used to going long stretches without seeing them, and days without speaking to them. For Nancy, it's a daily confrontation; she's been friends with my parents since she and my dad were in law school together.

After a minute of silence, I blurt out what we're all thinking. "This blows, huh?"

Nancy smiles faintly. "Totally."

Max pops his head up. "What does—"

"Hey, Max, wanna go see Pete?" asks Ty, glancing at Nancy for approval.

"Yes!" He downs the rest of his juice under my watchful eye and they head next door. I can hear Pete's playful yapping as soon as he spots them, and Nancy and I exchange a smile, but I can tell there's Real Talk coming.

Nancy doesn't disappoint. "How are you, sweetie?"

I shrug, my bagel rapidly losing its appeal under her watchful eye. "Fine. Sad. Which I think is pretty normal."

"Of course it's normal to be sad," she says, stroking my hair before picking up her mug to take another sip. "But are you sure you don't want to talk to someone professionally?"

I think about when Connor made the same suggestion, and how I snapped at him. I wonder if Nancy sees someone, if she had to after she lost her leg, or her husband left her. If she talks about my parents with some stranger. "I'm sure," I murmur, taking a sip from my own mug, even though I'm really not that sure anymore.

"Are your friends being supportive?"

Again, I think of Connor, but instead I just say, "Yeah. They make sure I get out of the house." And stick up for me against Trevor's asshole buddies, but there's no good way to bring that up. "Cait came with me to look at the apartment and stuff."

"Good," says Nancy with a smile. "I was a little worried when no one came down with you for the funeral."

"They offered. I told them not to." I take a napkin from the holder in the middle of the table and just kinda fiddle with it. I don't know why talking to Nancy is making me antsy, but it's just too…weird. I love Nancy, but she's not my mom.

My mom's met Cait and Frankie—last year, when she came up for parents' weekend and we did a whole girls' night thing because my dad had to work. My mom would've asked me about boys by now, would've dragged every single detail about Connor Lawson out of me the second she walked through the door.

But she won't be walking through the door, no matter how long and hard I stare at it. And, I realize as I feel Nancy's hand on my arm, that's exactly what I've been doing.

"Lizzie," she says softly, and that's all it takes for me to dissolve into a flood of tears.

Nancy immediately wraps her arms around me while I cry, but it only makes it worse. She doesn't wear my mother's perfume, her shoulders are broader, and her arm muscles are more prominent. Every soothing word she says in not-my-mother's voice is a stark reminder she's the most maternal person in my life right now. And while I really, really appreciate that she's here....

You're not Mom. Tyler said it to me last night, and I want to say it now. But I know how much it hurt when he threw it at me, and I have no desire to inflict any pain on Nancy.

The thing is, I realize as I use the napkin I'd been toying with to blow my nose, I'm not trying to be. And neither's Nancy. I had a mother, and she was wonderful, and she's gone.

I can't help wondering if Connor understood that being with me wouldn't have meant he had to be a dad.

"Better?" Nancy asks quietly as I wipe my eyes on the back of my hand and reach for another napkin.

"Relative term," I sniffle as I clean up the mess of my face, take a deep breath, and walk over to the sink to rinse off.

She waits until I sit back down and covers my hand with hers. "Talk to me, Lizzie, please."

So I do. I leave out the parts about Trevor and Sophie—the parts I probably wouldn't have told my mom either—but as I go on about forcing myself to pick up my grades and learning the wonders of carpool and meeting with the boys' therapists, I realize there's no way to omit Connor. He's been a part of everything for the past few months, and though I meant it when I told him I felt like we were surviving rather than living, I'm not even sure the former would have been possible without him.

"He sounds...torn," Nancy says when I finish.

I roll my eyes. "I guess that's a nice way of putting it. Anyway, he's not anymore. Decision made."

"Which sounds like it's for the best, given that he's your teacher," Nancy points out.

"He's just my TA," I mumble.

She raises an eyebrow.

"He is! I have a professor for that class. Seriously, it's not that big a deal."

"Spoken like a girl who hasn't quite let go of the idea of a relationship with this guy," she says wryly. "I thought that was off the table?"

"It *is*. I'm just saying, whatever's happened...it's not so bad."

"Sweetheart, I'm not gonna lie." She squeezes my hand. "If he's made you laugh at any point in the past few months, I don't care if he's Genghis Khan. But if he's hurting you...."

"He's not," I assure her, but I'm not sure it's true. "I mean, he has a right to say he doesn't think I'm worth the trouble. And I have to respect that, even if I think it's bullshit."

She laughs. "It *is* bullshit," she says, keeping her voice low, "and if he doesn't see that, he doesn't deserve you anyway."

"That's exactly what Mom would've said."

"Your mother was extremely wise. Good taste in friends, too." She grins and clinks her mug to mine before downing the rest of her coffee. "Now come on—if we're going to make perfect pie crust, we're gonna need some practice rounds."

• • •

It takes four hours, but by the time Nancy goes back home, we have gorgeous-looking apple and sweet potato pies, the latter of which is covered with perfectly golden marshmallows I know will make my brothers *very* happy. We also chopped up the vegetables for the stuffing to save time tomorrow, when I would attempt to cook my very first turkey.

But first….

I dropped both Tyler and Max off at friends' houses, and now it's just me, standing in the doorway to my parents' bedroom, looking around with dread at all of the belongings they'll never touch again. I don't want to let anything go, but Nancy keeps gently pointing out that other people can put the stuff to better use, and I know she's right.

I start with my dad's closet—the easiest. It's full of

suits, and there's an organization that takes professional attire and gives it to people who can't afford it so they have something to wear to interviews. I don't want them, and Max and Ty have no use for them. No-brainer.

Only it's not. Because I recognize the suit he wore to my high school graduation, the gray one he often wore with a white shirt and my favorite lavender tie. And there's the navy one my mother always teased him made him look like a politician. And that pinstripe one would be perfect for Tyler someday….

No. I shake my head, hoping it'll clear out all the doubts, and then grab as many suits as I can and haul them onto the bed, repeating the trip until all the suits, shirts, and ties are laid out and ready to be wrapped up. After another moment, I rescue the lavender tie. Next up is shoes, but I already feel so exhausted from the effort of purging my father's everyday existence from the house that I curl up next to the suits instead.

I don't even realize I've spaced out into a light nap until the cell phone in my pocket pings with a new e-mail. Fumbling with it, I squint into the bright light of the screen. The subject line is "Notes from today." The only message is, "Here's what you missed. –Connor."

Fuck you, I think immediately, surprising myself with my venom. He's the one who decided we were nothing but teacher and student. He's the one who walked out on me while I was asleep. I told him to stop being my white knight and he's *still* fucking doing it. It's like some crazy addiction, one that's supposed to be helpful but instead just turns my already fragile heart into a tortured mess of a bloody organ.

Thanks, I write back. *But you need to stop.* I'm about to hit Send, and then I add a *Please.*

I stare at my phone for a long time, waiting for his response, but when none comes after five minutes, then ten, I realize he's listening. He's backing off.

And I hate it.

On the bright side, now that I'm dying for a distraction, the idea of still having most of the room to go through no longer makes me want to claw my eyes out. I manage to separate my dad's shoes into ones in good enough shape to donate and trash—he loved his old slippers so much the right one had barely half a sole left—and then I do the same for my mother's.

I keep working—dividing, examining, hugging, crying—for hours and hours, getting lost in memories of the way my mother's dark waves looked in this white dress or wrapped in that blue scarf. And I'm lonely, so lonely that I can't stop myself from glancing at the dark screen of my phone every few minutes, praying that Connor will disobey my request while knowing he won't.

Eventually, the boys come back, and we order a pizza while we go through more stuff until we're too drained and exhausted to see straight. We all go to bed, and judging by the fact that I don't hear Tyler's computer or Max playing with his toys, the boys pass out right away.

I, of course, lie awake for what feels like forever, unwelcome images and memories of warm lips and hands running through my brain. If Connor's rejection hadn't hurt so badly, I'd almost be grateful for how much of my thoughts he's consuming, given that at least it's a break from mourning.

But it does hurt, and so does not being able to call him, and so does knowing that when I go back to my campus in just a few days, my biggest support system will be gone. I love Cait and Frankie, but life for Cait is *Lacrosse Über Alles*, and Frankie's a great friend, but it would never in a billion years occur to her to offer something like to watch Max for an hour.

At least it's looking hopeful my grades will keep me at Radleigh for another semester—straight As on my mid-terms.

I know being able to stay there is a good thing. I'm just having a hard time remembering why at this moment, when the very thought of being there, with things as they are now, makes me want to throw up two slices of Meat Lovers' Special.

Tomorrow's Thanksgiving. It used to be my favorite holiday, and now I can't think of a damn thing on earth to be grateful for.

chapter sixteen

We start even earlier the next morning, and this time we have all hands on deck—turns out, it's been a really, really long time since Nancy's made a turkey. "I did it when Sam and I first got married," she says, eyeing the defrosted bird every bit as warily as my mom used to eye Nancy's ex-husband before she got actual proof he was cheating on her. "But your mom's been making it for so many years, I'm just...out of practice."

"It can't be that hard," says Tyler. "Don't we just, like, stick it in the oven?"

I consult the recipe in front of me. "Was this turkey pre-brined?" I ask Nancy.

"I have no idea. I think so. Maybe." She frowns. "What if it wasn't? Do we have to brine it?"

"What does that even mean?" Tyler asks.

"I have no idea," I mutter, examining the massive

thing as if the information is stamped on the skin somewhere. "I think we should probably just proceed as if it was."

"So then what?" asks Max, obviously eager to get his hands dirty.

"Then we need to take the giblets and stuff out of the turkey," I say, reading the next step. "I think that's gonna be your special job, Max."

"Aren't we supposed to preheat the oven?" asks Nancy.

"Not yet," says Ty, looking over my shoulder.

"Well how does *that* make sense?" I ask.

"It *says*—"

"Yeah, but—"

"I think my hand is stuck!" yells Max.

"Max, your hand can't be stuck," Nancy says patiently, though her eyes widen and she watches him attempt to pull it out and fail.

"Oh, for Christ's sake, Max," I mutter as Tyler goes to work freeing him.

"Shouldn't someone be making the stuffing now?" Nancy muses.

"What about my hand?" cries Max.

We all start talking over each other, but then the doorbell rings, and we all fall quiet. "Ty," I sigh. "It's really not a good time to have one of your friends over."

"I didn't invite anyone," he insists.

"I'll get it," says Nancy. "You two work on getting Max's hand free."

It takes both me and Tyler, but we get Max's hand—and the giblets—loose just as Nancy calls, "Lizzie? Someone here for you."

"For me?" I mutter, giving my hands a quick rinse with a squirt of soap. I dry off on a hand towel and walk out. "Who—"

And then I freeze. Because there's nothing I can possibly say at the sight of Connor Lawson, standing in my entrance, a sheepish smile on his face as he says, "Any chance you've got room for one more at the table?"

• • •

It's fucking freezing outside. Connor's already offered me his coat, but other than telling Nancy I'd be right back before yanking his arm outside before the boys could spot him, I can't even form any words. All I can do is shiver and glare.

Connor's not doing much better than I am in the speaking department, but he's the one who finally breaks. "I'm sorry," he says, and his voice is so raw it hurts my throat. "I didn't mean to ambush you. I just…I got in my car, thinking I'd drive around to clear my head, and I was an hour south of Radleigh before I realized I knew where I was going all along. *Calisse.*" He scratches his head and looks away, anywhere but at

215

me. "This was a stupid thing to do."

"It really was," I mutter, apparently getting my voice back. "What the hell, Connor? How did you even know where I live?"

His cheeks flame at the question. "It's on the copy of the sublet agreement you gave to me with your keys."

"Oh." I fall silent again.

"That's it? I show up at your door and that's all you have to say?"

"If there's one thing I've learned from arguing with you, it's that I never get the answer I want," I point out coldly. "You've done a ton for me, and I'll always be grateful, but it doesn't give you the right to fuck with my head like you do. To *hurt* me like you do." I start to storm back to the house, and then whirl around.

"I don't know what the hell you're doing here," I declare, feeling my entire body shake, and not just from the cold. "But I don't want to have another conversation about how I'm too young, how I'm your student, how I come with too much baggage. I don't want to do this shit anymore, Connor."

"Good."

I blink. "Good?"

"Good," he affirms. "I don't either." He walks up to me, and before I can protest, he slides his coat off and wraps me in it. "I don't want to come up with

216

reasons not to be with you anymore. I just want to be with you. Period."

"And I'm supposed to be believe that now? After everything?" There's an edge in my voice, but the truth is that I want to, so badly that it hurts.

"I understand if you can't," he says, his breath turning to puffs of smoke in the air, "but I'm gonna do whatever I can to prove it. I thought driving five hours was a pretty nice start."

"What happened to not being able to handle my being a guardian?"

He squeezes his eyes shut, then opens them. "Emergency session," he says, and my stomach drops at the tinge of shame in his words. Shame I put there, when I had no business to. Especially when I see how much stronger it makes him, and has made Max, and maybe even Tyler. "You know what they say about daddy issues."

"You don't have to be their dad," I say softly, my earlier conversation with Nancy ringing in my ears. "I'm not trying to take her place, and you don't have to try to take his."

He nods wordlessly, but I can see he's still struggling with the idea. To be honest, though, so am I. "My shrink said the same thing. It's just hard to feel like I won't suck at it—whatever *it* is—when I have no idea what a decent father looks like."

"You're great with them," I remind him, seeking

out his hands and bringing them to my waist, inside the warmth of the coat. "You're already everything you have to be to be with me, if it's what you really want."

"Is it what you want?" he rasps.

"You showed up at my house on Thanksgiving morning and I haven't kicked you out yet," I say teasingly. "What do you think?"

He rests his forehead on mine. "I think it would be really nice to continue this conversation inside."

"Fair enough." I turn back to the house, but before I can take another step, I'm spun back around. And then his cold hands are on my cheeks, and his warm lips are on mine, and I swear, I'm melting in the thirty-degree air.

"Sorry," he says sheepishly when he pulls back just enough to speak. "I used up all my restraint waiting the last ten minutes to kiss you. That was all I had in me."

"You weren't kidding when you said we were in trouble," I murmur against his lips. "But if you come inside with me, you aren't gonna be able to run again. You don't have to be their dad, but you can't confuse the shit out of them either. And Nancy...she's the closest thing we have left to a parent."

He nods. "I can...I don't know...sit in my car or something while you talk to her, if you want."

Now it's my turn to feel my cheeks flame. "I think she's already got a pretty good idea who you are, given that we talked about you for a while yesterday."

"Yeah?"

I smile at his attempt to hide how pleased he is, like a kid on Christmas morning trying to pretend he hasn't sneaked a look at his present. "Yeah. But I should warn you—unless you know how to cook a turkey, I might have to trade you in for a guy who does."

"Well then," he says, laughing, "good thing I'm a fast learner."

• • •

The trembling isn't entirely out of my system as I walk back into the house, hand-in-hand with Connor. This conversation is far from over, and I know I'm letting my happiness that he's shown up cloud my judgment.

It's just really fucking hard to care.

I pause in the foyer and close my eyes, feeling his fingers intertwined with mine, the faint scent of his aftershave drifting to my nose, unobtrusive, just strong enough to remind me he's here. When I open my eyes again, he's watching me. "That nervous?" he asks softly.

I don't know how to tell him about the conversation in the car, that Ty and Max might not have the best feelings toward him right now. I'm not sure he realizes I've told Nancy he's my TA, nor do I know how he'll feel about her knowing.

But life doesn't give a shit about perfect timing, or perfect circumstances; it just happens. And by now, I've lived enough to recognize that when something pretty damn good is coming your way, no matter how inconvenient, you should just fucking embrace it while you still can.

"Nope." I squeeze his hand and pull him into the kitchen. "Hey, boys, say hi to our guest, will you?"

"Connor!" Max's face lights up, and he turns to Tyler. "I *told* you he likes me."

Ty isn't quite as welcoming, and the grin elicited by Max quickly drops when Ty asks Connor stonily, "What are you doing here?"

"Tyler!" Nancy scolds. "That's no way to greet a guest."

"He doesn't even wanna be here," Ty mutters.

Connor turns to me, eyebrows furrowed. "What's he talking about?"

"Ty," I say, clasping Connor's forearm. "Again, I'm sorry for what I said in the car. But he just drove all the way down here to spend Thanksgiving with us. You don't think maybe he's thought about it a little more and changed his mind?" *Please have genuinely thought about it more and changed your mind*, I mentally impart to Connor.

"You told them," says Connor, gently extricating his arm from my grasp, hurt and regret flashing across his face.

I just nod.

"Boys, why don't we go check on Pete," Nancy suggests.

Connor winces. "No, wait. Please." He turns to Tyler. "I'm sorry you had to hear that. I'm sorry I *said* it. It's just...I know you guys have had a hard year, and I was afraid to do something to make it worse. I don't know how to...." His face reddens. "I don't know what I'm doing. I just know I like hanging out with you guys, and I'm crazy about your sister, okay?"

My stomach flips like mad at the words, but I force a neutral expression on my face as I glance from Tyler to Nancy. Of course, that's when Max says, "Gross. Aren't you her teacher?"

Nancy's eyebrows shoot up. I don't blame her. I have not handled this well in the slightest over the past few weeks.

"Sort of," says Connor, his face darkening even further. "It's complicated."

Of all people, Tyler comes to the rescue. "He's not like Mrs. Yang," says Ty. "He's like Rita. The one who helps you with the scissors."

"I think I've just been demoted," Connor rumbles under his breath.

"Shut up and go with it."

Ty looks back at Connor, cocking his head. "So, you really like my sister? Are you, like, her boyfriend now?"

"Tyler!" I admonish him on instinct, but the truth is, I'm kind of curious myself.

Connor shrugs. "You have to ask her that, man. I'm just here because I heard you guys need help with turkey."

"That we do," says Nancy with a smile, snapping out of the little daze she'd been in, watching all the bizarre events playing out. "Max, honey, move over. I think maybe we'll let Connor handle the stuffing."

I watch as Nancy arranges all the testosterone-bearers in the room, giving them peeling, chopping, and microwaving tasks, and it strikes me with a pang in my heart that there's still a place in this house for family.

• • •

Dinner is sad. And sweet. And underseasoned. And full of reminiscing about the past and talking about the future. Connor takes a ton of gentle ribbing for being a Canadian on Thanksgiving, and responds by pedantically teaching us all about the "real" story of the first Thanksgiving. Everyone makes fun of him for ruining it, me loudest of all, but sitting there with my hand clasped in his, hearing everyone around the table laughing, I know he's saved this holiday for us.

When we're all stuffed full of apple pie with ice cream, and Max is practically asleep at the table, and Nancy's leg is growing stiff, and Tyler's getting antsy to chat with his friends, Connor and I announce that we'll take care of cleanup, and we send everyone on their way.

"Alone at last," I say with a smile as he wraps me in a warm hug. "So, you do okay?"

"You tell me." He drops a kiss into my hair. "I invaded your family Thanksgiving."

"It was nice to have some foreign blood," I assure him. "But I have to admit, I still kind of can't believe you're here."

He smiles against my forehead. "I can't really either. But there really isn't anywhere I'd rather be." Dropping one more kiss, he pulls away and takes a platter in each hand, starting to clear off the table. I do the same, following him into the kitchen.

"I have to ask," I say, watching him put the dishes down on the counter. "What made you change your mind?"

"I don't know," he says, but he seems to be concentrating extra hard on covering the leftover sweet potato pie with Saran wrap.

"You're a terrible liar."

"Isn't that a good thing?" He smiles ruefully, puts the pie in the fridge, and turns, leaning back against the counter. The sleeves of his gray sweater are pushed up to reveal extremely nice forearms, which feels like a dirty distraction tactic. "I never wanted to walk out on you that night, Elizabeth. I didn't even know I was going to. I got up to go to the bathroom and I tripped on one of Max's cars and I just…I don't know. It freaked me out."

He walks over to where I'm standing and takes the platters from my hands, putting them on the counter. "It still freaks me out, thinking about it, sometimes," he admits hoarsely. "But not getting any more pissed-off texts from you, or homemade mac 'n cheese, or fashion tips is so much scarier. *Crisse*, just the fact that you ask about my family. No one asks that. No one declares 'daddy issues' like it's her right to crawl into my brain, but there you are. Just thinking about losing you for good was so much scarier than anything else.

"And I *do* like your brothers. A *lot*. I'm glad to spend time with them, to have them around. And I know they don't need or want another dad-like-person. I just don't want to fail at whatever I'm supposed to be to them, the way my dad did with me."

I reach for his hand, run my thumb over his knuckles before intertwining our fingers. "You've already done infinitely more for them, and for me, than your asshole father ever did for you, Connor. You could fuck *everything* up from here on out and still put your dad to shame. You know that, right?"

He doesn't answer, but he does kiss me.

"It was last night," he murmurs against my lips. "When you said 'we like each other.' That's what did it. It was just simple and right and equal and I thought

'I would have to be a fucking idiot to let go of a girl who makes me excited to get up in the morning and who feels perfect in my arms falling asleep.' Happy now?"

"Very," I say our mouths find each other again, but it feels like the understatement of the century. My body feels suffused in warmth from his words, and it's only growing hotter as the kiss grows deeper. His hands slide up the back of my dress, toying with the zipper, as mine encircle his neck.

"Are you kissing? Ew."

We jump apart to see Max standing in the doorway to the kitchen, in his pajamas, looking rumpled and sleepy. "What's up, buddy?" I ask sheepishly, smoothing my dress as Connor runs a hand through his hair.

"Can I have water?"

I pour him some and get him back to bed while Connor continues to clear the table. It takes a good half hour to get everything in the refrigerator, dishwasher, or garbage, and I don't even bother dealing with the tablecloth or the recycling; it can wait.

The end of this conversation, and whatever comes afterward, can't. Not anymore.

chapter seventeen

Connor's been in my bedroom in my apartment at Radleigh, but bringing him up to my bedroom at my parents' house feels a thousand times more intimate. I watch, closing the door behind me, as he does a slow walk around the room, taking in old spelling ribbons, pictures of me and the girls I called friends a million years ago, and shelves spilling over with books.

"Very different from your room upstate," he observes.

"Very different life upstate."

He does one last scan of a collage frame before taking a seat on my bed. "Why?"

"I wish I knew," I admit, exhaling sharply. I'm still leaning back against the door, not ready yet to join him on the bed. "I just found high school easier, I guess. It was comfortable. Home."

"So why didn't you stay here for college?"

I snort. "That was the last thing I wanted. I was valedictorian, Connor. I was gonna go places. I was gonna go to Cornell and kick some ass and then go to Harvard fucking Law."

"But?"

"But I went to visit Cornell and all the prospectives started talking about the suicide gorge and I freaked the fuck out and had a panic attack in front of my entire tour group. When I got home, I deleted my Cornell application and applied to Radleigh instead. Same weather; less pressure. My friends thought I was pathetic and couldn't ditch me fast enough, but I got a scholarship that pays three-quarters of my tuition—a scholarship I can't believe I'm maintaining, though you get lots of thanks for that this semester—and voila."

"That's it?" He furrows his brow.

"That's it," I say, lifting my chin defiantly. "Still think I'm hot, knowing I'm just some chick who couldn't hack her original plans?"

"If you'd clung to your original plans, you'd still be in the position you are now," he points out. "You'd just have your brothers at Cornell instead of Radleigh."

I snort. "Guess I got lucky, then."

"That's not what I meant," he says, rising.

"I know."

"If you're trying to turn me off, it's not going to work. I'm just gonna warn you of that right now."

My lips curve up a little at that. "I'm not trying to turn you off. I'm trying to be clear about who I am before we make a decision that could affect your career."

"I know who you are." His voice is husky as he closes the distance between us and cups my face in his palms. "You are smart, and you are strong, and you are brave. And you take great care of your brothers, and you rise to challenges like no one I've ever seen. So you can beat yourself up about choices you made when you were in high school, or you can see what I see, which is a woman who's strong enough to do anything she puts her mind to."

"You overestimate me," I say quietly. "I let myself be selfish until now, and all day, but as much as I want this, I can't let you throw your job away over me. I promise you, Connor—I'm not worth it."

"I think I estimate you just fine, and you're plenty worth it, but I'm not throwing away my job. I hope not, anyway." He hesitates before saying anything else, then pulls me slowly to the bed, where we lie down facing each other, close but not touching. "There's only one month left to the semester. I know it's still not exactly the height of ethics, but…as long as we're not actually sleeping together…" He takes a deep breath. "I can wait a month if I know we'll be together at the end of it." A hint of pink rises into his cheeks. "*Be* together, I mean. Not…I'm not trying to put a date on when we have sex or anything. *Tabarnac*," he mutters. "I'm really not saying any of this right."

I can't help laughing at the sight of him all flustered. "I get it," I assure him. "I can do a month."

"Are you sure?"

"I'm sure." He looks so earnest as he asks, and I cup his jaw in my hand, trace my thumb along the curve of his lower lip. "I trust you'll still love me in a month."

His eyebrows shoot up. "Well, that's presumptuous. I don't recall using the L-word."

I roll my eyes. "You just drove five hours to come spend Thanksgiving with me and two tween boys, but sure, whatever. Will you still *like* me in a month?"

He smirks as he reaches up to tuck a wave of hair behind my ear, gently caressing my cheek as he does. "Yes, Lizzie, I'll still love you in a month."

Even though I was the one who put the word in his mouth, hearing it emerge in his voice jars something in me, makes my heart explode against my ribs and then put itself back together, fuller, stronger. I grab hold of his shirt collar and smash my mouth fiercely against his, devouring him, swallowing his words so deeply I can feel them imprinting themselves on my insides.

Fuck waiting.

My fingers fly over his buttons while his tangle in my hair, releasing me only to let me slide his shirt down his arms and off. "What happened to 'I can do a month'?" he pants as I slide his undershirt up and toss it onto the floor.

"Declaration of love trumps all," I inform him, sliding my hands over the hard planes of his chest, the pale expanse of his stomach. Trevor might've had a tan and a six-pack, but I can't imagine anything sexier than the man in front of me now. I press my lips to his neck and suck gently, and his responsive moan is so hot, I do it again, and again, and again until I've dotted his throat with little suction marks. "At least while we're here, far, far away from Radleigh."

"Is that so?" he utters as I reposition for better access to the other side.

"Mmhmm," I murmur against his skin before giving him a gentle nip. "It's in the rules."

There's no argument from his side; he gives in completely, kissing and touching every inch he can, desperately trying to get my clingy dress away from my body. Finally, I roll off of him until I'm standing on my bedroom floor, and I see his expression change from puzzlement to disappointment.

"Okay," he says as he tries to control his breathing. "I'm sorry. You're right."

"About what?"

"That we should stop," he says, gesturing to the space I've created between us.

I can't help it; I snort with laughter. "You idiot. I got up to take off my dress, because you suck at it."

"Oh, thank God," he mutters so quietly I'm not even sure I was supposed to hear it. "So this is love, huh?" he says in a louder voice of mock wonder as I reach behind my back and unzip. "I always wondered. It's less…sweet than I imagined."

"Smartass," I mutter, and he laughs. At least until my dress drops to the floor.

Then his laughter abruptly cuts out and he murmurs, "*Sacrement.*"

"What?" I ask in a panic, instantly dropping to a crouch to grab my dress and use it to shield my body.

"Drop the dress, Elizabeth," Connor practically growls. Instinctively, I do. "Come over here." Again, I do. I'm not typically the obedient type, but my libido's calling the shots right now and its response to Connor's molten glare is too strong to override.

He runs a hand slowly up the back of my thigh, cups my ass through my striped cotton underwear—not what I would've packed if I'd known to expect company—slides it back down. "I was absolutely positive I'd built up your body in my head," he says hoarsely, his eyes raking my body up and down. "I didn't even think it was possible for a real person to look like this." He shakes his head as he strokes me again.

"Oh." I don't even know what else to say. Compliments—still not my forte.

This time, he slides between my thighs on the downstroke, so slowly I think it's meant to torture me into insanity. "You're drenched," he observes with a groan.

"I can't imagine how I got that way," I reply, shuddering lightly with each pass of his thumb.

He keeps up the brutally slow pace, and I can feel his eyes on me as he does it, though mine are closed. "I can't believe you get this wet for me." He dips a finger inside the edge of the lining and caresses me slowly, so slowly. "You're so hot it's fucking maddening. You realize I'm just an older history nerd, right?"

I look down at him, propped up on the bed, his lean body, his slightly too-long hair falling in his those midnight eyes, and a smile curls my lips. "A sexy older history nerd," I correct him. "Doesn't hurt that I happen to know you know how to use that tongue. Think you're the only one who regularly rubs one out thinking of that night by the parking lot?"

Now Connor's lips curve upward to match mine, as if we're partners in crime, and he slips in a second finger. "We should probably create some newer material."

He's massaging my clit now; a pathetic "uh huh" of agreement is all I can muster.

"Come here," he murmurs, reclaiming his fingers.

"I'm already here," I reply petulantly. "Put them back."

He laughs lowly. "No, Elizabeth. Come." He brings his fingers to his mouth, sucks them clean. If I wasn't dripping before, I certainly am now. "Here."

Mother of God, I am going to explode before he even touches me. I take a step toward him, but stop when I see the amusement twisting his lips. "What?"

"Maybe lose the underwear before you mount me," he suggests helpfully.

"Who's the smartass now?" I grumble, shoving my panties to the floor. I unhook my bra and slip it off too, and greatly enjoy the way all traces of smugness disappear from him face when I do.

"*Tabarnac de câlisse*," he swears under his breath, looking me up and down.

God, I love Canada.

"This better?" I ask sweetly.

"Get over here," he growls, grabbing my wrist and pulling me on top of him. We share a long, hungry kiss, breaking off only when his fingers find my nipples and I cry out.

Immediately, I cover my mouth. "Shit," I whisper through my fingers. "We have to be quieter."

"That's not really your greatest skill," says Connor with a smile, earning him a whack on the arm. He glances around the room. "How about the air conditioner? Window units are pretty loud."

"It's freezing outside!"

"I promise to keep you warm."

The husky way he says the words sends shivers down my entire body. I decide not to share that irony. "You better." I climb off and scurry to the AC. "And lose the pants," I call back over my shoulder.

I'm pleased to see he's complied by the time I return, and I climb back into bed. "Now," I say as I straddle his boxer-clad hips. "I believe you were about to get me to make some noise."

"That I am." He strokes my legs up from my knees, then cups my ass to nudge me closer. And closer. And then I'm straddling his shoulders, and he's holding me in place with big, strong hands, and—

"Oh, fuck!" The first stroke of Connor's tongue is firmer than I expect, and by the time it hits my insanely sensitized clit, I know I'm about five seconds away from an orgasm. I try to maintain some semblance of control, keep my hips at a slow roll, but Connor's not having it. His hands tightly grip my ass, pushing my hips forward in time with the thrusting of his tongue. I give up any attempt at restraint and simply brace myself on the wall behind his head while I ride his hungry mouth like a woman possessed. I fall over the edge all too soon, crying out while I try to gain purchase on the unyielding surface, Connor greedily imbibing every last drop until the last shudder goes through me and I collapse into his arms.

"*Câlisse*, you are delicious," he murmurs, brushing a hand idly over the top of my head. "I will never get sick of that."

I laugh softly into his chest. "This is only the second time, Connor," I remind him, though I can't really imagine getting sick of it either.

"Doesn't matter." His voice is infused with so much confidence, it almost convinces me too. "I've seen your life become this monumental struggle to gain control over every moment. To watch you willingly lose it, even for just a minute…you don't know what it does to me." He tilts my chin up so I have no choice but to meet his glittering gaze in the dark. "To have you lose it with me…."

There's so much emotion suffusing this room right now, I'm not sure I can handle it. "Fuck, Connor—"

"Yeah, now's good for that." His mouth closes over mine, and it's clear the feelings-sharing portion of the evening is over. I don't know whether the chills running down my arms are from the air conditioning, but he makes good on his promise to keep me warm, and then some.

It's so easy to get lost in all of it—the caresses on my skin, the erotic sweep of his tongue, the soft firmness of his lips—but I force myself to pull back. "It's my turn."

"Your turn?" He kisses me again. "I mean, fine with me, if you're ready for more—"

"No, jackass." I push him down to the pillows, and he laughs. "My turn to see you lose control. You've watched me come twice now. It's my turn." I press my lips to his neck, sucking gently, and his laughter fades into a soft moan. I keep going down his chest and through the smattering of soft brown hair there, stopping to take a nipple between my teeth. He hisses out a soft curse, which only spurs me on.

I nip the other one too, then continue on down with slow swirls of my tongue that leave Connor panting. "You've really perfected the art of torture," he observes breathlessly, arching into my mouth.

"Consider it revenge for all the red ink on my first paper." I realize as soon as the words come out of my mouth that I shouldn't have mentioned class, but Connor's already too far gone for it to matter. His fists are clutching the sheets at his sides, and he's watching me through partially closed lids, and I wonder which one of us is more anxiously anticipating what comes next.

It takes all the patience I possess not to simply yank down his boxers, but eventually, my mouth makes it to the waistband and I pull slowly, slowly, like unwrapping a Christmas present, forcing his hips off the bed. Then I slither back up his body and engulf him in my mouth.

"*Sacrement de calisse de tabarnac!*" Connor writhes beneath me, streams of beautiful profanity slipping breathlessly from his lips as I take him further and further into my throat. I know exactly what he means about the wonder of seeing me lose control now, because I feel it as I watch him, and it's so fucking hot I feel like I'm halfway to the edge all over again.

Moving up and down on his shaft, I let my long hair swish along his inner thighs, and add my hands to the mix, cupping and stroking while he bucks and moans and swears incoherently. Finally, he groans, "Lizzie, stop, I'm gonna come."

I lick slowly upward and swirl my tongue around the crown, loving the way his entire body shudders in response. "That's sort of the point."

He shakes his head and pulls me up to kiss me fiercely. "I want to be inside you." He rolls his hips against mine, as if I could possibly miss his meaning, then slides a hand down my leg and wraps it around his waist, pulling us closer but still not close enough. His cock is so hot and so hard it's practically branding me, and each time it brushes against my clit, it brings me closer and closer, but it's not enough, it's never enough.

I reach out clumsily for my nightstand, but this isn't college; I have no condoms in there. I graduated high school a virgin. It was only at Radleigh that condoms became a nightstand staple.

"My pants," Connor murmurs before sucking my bottom lip into his mouth. "There's a condom in my wallet."

A white-hot streak of jealousy zips through my insides as I fumble for his pants on the floor. I know he didn't have one in his wallet the night he went down on me by my parking lot, and he didn't plan to sleep with me before the semester was over. It never even occurred to me he might be fucking anyone else, but it's sure as hell occurring to me now. I so, so want not to give a shit.

I retrieve the condom and drop his pants back on the floor. "You sure no one's gonna miss this?" I ask coolly, handing it over.

"What?" He stops kissing me long enough to look me in the eye. "Oh, Lizzie. I put it in there after...that night. Just in case we ever got there again. I know it was stupid, that it was probably better—"

"Shut up, Connor." I kiss him, hard. There's no one else. Of course there's no one else. I'm not The Other Woman with Connor; I'm it, the same way he is for me. "Put on the condom and fuck me. Now."

He's sheathed and ready to go in about two seconds, and he rolls me over so he's on top of me now, looking into my eyes, covering me with his warmth. "Are you sure about this?" he asks softly.

I take his face in my palms and bring his mouth to mine for a long, slow kiss that leaves no room for doubt on my end. "Are you?"

"More than I ever thought possible." And then I feel him nudging me open, and the penetration is so welcome I could weep. It comes out more like a whimper, and he waits for me to assure him I'm okay before pushing in, inch by inch, so slowly I could scream, so hot I probably will. "You feel so fucking good," he murmurs as he buries himself up to the hilt, his lips a whisper away from mine until he closes the gap between us.

"Not so bad yourself," I try to tease, but it comes out on a moan as he rolls his hips. His mouth reclaims mine as he begins a slow slide in and out, then kisses a damp trail down to my nipple. He takes it into his mouth on a harder, faster thrust, and I cry out, all the sensations racking my body too much to process at once.

I'm so close, I can feel the coil of tension building, sweat beading on my skin despite the blasting air conditioner. I'm probably digging into Connor's muscled back firmly enough to draw blood, but it's not enough. I want him deeper. I want to see more of him. I want *more*.

I wrap my legs tightly around his hips and roll us over, careful to keep him inside me. On top now, I can see the scratches I've left on his chest, the slightly sweaty sheen of his skin, lust-dark eyes boring into mine. I lean down, bracing my palms on either side of his head. "I wanted to see you," I whisper, my hair brushing his broad shoulders. "Is this okay?"

He laughs breathlessly. "I'm buried inside you, with a great view of your incredible body. Yeah, Lizzie, I think that's okay." He cups my face in his palms and kisses me, long and slow and deep. "I should've known you'd prefer to be on top."

"Don't make me get down from here."

"You wouldn't dare." He takes one nipple in his mouth, the other between his fingers, until I whimper helplessly. "Still want to get down?"

"No."

"Good." His eyes flash fire. "Now ride me like a fucking pony."

Fucking hell. The words set me off, and I tighten around him until he grunts and his eyes roll back into his head. I want to go slowly to prolong the pleasure of having him inside me, but my hips lift up as if following Connor's command of their own volition. After a few seconds he opens his eyes and I watch him drink me in as he meets me stroke for stroke. The naked lust in his eyes nearly does me in, and I tighten around him again, trying to prevent myself from coming too soon.

He groans and pumps harder, grasping my back with desperate fingers and pulling me close to suck a nipple into his mouth. Our pace speeds up, approaching frantic, and the electric tension building up in my body is coiled so tightly, is so densely present, I can't even imagine how it'll feel to snap. I'm on the edge of exploding on such a grand scale I'm not entirely sure I'll ever be able to piece myself back together.

His hands drop to my ass, gripping it so tightly as he thrusts that I swear he might go right through me. "I am so fucking close," he pants, his breath hot on my damp skin. "I can't wait to come inside you."

I pull him close enough to whisper into his ear. "Then don't wait." I tighten on him one more time and snap my hips just enough to make him roar with the power of his release, then grind down in just the right spot to take me with him. Our shuddering climaxes feed each other in ripple effects, and it takes forever but somehow not nearly long enough for us to come down.

I collapse on top of him and roll off to his side. Both of us are breathing too heavily to speak, staring at the ceiling as if making eye contact now would be too much. Finally, I break the silence.

"*Sacrement.*"

His lips twitch. "Funny, I was just about to say, 'Holy shit.'"

Propping myself up on an elbow, I watch his heaving chest as his breathing works its way back to normal. "You are *dirty* in bed, Mr. Lawson."

His cheeks flush slightly; it's adorable. "Not usually. You must bring it out in me."

"Trust me—I'm not complaining." I lean over and give him a long, languid kiss. "It's hot as fuck. I've never come that hard in my entire life."

"Oh good; it's not just me." Connor huffs out a breath. "If that's sex, I have no idea what the hell I've been doing for the last decade, but I should've just spent it studying."

I drop back onto the pillow and laugh. "I just assumed that's what you *had* been doing. Honestly, it crossed my mind more than once that you might be a virgin."

"And what if I was?"

I freeze. "Shit. Were you?"

He doesn't respond.

I prop myself up on my arm and turn to him. "Connor—"

"No, Elizabeth, I wasn't a virgin, but I'm flattered. Really."

"You're such a dick."

"Ah, there's that romance I missed." He reaches out and smooths a few sweaty strands of hair out of my face. "And sorry, but my high school prom date got there first."

I shouldn't have wanted to kill the bitch, and rationally, I knew that, but still.

"You were trained well," I admit grudgingly. "Even if you're a total cliché."

"I think that might be the highest praise you've ever bestowed upon me."

"Don't get used to it," I warn, though even as I do my mind fills with all the things my lips can't seem to say. Like how much it means to me that he drove down here. And how mind-blowingly gorgeous I think he is. And how right now, I feel a kind of happiness I'd assumed would be off limits to me forever.

I pull him toward me for a kiss instead, hoping that somehow, I'm getting it all across without having to say a word.

chapter eighteen

I wake up naked, alone, wrapped in a blanket like a burrito, and completely confused. It takes a minute for the pieces to fall into place. *Thanksgiving. I'm in my house. My parents aren't. They never will be.*

And then, *Connor.*

I jump out of bed, nearly killing myself in the tangled sheets, and am immediately hit by a gust of freezing air; we'd forgotten to turn off the air conditioner last night. I dash across the room to shut it off, then yank on a sweatshirt to quiet my shivering.

I cannot believe this is happening again. I cannot believe he took off after last night. I jam my legs into a pair of underwear from my suitcase and then into the warmest pair of flannel pajama pants I can find in my drawers. How fucking stupid am I to have thought things would be different?

I look wildly around the room, but there's no note,

not so much as a text. What a fucking asshole. So much for being thankful. The only thing I'm grateful for this holiday is that there's still scotch in my dad's study.

Stalking out of my room, I can practically taste the smoky liquid relief on my tongue. But I can also smell...bacon?

I continue down the stairs, more softly now, and freeze on the bottom step, my hand gripping the bannister for dear life. Connor is standing at the stove in a hoodie and drawstring cotton sleep pants, whistling as he tends to a pan with a spatula.

He didn't leave me.

He still hasn't noticed me there, and I don't move to announce myself. I can't. There's an ache in my heart that's rapidly climbing up my throat and destroying all powers of speech.

Connor makes this place look like home again.

The tears come without warning, and I sniff instinctively to keep them at bay. He whirls around, and his face brightens—it fucking *lights up*—when he sees me, for a second before he realizes I'm crying.

"Lizzie, what's wrong?" He turns off the burners, ever practical, and hurries over, taking my teary mess of a face in his hands. "Are you okay?"

"I thought you left me," I say hoarsely. "Again."

"I didn't. I *wouldn't*," he assures me firmly, pulling me close, not even flinching as I dig my nails into his back. "Not again. I swear, Lizzie. I'm not going

245

anywhere." He kisses the top of my head, and rests his chin there. "I just didn't want the boys to see me coming out of your room in the morning. I slept on the couch, and I woke up when Nancy let herself in to put some groceries in the fridge. Hence the bacon."

"So you're really here. In my house. With me." I want to pinch myself. Or him. Maybe both.

He smiles against my hair. "Yes, beautiful. I am very much with you."

The complimentary endearment makes me squirm. "God, how do you just…say that?"

"Say what?"

I can't even. "The B-word." Heat rises into my cheeks as I pull away. "Especially when we both know I look like shit."

He throws back his head and laughs. It's rich and warm and even at my expense I think I could live off that sound forever. "I have never seen such a confident woman hate compliments so much." He rests his hands on my hips but doesn't pull me back into his arms. Instead, he presses his forehead to mine, his dark-blue eyes focusing intensely. "And I say it because I think it, every single time I see you. This morning's not even close to an exception. You are beautiful, Elizabeth—in pajamas, in jeans, and definitely in nothing at all."

My heart pounds in response as I remember the way he looked at me last night when I pulled off my dress. He means it. This gorgeous, intelligent, and good man actually means every word he says.

"Fuck, my parents would've loved you," I whisper around the lump forming in my throat. "Not that comment about my naked body—my dad would've taken up hunting for that one—but just...you. I hate that they'll never see me finally get life right again."

Connor swallows hard, his fingers tightening on my waist. "They know," he assures me quietly. "They knew you'd be fine. Better than fine. Amazing. They wouldn't have left the boys to you otherwise. They knew you'd find your way eventually, Lizzie."

I slip my arms up around his neck, marveling at how he always knows what to say to make me feel like life will be okay, at least for a little while. "Where are the boys, anyway?" I ask, eager to change the subject I'm embarrassed I've brought up. "Max is usually up at the crack of dawn."

"Nancy took Max," says Connor, fingertips inching under my sweatshirt. "And Ty biked to a friend's house."

"So we have the house to ourselves," I clarify slowly, blinking in disbelief.

He kisses the spot right under my ear, setting off a shiver throughout my entire body, despite my warm pajamas. "That we do."

I reach past him to grab my keys from the countertop. "Let's go," I order.

"Where?"

"To get a megabox of condoms for the next three days."

He pulls me back, wrapping his arms around my waist from behind and resting his chin on my shoulder as he slides the keys from my hand and returns them to the counter. "Already taken care of," he murmurs into my ear. "I told Nancy I forgot my toothbrush and she gave me directions to the drugstore."

I've never found forethought so sexy. "Impressive." I grind back against his growing hard-on to give the word double meaning.

"I thought so." His hand drifts lightly over the front of my pants, and I resist the urge to grab it and shove it exactly where I need it. We only have three days before we have to quit cold turkey for the rest of the semester, and I want them to count.

The touches become more deliberate, and I groan before finally biting out, "Back to my room. Now."

"But what about breakfast?" he asks innocently, leaving a searing kiss on my neck.

"Unless you're going to eat it off my naked body, leave it."

He shrugs, grabs the pans, and follows me upstairs.

• • •

We have a few blissful hours together before the boys return, and then we reluctantly put our clothes back on for an afternoon of watching TV, throwing a football around in the backyard, making turkey adobo out of the leftovers, and then collapsing on the couch with a movie and a crackling fire. It ends up being a really nice day, and as I look around at Max asleep on the floor and Tyler curled up on the loveseat, texting his friends, I think I'm actually doing okay.

"You know what we haven't done?" Connor says, his fingers gently stroking my thigh under the throw blanket we're currently sharing.

I raise an eyebrow. Tyler doesn't look up, but he's definitely in hearing distance. The boys may know Connor's more than my teacher by now, but there are limits.

"Looked at your old photo albums," he says pointedly, giving me a playful swat, and I laugh. "Get your mind out of the gutter, Elizabeth," he murmurs much more quietly. "At least until we're alone."

"You guys are gross, by the way," Tyler calls without so much as glancing up from his phone.

I toss a throw pillow at his head, and he ducks, laughing. "You're the one who asked if he was nailing me," I remind Tyler. "Well, now you know."

"Elizabeth!"

Connor's horrified expression cracks me up. Tyler mock vomits into his lap, then swings his legs around to stand. "Just for that," he says, walking over to the cabinets under the TV where all the Brandt family albums are located, "I'm showing Connor the green one."

All traces of snugness disappear from my expression in a heartbeat. "Tyler, no."

"Lizzie, yes."

"What's the green one?" Connor asks, practically salivating at the promise of my misery.

"Oh, you'll see," Ty says gleefully as he locates the offending thing and dances over to the couch with it. Connor all too eagerly shifts closer to me to make room, and I'm tempted to snatch the album and toss it into the fire. Only it was my parents' all-time favorite, and I know I could never.

I turn to Connor, who's pulling the album onto his lap. "Just remember," I plead, stilling his hand on the cover, "this was a long time ago, and I was a very different person, and you really, really like me."

"All things duly noted," he replies, eyes twinkling. "Now, move your hand."

I do, and cringe as he opens it up.

His jaw drops as he takes in the pictures in front of him. "*Sacre*...." He glances from them to me and back again. "Lizzie, what *are* these?"

That's all it takes for Tyler to break out in hysterical laughter. "It was a phase!" I cry.

"A baby hooker phase?"

My face is flaming, which only eggs Tyler on. "She wanted to be in beauty pageants," he manages as tears of laughter stream down his cheeks. "She *begged* our mom to get her hair done like that, and for one of those denture things."

"They're called flippers," I say defensively, but then I lose it too. Ty's too young to actually remember any of this—I was Max's age, and he was just a toddler—but my mom loved sharing these pictures and stories with anyone who'd listen, and they'd always been Ty's favorites.

"And the outfit?" Connor asks, eyes wide as he turns the page. "Or should I say outfits?"

"Aunt Lily used to buy them for her," says Ty, pointing to the blonde smiling next to me in one of the pictures. I'd forgotten Lily used to love this stuff, or anything at all that didn't come in a glass bottle, back before her divorce, and her bitterness at my parents for having three kids when she couldn't have any.

"Except that one," I say, pointing at a ruffled red one with gold sequins. "That was my favorite. It was my mom's when she was a kid. She brought it with her from the Philippines."

"We still have it here somewhere," says Ty as Connor turns another page. And then my heart cracks a little, because these next pictures are all of us smiling brightly as a family. My dad's actually trying hard not to crack up in most of them—an admirable effort, and one he never managed to pull off on pageant days—but my mom is pure joy, baby Ty in her lap, her hand squeezing mine, my father's arm around her shoulders.

"She looks so young here," Ty marvels. "I forgot how much she used to look like you."

"She really does." Connor looks at the picture, then me, then the picture again. He taps her face in the photo and smiles. "Thanks for passing along the great genes."

I laugh, my heart squeezing in my chest. My parents should be here for this. They would've loved to see this album viewing, and sibling bonding, and meet Connor. This should be when my dad grills him on his intentions. I should have to sneak into the guest room for some alone time after everyone's passed out.

Instead, it's on me to figure out exactly what his intentions are, and to make the decision that Connor will sleep with me tonight and be there when I wake up.

Given the choice, I'd take the third degree and forced sneaking around any day, if it meant getting my parents back. But I don't have that choice, so damn if I'm not going to take a little advantage of being the head of the household sometimes.

"Who do you look like, Connor?" Ty asks, turning the page and grinning at a picture of me in a ridiculous ballerina get-up.

"My dad, apparently," Connor says wryly, raking a hand through his hair. "That's what my mom says, anyway."

"You don't think so?" Tyler asks.

Connor glances at me, and I squeeze his thigh

under the blanket. He looks back down at the album, but I can tell he's turning pages without really seeing them. "I think it's harder to see that sort of thing in yourself."

Ty shrugs. "I guess. I don't really see either of my parents in me."

It's true Ty doesn't as obviously resemble either of our parents as Max and I do—he doesn't have any of the Asiatic features my mother and I share, and his skin is paler than both mine and Max's—but I've never heard him sound so sad about it. "You have Dad's eyes," I say, reaching across Connor to brush Ty's milk-chocolate brown hair out of them. "You probably have his mouth and chin, too; it was just hard to tell with that crazy mustache of his."

"Yeah?"

"Yeah," I say with a smile. Then I tap a lens in my glasses. "But I, of course, am the one who got his eyesight."

"You're lucky you're not blind."

"There's still plenty of time."

We finish the album, and then Ty yawns and announces he's going up to bed. "Really?" I ask. "It's still pretty early."

He smiles sheepishly and holds up his phone. "Amy texted and asked if I wanna video chat, so…."

"Got it. And Ty, if you and Amy need a ride to a movie or something tomorrow night, lemme know?"

"Yeah?" he asks, blushing adorably.

"Yeah."

"Cool." He stoops to wake up a drooling Max and the two of them shuffle upstairs.

"Well," says Connor once they're out of earshot, "that was brave of you, encouraging a teenage boy to spend a night in a dark room with a teenage girl."

"Oh, come on. He's thirteen. What were you really doing at thirteen?"

"Uh, masturbating myself blind because my big sister *didn't* drive me to the movies with girls?"

I shake my head, laughing. "God, teenage Connor. Were they Anne Boleyn fantasies?"

"Catherine Howard, actually. I've always had slightly off-the-beaten-path tastes."

"I'm flattered."

He leans over and kisses me gently. "You should be."

I genuinely am, but it's too odd to say so. Instead, I ask, "So how'd you get from the Tudors to the Byzantines?"

"Hard to say." His fingertips trace patterns on my thigh under the blanket as he speaks, giving me pleasant chills. "I think I got into history in the first place because I was so fascinated by the concept of people being able to make that strong a mark on humanity. I liked the idea of these incredibly important, unforgettable people, especially given how easily I was left behind."

"Oh, Connor...."

There's only a tinge of bitterness in his laughter. "I know, I know—daddy issues. So sue me. Anyway, at some point, I realized *everyone* was into Anne Boleyn—there were books about her, movies about her...she was already a star. And I guess I grew out of the legend of the celebrity. I wanted to know about the huge players who didn't get quite as much attention. I started with Mongol history and eventually I just clicked with the Byzantines."

"Well, I'm glad for it," I say with a smile, linking my fingers with his. "And for whatever it's worth, you've obviously made your mark on the remainder of the Brandt family." I snuggle into his side and close my eyes for a moment, enjoying the warmth of his touch and the crackling fire and the comfortable silence that comes with both boys having gone upstairs for the night. But I can feel his gaze on me, intense and unyielding, and my eyes flutter back open. "What?"

His smile softens as he tucks my hair behind my ear, and so does his voice. "I really do love you. I just wanted to say that, on my own, out of bed."

The words tingle my insides until they melt, and I wrap my arms around his neck and kiss him with everything in me. I can't say the words back, even though I feel them; having never been in a serious relationship or had the kinds of friends who freely exchanged such sentiments, they'd been reserved for my parents. I'm kinda rusty on that particular vocabulary with them gone.

If he minds, he doesn't show it.

I pull back, just slightly. "So," I say, bringing a leg over his lap until I'm straddling him, perched on his solid thighs. "Let's say you got a ride to the movies."

"Uh huh," he breathes against my lips as his hands cup my ass.

"You and me and a dark room." I rock my hips forward gently; he's already most of the way to hard. "What do you do?"

"If I'm thirteen? Probably come in my pants the second you touch me."

"Hot," I murmur against his mouth, and our tongues dance around each other.

"Yes, you are." Warm hands slide up my shirt to caress me through my bra, and he sucks my lower lip into his mouth. "I would've had no clue what to do with a girl like you at that age. Hell, probably not when I was your age, either. Maybe it's a good thing we didn't meet until now."

It's the first time I've ever heard him say anything positive about the age gap between us, and a fresh wave of hopefulness sweeps through me. "Maybe," I murmur, kissing him again before pulling my shirt up and over my head.

Connor's eyes widen. "Uh, Lizzie?" He gestures to

the open entrance.

"Oh, right." I hop up and close the pocket doors to the den, then reclaim my spot on Connor's lap. "Now, where were we?"

"I think we were talking about what we would do if I had you alone in a dark room." He kisses my shoulder. My collarbone. My throat. "Though I'm pretty sure they don't let you sit like this at the movies."

"The quality of Hollywood entertainment really has gone down." I roll off until I'm sitting next to him, movie seat-width apart.

"Mmhmm." He leans in to my neck again, kissing with light suction that drives me crazy. "And obviously I'd have to play it cool, just holding your hand at first." His hand takes mine, places them both on my thigh. "I'm very innocent, you know."

"I'm well aware."

The logs continue to crackle in the fireplace, bits of ember dropping into the ash. I love the smell of the burning wood, the intense natural warmth.

Connor's fingertips are stroking my thigh now, inching closer to the fly of my jeans.

"Subtle," I whisper.

"That's my game," he whispers back.

The wait feels interminable as his fingers move mere centimeters every few minutes, and by the time the tip of his pinky skates over the zipper I'm about ready to explode. But I let him take his time as we watch the fire, brushing over the denim and metal as if unsure whether I'll let him inside.

"Mmm, you smell good." He's nuzzling my ear now, nipping the lobe, and despite the heat emanating from the fire, chills dance down my spine. "Taste good, too."

My eyelids flutter closed. His hand covers my fly now, and he rolls his palm over the stiff denim so it hits me in all the right places. A whiny little whimper escapes my lips, and he whispers "Shh" in my ear. "People are trying to watch the movie."

"I'm probably going to kill you."

"I have a lot of celibate teenage years to make up for."

"Teenage Connor didn't have game. Adult Connor's got some."

"Some?"

"A little bit. Don't let it go to your head."

He cups me through the denim. "Those are some awfully damp jeans for a little bit of game."

"I hate you."

"I don't think you do." He resumes the rough stroking, and I grit my teeth through it. "I actually think you rather like me, even if you'd only admit it under extreme duress. And maybe not even then."

I open my mouth to respond, but the feeling of his fingers working the button of my jeans shuts me up.

"Teenage Connor moves slowly," he continues, "because he is respectful of teenage Lizzie and wants to be clear she is free to stop things at any time."

"You gave a lot of thought to how chivalrous you'd be if you ever got this far, didn't you?"

"I did. How am I doing?"

"A little torturous, but I suppose it works under the guise of chivalry." I let my head loll back onto the couch cushions and look up into his slightly glassy gaze. "You know I'm still Teenage Lizzie, right?"

"I know," he says quietly, and then he kisses me again, his free hand stroking my cheek as the other one tugs my zipper down so slowly I swear I can hear it release every single one of its teeth.

I pull back, because I have to ask. "And you're okay with that now?"

He presses his lips together, obviously choosing his words carefully. Finally, he says, "I just want exactly who you are."

"Good answer." I slide my hand through his hair to pull him back into a kiss. His fingers return to their work, stroking the little triangle of underwear revealed by the open zipper, and I shift to give him better access.

"You are completely soaked," he groans, slipping two fingers inside me.

"Shhh." I nip his earlobe. "People are trying to watch the movie."

Connor nods and turns back to the fire, pulling his

fingers the shallow distance allowed by the confining jeans, then thrusting them back in. "Didn't mean to disturb everyone," he says pleasantly, as if completely unaware he's fucking me with his fingers. I want to give a smartass answer but I'm too far gone, my hips rocking into his hand, desperately trying to take in more than the jeans will allow. Then his thumb finds my clit, and I'm gone, coming all over his hand while he covers my mouth with his and swallows my cries.

When the waves have passed and he releases me, I feel completely wiped out. "I don't think I've ever come so many times in one day," I moan sleepily. "I've actually lost count."

"That was five. And if I have my way, there'll be a sixth. Maybe a seventh."

I regard him from beneath slitted lids. "You're keeping track?"

"I don't think you understand," he says, cocking his head as he slips his hand free. "You are literally the sexiest woman I've ever known, and I don't buy into that 'you can use literally to mean figuratively' bullshit. If you don't think I'm committing every fucking second of this to memory, you're crazy. This is basically every fantasy I've ever had, come to life."

Suddenly, I'm a little less sleepy. "You always *have* made very compelling arguments, Mr. Lawson." I pick up the blanket and look underneath; the tent in his jeans could house a village. Yup, I'm awake. "I don't know that we're really covering fantasy ground, though. I haven't worn any costumes, there's only one of me...tell me what you really want."

"What I really want?" he asks, eyebrows raised.

"What you really want," I confirm.

"Fine, but you're gonna laugh at me."

"Well now I'm just curious. Is it something with rubber gloves? Want me to call you by the name of a childhood pet?"

He rolls his eyes. "Never mind."

"Oh, no you don't." I reach under the blanket and grab his cock as if holding it hostage. "Out with it, Connor," I demand as he grunts.

"This is messed up."

"That's not an answer."

He sighs and loosens my grip. Then he scoops me up from underneath, blanket and all, and deposits me gently on the floor. "This," he says.

"This?" I glance around. "I'm not even sure what this is."

He gets up, turns off the light, then comes to lie down next to me, illuminated by the flames. "I want to make love to you by firelight. Yes, that's a real thing. Yes, I said 'make love' and not 'fuck.' And yes, it's what I want, just this once. Indulge me, will you?"

I don't even know what to say. It's cheesy, and it's not my style, and for some reason, I really, really want it too. Just this once. So I don't say anything at all, just

261

nod once, and lift my hips.

Connor takes the cue to slide my unzipped jeans down my legs, taking my underwear with them, before kissing his way back up my calves, knees, and thighs. Then I pull off the rest of my clothes, and help relieve him of his.

True to his word, there's a sixth, thanks to his talented mouth, and then he covers me for number seven, warm and protective and solid and *there*. I can't imagine Connor running away again, can't believe I thought he had this morning. As he seats himself inside me, murmuring about how beautiful I am, I realize I'm an entirely new kind of happy from any I've ever been.

And then he begins to move, our hips rocking together slowly in a smooth rhythm that feels far more practiced than it is, and I realize just how much crushing sadness I had to suffer in order to get the man currently holding me in his arms.

While I can't say it was all worth it, I do feel for the first time, in the late-autumn darkness, like the sun is finally starting to shine again.

chapter nineteen

Spent and sated, we both fall asleep in front of the
fire, but I wake up not long after. Next to me, Connor is
still comatose, his torso bared by the blanket having
slipped down to his hips. I watch him for a minute, but
I feel like a creep and cover him up. Then I slip my
clothing back on, grab another one of the photo albums,
and curl up on the couch.

This time, it's my parents' wedding album, and I
handle it gingerly as I flip the pages. I used to love
looking through this thing as a kid, teasing my mom
about her way-overcomplicated updo. My parents were
so young when they got married—Mom was still in
college, a senior, and Dad had been out just a year,
working as a paralegal to save up some money before
law school.

My mom once told me people had assumed it was
a shotgun wedding, though she didn't learn quite how

prevalent that assumption was until they had me three years later. "And if they didn't think I was pregnant, they assumed I needed a green card, even though I was in the U.S. on a student visa. Bored people love to gossip," she'd said. "It didn't matter what anyone thought. We loved each other and we didn't want to wait. That's all there was to it."

I glance back at Connor, lying peacefully on the floor. People are going to talk about us, that's for sure. After the whole mess with Trevor and Sophie, I'm pretty sure I can handle any idiotic rumor. But will he be able to? Yes, he'd come here and apologized and told me he loved me and wanted to be together when the semester ended, but who knows if he'll still feel that way under the scrutiny of the other students, and his grad student classmates, and "Jess," and, oh God, Professor Ozgur....

But I'm getting ahead of myself. We have a month to make it through first, and before that, we still have another full day here, away from Radleigh and classes everything else I'd just as soon drop forever if I could reasonably do so. There's plenty of time to stress about how difficult things will be when we return, but why spend time doing it on the last blissful day we have together?

I force my attention back to the album. My mom really did look like me back then, minus the glasses. But there's more. You could tell she was good, and kind, a few other choice things I didn't inherit. I think of what Connor said about Sophie, how she didn't deserve me sleeping with her boyfriend. He's right, and it kills me that I didn't care on my own.

There's a part of me that hopes being with him makes me a nicer person.

"Hey."

I glance up from the album to see Connor sit up and reach aimlessly for his boxers, his longish brown hair disheveled, deep-blue eyes sleepy. *You're beautiful*, I think. "Hey," I say.

"Whatcha got there?" He locates his boxers, pulls them on under the blanket, then throws his undershirt back on before joining me on the couch. The fire's been out for a while now, and he covers us both with the blanket.

"Just more pictures. Wedding album."

"Getting ideas?" he teases, but despite the way he raises his eyebrows, it doesn't sound like it'd displease him all that much if I said yes.

"I thought about it, but then I realized how terrible Lizzie Lawson sounds. Oh well."

He laughs as I snuggle into the crook of his arm. "Elizabeth Lawson sounds nice," he murmurs, kissing the top of my head.

"Give it up, Connor. You can save 'Elizabeth' for when you're mad at me."

His lips curve into a smile against my hair, and he turns the page. "Who's that?"

"My mom's cousin Espie. She's the only one who came in from the Philippines for the wedding, but they lost touch after a little while."

"Literally the only one? What about her parents?"

I snort. "Her parents stopped talking to her the day she announced she was marrying my father and staying in America."

"You've never met them?"

"Never met them, never spoken to them, honestly don't even know if they're still alive. My mother tried straight up through when Tyler was born, even wanted to bring me to visit, but they wouldn't have it."

"So they don't even know?"

"Wouldn't know how to tell them even if they weren't assholes."

He sighs and hugs me tight around my waist. "Whatever happened to the whole 'unconditional love of family' thing?"

"We don't choose family," I say, curling into his warmth. "We're born into it. It's like…if someone else picked my clothes every day, there's a chance I'd like some outfits, and there's a chance I'd hate them." Reaching up to cup his jaw and lower his mouth to mine, I add, "But it's the clothing *I* choose that I want to wrap myself in every day."

"Mmm." His lips brush mine. "I'm very new to this whole fashion thing, but I think I approve of your metaphor."

"And you're okay with the fact that I've picked out clothing for you?"

He pauses. "Are we back to the flat-front pants or still on the metaphor and referring to your brothers?"

"I was still on the metaphor, but now I'm curious about both."

He grins, kisses me again. "I'm happy with all the clothing you've picked out for me. Especially when I catch you staring at my ass in them. And yes, now I'm just referring to the pants."

"I do not," I lie.

"Yeah, okay." His tongue teases the seam of my lips and I open up and let him in, falling back on the couch and taking him with me. It's addictive, being with him, touching him, kissing him, and though a month didn't sound like a big deal when he first mentioned it, now it sounds on par with climbing Everest.

"I'm gonna miss this," I say, sliding my hands up the back of his shirt, feeling firm muscle and soft skin. "I might've been a little overconfident about that whole 'month' thing."

He chuckles softly and rests his forehead on mine. "I'm already having a hard time knowing my bed won't have you in it on Sunday night. You'd think I'd have learned not to overestimate my restraint when it comes to you."

"Well, for what it's worth, I wouldn't have been in your bed Sunday night anyway," I point out. "I can't exactly leave the boys for a night to stay with you. Ever."

"Right," he mutters. "And staying at your place...."

"Probably not the best idea. No wall units," I add with a rueful smile.

He lowers himself while rolling me over so now he's lying on the couch and I'm on top of him, his arms holding me in place. "We really like a challenge, huh?"

"Do you?" I ask, tousling a wayward strand of hair. "Because we don't have to do this. Jess—"

"Is not you," Connor says firmly, lifting his mouth to mine. "We'll figure it out, Lizzie. All of it. One way or another."

Once again, his voice holds enough confidence and conviction to make me a believer. I shimmy down a bit to rest my head on his chest, and this time, when we close our eyes and fall asleep, we don't wake up until morning.

• • •

Saturday morning breakfast is long and leisurely, with Connor doing the cooking for everyone as we huddle in the kitchen, wrapped in blankets and coming up with gross ideas for omelets using Thanksgiving leftovers.

Afterward, Ty and Max take Pete for a walk, Connor holes himself up in my room with some work he hasn't yet touched this weekend, and I walk over to Nancy's as we'd planned on the phone earlier that week. "Okay," I say, taking a deep breath. "I'm ready for this round of lessons on 'How to Be an Adult.'"

Nancy grins. "You're doing great, Lizzie. Do you want to start with balancing a checkbook, dealing with car payments and insurance, or paying off the mortgage? Or," she adds with a tip of her head, "now that I have you alone again, do you want to explain to me how you plan to deal with the fact that your boyfriend—whom you neglected to reveal is *extremely* good-looking, by the way—is your Teaching Assistant?"

My cheeks flame at the question. "He's not my boyfriend," I mumble, as if Nancy doesn't have a finely honed bullshit detector.

"Oh, really? So he drove five hours for a free dinner and some tutoring?"

"I mean, I guess he *is*, or will be...." I drop my head into my hands. "I have no clue what we're doing, Nancy. Neither of us does."

She reaches out and strokes my hair, so much like my mother used to do. "It's not ideal, sweetheart. But you already knew that."

"Yeah, but I also didn't think it would actually *happen*," I admit. "Even when we were...getting to know each other up at Radleigh, I just thought...."

"You didn't think you'd fall in love with him?" she ventures gently.

I stare down at my hands on her kitchen tabletop, bite the insides of my lips, shake my head.

"But you did."

I nod. I'm a fucking marionette.

"And he feels the same way about you?" She pauses. "Well, never mind. That's a stupid question. I've seen the way he looks at you."

I smile a bit at that, but I still can't meet her eyes. I'm so stupid. So, so fucking stupid.

She wraps an arm around my shoulders and pulls me into her so my head is resting against hers. "Everything's going to be okay, Lizzie."

"How mad at me do you think my parents would be right now if they knew?"

She laughs lightly. "Your mother would not be thrilled. Your father...would at least be able to empathize a bit."

At that, I jerk upright. "I'm sorry, *what*?"

"Oh, it's nothing like *this*," she says, a teasing tone in her voice, "but your father had *such* a crush on one of our professors in law school. I dare say it actually made Manuella nervous, except there's no way he would've acted on it. Nor would the professor, who turned out to be partnered to a rather lovely woman."

"Whoops."

"Very oops." She tucks a piece of hair behind my ear. "Your brothers seem to like him, at least. And it would appear that is mutual."

"It does appear that way, doesn't it? Is that good? Bad? Does it mean I made this whole weird thing happen too fast?"

"Lizzie, darling, you didn't *make* anything happen. It *happened*. That's love. But have you thought about what you'll do when you get back to school?"

"Not much we *can* do," I say with a shrug. "Stay apart for the next month, then figure it out from there."

"How stupid do you think I am?"

"Hey, I'm wishful thinking."

She laughs and kisses my forehead. "Whatever you do, Lizzie, just be careful. His career is important, but so's yours. I'd warn you about your heart, too, but somehow I have a feeling it's safe with that one."

"Somehow, I have the same feeling," I say, my insides suffusing with warmth. "But forgetting about Connor for a second, I have to ask you—do you think the boys are doing okay?"

"They seem to be. Why, has Max had more nightmares?"

"No, but…I guess I want them to be more than okay. I want them to be happy. And I'm afraid that's not gonna happen up there." I lower my voice, in case the boys return. "I think they miss it here, and I'm afraid I'm being selfish, keeping them up at Radleigh."

"Do you want to come back here?" Nancy asks.

I bite my lip. "Well, no, but...I don't know. It's not just about what I want."

"Your parents didn't ask if this is where you want to live. It's what worked for them, for their jobs."

"Yeah, but I'm not them. I don't even have a job."

"Going to school *is* your job. And anyway, what would it be here? Something at the mall?"

There's no point in responding; we both know I don't have better answers to this than when we first talked about it in September. "I just feel like there has to be some sort of happy medium."

"There isn't always. Sometimes, life just gives you cancer and a cheating husband and takes your leg, you know?"

My mouth drops open; I've never heard Nancy talk that bluntly about...well, any of that before. "Nancy—"

She laughs. "Yeah, I know, I'm supposed to be over all that. Some days I am. But most days I was, it was because I lived next door to my best friends."

I squeeze her hand as tears fill my eyes. Sometimes, I forget that Ty, Max, and I weren't the only ones who lost family when my parents died. "Maybe you should move up to Radleigh," I joke. "We'd love to have you."

She squeezes my hand back. "Pretty sure my college days are over, but it's nice to have you three back again, even if just for a long weekend. And it's nice to meet Connor, too. He really is a nice boy. Well," she amends with a grin, "a nice *man*, anyway."

A blush fills my cheeks again, but it's a good kind of blush. A happy one. "How about you teach me that whole checkbook thing now," I suggest, ducking my head, and when she laughs, I think, *You may not be my mother, but I am so, so lucky to have you.*

· · ·

I do learn how to balance a checkbook, though I'm sure I'll be calling her for refreshers, and I get pretty well versed in car payments, insurance, paying utilities for my parents' house via internet, and a whole bunch of other fun things. It feels good, if a bit daunting, to finally be able to take some of the responsibilities Nancy's been juggling. And while I'm sure I'll screw up plenty, I've already screwed up plenty in the past, and I'm learning there's not a whole lot you can't come back from.

We decide to leave on the early side of Sunday, to make a fun day out of the long ride back to Radleigh. Both our car and Connor's are packed full of stuff we didn't bring back with us the first time around— warmer clothes, a few things of our parents', and, despite my overwhelming objections, the notorious green album.

"Who's riding up with me for round one?" Connor asks as the boys put on their coats while I take a final look around the house, making sure we didn't leave anything behind.

"Can I sit in the front if I do?" Max asks excitedly.

"Definitely not." I find his gloves and hat in the closet and make sure he's fully suited up. "But I bet Connor would love listening to that song about the trains a couple hundred times."

Connor raises his eyebrows at me, and I smile sweetly.

"Yeah, Connor?" Max looks up at him with those big brown puppy-dog eyes and I know without a doubt my boyf—whatever—is about to get suckered in.

As expected, Connor smiles. "Sure, buddy. Sounds great. You have the CD?"

"It's in our car. I'll go get it."

"Ty, go with him, please. Make sure he doesn't run into the street."

"Yes, boss."

The boys go out to the driveway, leaving Connor and me alone for our last few moments before everything changes again. "Sorry about that," I say impishly, not really all that sorry. "I just can't take any more of that thing."

He laughs and wraps his arms around my waist. "Well, I really appreciate that you're willing to subject me to the torture, then."

"Always," I murmur as my arms encircle his neck and I pull him down for a kiss. "Besides, it's only for an hour, and then we'll meet up at the bowling alley near Monticello."

"Okay, but I should warn you. I'm probably going to judge your fashion sense the second you put on bowling shoes, just because I can."

"Bowling shoes are cool," I tell him as I lay one more soft kiss on his lips, just before the boys come slamming back into the house. "It just takes someone as hot as I am to pull them off."

He looks me up and down appreciatively, but keeps his thoughts quiet as Ty and Max charge back over to us, that horrid album in hand. "All right," I say, just like Dad used to. "Let's get this show on the road."

• • •

It's late at night by the time we get back, both boys passed out in my car for the final leg of the trip, but I can't imagine any of us have any regrets. We bowled near Monticello, went to the mall in Binghamton, bundled up together to watch the sun set at Sandy Island Beach, and went for dinner in Watertown. It was only there, twenty minutes from Radleigh, that I realized how much closer school is to Montreal than to

Pomona. I didn't say anything about it then, but after the boys are in bed and I'm washed up and ready to do the same, I call Connor.

"Miss me already?" he says with a smile in his voice.

"Yes, but that's not why I'm calling."

"Well, this sounds ominous."

"It isn't," I assure him. "I don't think it is, anyway. I just wanted to know—I know you don't celebrate American Thanksgiving, but Montreal is only, like, three hours away from here. I can't believe I forgot that, considering Frankie was always trying to get us to go for the weekend last year, but none of us had cars and we didn't feel like taking the bus."

"It is about three hours, yes."

"So, why weren't you going home anyway? Like, just to *be* home for the long weekend? You obviously could've driven there no problem."

He's quiet, and I wonder if I've ventured into too-personal territory.

Do we still *have* too-personal territory?

"You know what you said about how we don't choose family?" he says finally.

"Yes."

"Well, let's just say that no one in my family chose me."

The bitterness in his voice squeezes my heart. "But your mom called, that first week I was in your office—"

"She calls sometimes," he concedes. "She's usually drunk, or wants to know if I've heard from my sister, or both. Mostly I'm just the kid who ran off her boyfriend, and I always will be."

There's a horrible irony in that my parents, who would've loved us both enough for a billion parents, are gone, and his still walk the earth as cruel, heartless assholes.

But I don't know if that's okay to say—I'm still sort of working on the whole "tact" thing. And now that we're back at Radleigh, I'm scared that everything that's happened over the past few days was just some sort of Pomona-centric fairytale. Insecurity, especially over a guy, isn't usually my color, and yet despite the fact that he's told me he loves me, and we've spent a major holiday together, and had a *lot* of incredible sex, it all feels so...fragile.

"I still choose to wrap myself in you," I say quietly, both because he needs to know someone does and because I need to know he feels the same way, still, even though we're back in a scarier place to say it.

"And that's why I'd drive five hours to you any day over three hours to her." His voice sounds warm again, and it travels straight to my toes.

"Good thing you don't have to do that to see me."

"A very good thing," he murmurs back. "Though my bed feels ten sizes too big right now without you flinging your arms in my face."

"Funny, I was just thinking how quiet mine is without your snoring."

His low, brief laugh makes my skin buzz with longing, which is only compounded when he says, "Goodnight, Elizabeth."

"Goodnight," I manage back, but when I hang up, it takes me far too long to fall asleep in solitude.

chapter twenty

When I wake up the next morning after a restless night's sleep, my first thought is that I need to see Connor again, need to know where we stand now that we're back at Radleigh. But all of that slips out of my brain in a heartbeat when I hear moaning and realize it's Max begging for "Mommy" from his bed.

He's only had one nightmare since he started going to therapy, and even that one was considerably calmer than the first, but this time, he sounds miserable. So miserable that I'm shocked to see he's actually awake when I slip into his bedroom.

"I think he's sick," says Tyler from where he's standing across the room, as if Max is shedding cooties. "His forehead is hot and stuff."

Shit. It really is. "Do we have a thermometer?" I ask Ty.

"How should I know?"

Right. That's my job. Which means we definitely don't. "Crap," I mutter. I'm about to ask Ty to fetch the Tylenol when I realize Max probably needs some sort of children's kind. The kid's seven; pretty sure swallowing pills is out of his domain.

Kind of like parenting is obviously out of mine.

How am I still so bad at this? Nothing calling Nancy can do for me now; I need to get to a drugstore, and I can't exactly leave Max here. But do I send Ty and have him miss school? Do I leave Ty here to babysit while *I* go? I'm obviously missing class either way, a fact I need to communicate to Professor Ivanova as soon as possible.

I'm itching to call Connor; I know he could and would help in a heartbeat. But I also know if I get within ten feet of him, I won't be able to be held responsible for my actions, and I—we—promised a month.

Besides, *he's* not their guardian; I am. And I need to be able to do this stuff on my own.

Executive decision time. "Ty, you should go to school; I don't want you to miss your first day back, and I don't need Max getting you sick, either. Do you have any friends you can ask to pick you up? It's too cold for you to bike."

He looks a little uncomfortable at the question, and my heart aches at the realization the answer might be "no." Is it possible Ty's been at school here two months without making any real friends? Jesus; I thought having only two was bad.

"Okay, forget it. I'll drive you, and we'll just have to bundle Max up in the backseat." I hate the idea of taking Max outside, but I honestly have no idea what else to do. By the time I drop Ty off, Max is burning up and whimpering, and I still don't have medicine.

I do, however, have all the respect in the world for single parents.

I drive us to the health clinic and tell Max to put on his cutest, most pathetic face imaginable.

Thankfully, it only takes us twenty minutes to get inside, and once we're there, Max gets in relatively quickly. He doesn't want me in the room—apparently he's a very tough, old seven now—so I give him a kiss on his burning forehead and leave him with the doctor while I go upstairs to the pharmacy to stock up on all the children's medicine I should've already had on hand.

I'm waiting on line at the counter when I notice the rows of colorful condoms lining the walls. I have a few on hand between my purse and my night stand, and Connor took back all the extras from Thanksgiving— not that there were many left over—but I'm definitely low enough that the promise of regular fornication would be leading me to buy some right now.

I won't need them for a month, but there's no harm

in being prepared, right? Or will I look like a total perv, buying condoms along with children's Tylenol?

"Miss?"

I blink, and realize there's no one standing in front of me, and I'm holding up the line. To buy or not to buy?

"Um, you're next," says the girl behind me.

Thank you, Captain fucking Obvious. "Sorry, you can go ahead," I say, quickly stepping behind her. I don't know why I'm so hung up on this. They're just condoms. I've bought them a zillion times. Well, more like four or five—Trevor was actually really good about it, and before him, there were just random guys here and there, most of whom optimistically carried them in their wallets.

She gives me a weird look but moves forward, empty-handed. "I'm just here for a refill," she says to the guy behind the counter. When she gives the name of the medication, it actually sounds familiar, and then I realize that's because it's Cait's birth control pill.

I've never been on the Pill before; I've never really trusted myself to do the whole "take it at the same time every day" thing. But now I have an actual, daily routine…one that will hopefully involve copious amounts of sex starting a month from now. Really, really good sex. Sex involving a man who's quite skilled with his tongue and—

"Next!"

I shuffle up to the counter and put down the bottles of chewable pills.

"Just these?"

I glance up at the condoms on the wall behind him one last time. "Just these."

• • •

By Thursday morning, Max is back in school and I'm an anxious mess. I contacted Professor Ozgur rather than Connor to tell him I'd be missing class on Tuesday, and Connor had the assignment sent to me through someone else as well. After going on four days with no communication, not to mention the fact that I've barely left my apartment and Ty's been super ornery since we got back, I'm going a little crazy and a *lot* paranoid that he's changed his mind.

I hope not, both for obvious reasons and because I've got an appointment at the clinic later this afternoon to get tested and get a prescription for the Pill. Just thinking about seeing him in class this morning fills me with nervous butterflies, and I'm not sure I can wait. *After all*, I reason as I change from the outfit I wore to drop off the boys this morning, *we should probably see each other in private first. Just to make sure we're okay.*

It's a stupid idea, and I know it, but I need it for my own sanity. Connor's office hours are officially on

Tuesday and Friday mornings, but I know he's always there for the hour or two before class on Thursday on as well. I take a little more time with hair and makeup than usual, add a little of the jasmine perfume I know he loves, and head over to the history department on what feel like strangely unsteady feet.

As I near his office, I start to get flashbacks to the day I let myself into his office to kiss him, and I'm tempted to turn and run. I'd been so confident that day, so sure of where things were gonna go, and I couldn't have been more wrong. Well, I suppose I could've been a *little* more wrong...but if he pulled the same initial freakout now, after Thanksgiving....

No. I shake my head as I turn the corner to the hallway to his door. *He wouldn't. Not again.*

And then I freeze in my tracks. Because there's an actual line of students tracking from his office. A conspicuously all-female line. In all the times I've been here, I've never seen more than one student waiting for Connor, and that was usually when we had to run paper topics by him. What the hell is going on?

"Did I miss a paper assignment?" I ask the two girls chatting at the back, both of whom are wearing miniskirts with their Uggs despite the fact that it's a billion fucking degrees below zero outside.

"Nope," one of them—Cecily, I think—responds, flipping long cornrows over her shoulder. "Just hoping for a little extra help before the final."

The other girl, a skinny redhead with a cute rash of freckles across her nose, just smiles cheekily, and the two exchange a glance and dissolve into giggles. There's clearly a joke everyone else here is in on, and I don't get it.

Then Connor's door pops open, and a girl with flawless peaches-and-cream skin and a smirk I wish I could literally pull off her face with my stubby nails walks out. *So fucking hot,* she mouths at my new friends as she walks toward us down the hall, and Cecily laughs and gives her a behind-the-back high five as she passes.

What the hell?

"Is she talking about *Connor?*" I ask the redhead. "Am I in the right place?"

Both girls look at me like I've gone insane. "Uh, duh," says Cecily. "Girl, where have you been?"

Underneath him! I want to scream, but I settle for clenching my fists at my sides as I watch the next girl prance inside and close the door behind her. "I just...never really thought of him that way," I lie.

"I didn't at first either," the redhead admits, "but he's become a serious babe lately." She nods down the line. "Pretty sure we're not the only ones who've noticed."

If my insecurities about our relationship were playing just below the surface before, now they're pinging around everywhere like pinballs, threatening to burst out of my skin. Especially when I hear flirtatious laughter coming through the door, and it doesn't all belong to the girl.

"I thought he was a total tightass," Cecily adds, "but then he was really fun when he led class on Tuesday, and—"

"Wait. He led class on Tuesday? Not, like, discussion session, but actual class?"

Cecily and Redhead laugh. "Guess you skipped, huh?" says Cecily.

"Not on purpose," I murmur, and then the door opens again, a shotgun blast stirring everyone into silence. The girl walks out slowly, wearing her two minutes alone with Connor like some weird badge of pride, and I grit my teeth so hard they might actually crack.

Then, suddenly, Connor himself steps out of his office, and I suck in a breath through my teeth. *Holy shit.* He *does* look different, I can see now that we've been a few days apart. He's sticking with the flat-front pants and slim-fitting shirts, but they look more sexy-casual on him now, with his sleeves rolled up to reveal those solid forearms, and an extra button open up top. His hair looks different too, not like he's cut it but like he's actually spent three seconds with it. And he's smiling, something that used to rival unicorn sighting in its rarity.

The overall effect is fucking gorgeous.

"Seems like she gets it now," I hear either Redhead or Cecily murmur to the other, and a deep, visceral longing for the days when I was the only one who did—other than Frankie, admittedly—jars me.

"I really appreciate how many of you are making an effort to come to office hours," says Connor, "but I'm afraid most of you are gonna be late—" His eyes flicker on me then, standing on line like all the other horny losers in his class, and I can feel my face reddening. "I'm gonna have to close up shop now. But feel free to come back tomorrow morning at nine."

There's some grumbling and a little just-shy-of-pathetic begging, but eventually, the line dissipates and girls start to shuffle off. I genuinely don't know if I'm supposed to shuffle off with them, but when I glance up at him, there's a hard, hot look in his eyes that makes me think I need to find an excuse to stick around just a minute longer. I pull out my phone and pretend to text someone, as if I'm not quite ready to move back out into the cold without a new plan, and stay put while everyone else drifts out around me. Finally, when I can no longer hear the chattering of voices, Connor jerks his head toward his office and disappears inside.

I look around one last time, and, satisfied that we're alone, I follow him in and close the door. "Hi," I say as we take our usual seats on opposite sides of his desk.

"Hi."

"You taught class on Tuesday."

The corner of his mouth curves up. "I did."

"Apparently, you were great."

"I thought I was pretty good, yeah," he says bashfully, but I can hear the pride coloring his voice.

"I'm sorry I missed it," I say, and I mean it as much as I've ever meant anything.

He laughs sheepishly. "I was too, until I realized I probably would've been twelve times as nervous if you'd been there. Probably for the best."

I just nod. Ordinarily I would've taken a lot of pleasure in the fact that I make him nervous, but right now, he's making *me* nervous, and it's more than a little unsettling. I don't want competition when it comes to Connor. I just want him to be mine. The image of his body beneath me, biceps flexing as he held me firmly, flashes through my brain, and the need to claim him again is so strong I have to dig my heels into the carpet.

"Stop looking at me like that," he says hoarsely.

"Like what?"

"Like you know what." He swallows, hard, and it's a relief to see I still have this effect on him.

"Like I want to fuck your brains out?" I ask innocently, feeling a little more in control again. "It's okay to say the words, Connor."

He groans but offers no other articulate response.

"You're looking at me the same way, you know."

"I know," he says, voice low. "Trust me, I know." He drops the pen he'd been unconsciously clicking and pushes back from his desk. "Did you have to wear...that?"

"What's wrong with my outfit?" I'm being an asshole. I may not be wearing a miniskirt, but my boobs look insanely good in this shirt, and the neckline ensures you can see as much as you like. Especially when I lean over his desk. The red lace bra I'm wearing underneath probably isn't helping.

"You *want* to ruin me, right? That's your plan? Revenge for the first month of middling grades?"

He's not angry. I know his face, his voice, when he's angry. The fact that he can't keep his eyes out of my shirt isn't a bad sign either.

"Of course not, Connor," I say honestly, getting up to check and see if there's a lock on his door. There is, and I click it. "I definitely don't want that."

This time, I can hear his swallow from across the office. "Elizabeth—"

"You had it right the first time," I say as I sashay over to him and drape myself in his lap, wrap my arms around his neck, smile. "I just want to fuck your brains out."

His cock jumps up behind his fly—poor restrained thing—a split second before he thrusts a hand in my hair and pulls our mouths together. He tastes like his strong coffee, which explains the delicious buzz I feel as his tongue strokes mine. A little purr of contentment rises from my throat, and tapers off into a whimper as he nibbles my lower lip. Then he moves to the hollow below my jaw, and when I feel his gentle sucking at my skin, I can't stop myself from moaning.

"You're making me too loud," I pant as he slides a hand up my shirt.

His lips curve into a smile against my neck. "I know." He leaves a trail of hot, wet kisses on my throat and along my collarbone. "But you make the sexiest sounds." Dipping his head, he kisses down the skin bared by my wide-open collar. Both his hands are massaging my breasts now, lazy thumbs caressing my nipples until they could cut glass.

"Jesus, Connor. You used to be such a good boy. What happened to you?"

"Extremely good sex," he responds without missing a beat before mouthing a breast through my top. "It's a terrible impediment to making good decisions."

It feels so good I can't even form a coherent response, but I know I should stop this, shouldn't even have started it, not in here. But the warmth of his mouth and delicate grazing of his fingertips on my ribs feels so damn good, and it's becoming increasingly difficult to remember why I want to stop this.

Because in all honesty, I don't.

But I also know Connor. I know if he bends me over his desk like I want him to, he'll feel nothing but self-loathing when he sits down at it in the morning. Some teachers get off on the idea of fucking students, but to him, the fact that I'm in his class is probably the biggest turn-off about me.

And I know that not so deep down, despite that he's officially made his peace with it, the fact that he's fucking a student is probably his least favorite thing about himself, too.

So even though I know I'll be spending the entire night with my vibrator as a result, I cup Connor's cheek in my hand and lift his head up until our foreheads are touching. "I'll still love you in a month," I say softly.

He collapses against me, his gentle laughter ghosting over my lips. "You sure know how to take the sting out of rejection."

"I'm not—"

"I know, I know." He brushes my forehead with his lips. "I'm sorry. And thank you."

"*I'm* sorry I started it. I'll try to be good." I tip my head. "Well, at least for the next month. Then all bets are off."

His lips curve up slyly as I extricate myself from his lap. "I wouldn't have it any other way."

"I sincerely hope you plan to be good too," I warn

him, motioning toward his door. "If I'd known half the girls in the class wanted to fuck you, I might've been a lot less amenable to this whole 'month' thing."

He laughs. "Your jealousy is cute, but those girls were just here because the final's coming up."

"Oh, Connor." I roll my eyes. "My jealousy isn't half as cute as your absurd naïveté, but okay. Every girl who was here wants to bone you."

I can tell he thinks I'm kidding, but when I don't crack a smile, his eyebrows shoot up. "Seriously?"

"Don't get too excited about it." I lean over and take his lower lip between my teeth, sucking it into my mouth for a couple of seconds before releasing it. "I can guarantee I'm a better lay than any of them, and I'm not doing the sharing thing anymore. Plus," I add, thinking about the appointment I have scheduled later, "I have a surprise for you, once the semester's over."

"Is that so? Do I get a hint?"

"'Once the semester's over' *was* your hint." I smooth my top and roll my shoulders back. "I should go. I've got class in a few minutes, and I don't think my TA would like it if I showed up late."

"He sounds like a hard-ass."

"Emphasis on 'hard,'" I say lightly, glancing down at the glaring bulge behind his fly. "Sorry about that."

"No you're not."

"No," I say with a grin, "I'm not." I give him one last peck on the lips, but he surprises me by burying his hand in my hair and pulling me close for a long, deep, hungry kiss.

When he pulls back, I swear my mind has gone completely blank, and I know my lips will be too puffy for anyone to miss. "Just wanted to clarify that I'm not, nor will I be, holding these kinds of office hours with anyone else. Ever."

I can only nod in response.

I've never been so excited for a doctor's appointment in my entire life.

chapter twenty-one

It's damn near impossible to keep my focus during class, but at least Professor Ozgur is back at the helm. When the bell rings, Connor leaves almost immediately, and I rush out pretty close behind him, eager to make my appointment. Well, more accurately, I'm eager to get it over with. Although I've always been diligent about using condoms every time and with every guy, the fact that I've never been tested makes me anxious about the results.

Thankfully, the entire process is relatively painless, and when I step out of the OB-GYN's exam room with a clean bill of health and a prescription of a year's worth of birth control pills in hand, I'm feeling pretty good.

Until I nearly smack into Sophie Springer, right there in the office.

"You've got to be kidding me," she utters with

more disgust than I'd previously thought possible to express over someone who's never been convicted of war crimes.

It's hard to blame her for not being thrilled to see me. Connor's right—I wronged her, period. The fact that she's an unbearable bitch doesn't mean it was okay for me to sleep with her boyfriend. I take a deep breath—*nothing* comes less naturally to me than apologizing, especially not to someone I'd just as soon see transfer to Mogadishu University—and force the words out. "Listen, Sophie, I want to apologize. I'm sorry for hooking up with Trevor. It was wrong, and I shouldn't have."

Her eyes widen, her mouth dropping open slightly. "What are you going for here?"

"Nothing," I say, hoping the honesty of my statement comes through. "I'm apologizing. For real. I was wrong, and I'm sorry."

She laughs. Throws her head back and cracks up so loudly it draws the attention of every single other woman in the office. "Are you kidding me? You think I want or need your *apology*? God, you *are* delusional. You can keep that to yourself, thanks."

"Okay," I say stiffly, feeling my face reddening at all the scrutiny on us right now. "Well, I tried." I turn away from her, toward the door, but then I feel her talons clutching my arm.

"I'm going to give you a choice as to how I'm

going to ruin your life," she hisses in my ear. "Which I think is pretty generous, since that's certainly more than you gave me."

"What the hell are you talking about, Sophie?"

"Your boyfriend," she coos, her voice still low, turning the blood in my veins to ice. "You really think I'm going to let your disgusting relationship continue after you destroyed mine?"

"There was nothing in *your* disgusting relationship that hadn't already been destroyed by Trevor being an asshole."

She narrows her flint-gray eyes. "Maybe I won't give you a choice after all. Maybe I'll just tell your professor, and the administration, and your social worker, and let shit fly."

Oh my God, she knows. She knows a *lot*. How is that even possible?

I force myself to keep a neutral expression on my face. "Whatever you think you know, you're wrong."

"Oh, don't even. I've seen the two of you."

"The two of who?" I ask innocently, hoping against hope she's bluffing out of her ass. I've barely touched Connor anywhere people could've seen us.

"I *was* going to be more subtle about it in public," she says dramatically, as if doing me the world's greatest favor, "but apparently you *want* me to announce that you're fucking Con—"

I yank her outside the office before she can finish,

and her cackling echoes into the external hallway. "You little whore," she marvels, shaking her head. "Aren't you even the tiniest bit embarrassed at how many guys you let use you for sex? Especially when you're supposed to be acting like a role model to those two little boys?"

"Leave my brothers out of this," I spit. "What the fuck do you want, you psycho?"

"I told you—I want you to destroy yourself. Take your pick. Either you can tattle on your TA to your professor and everyone else, and get him booted, or you can drop out and move back to your sad little house in bumblefuck. See? Your choice."

"You are so fucked-up—"

"*Knocked*-up, honey. The term is knocked-up."

Oh. Shit. "You're not."

"Oh, I am," she says, holding out the paper I hadn't noticed in her hand until now, which is most definitely a positive pregnancy test with her name on it. "In case you weren't sure just how much I despise you."

"*I* didn't get you pregnant!"

"No, you just fucked my baby's father, then told the whole world about it."

This conversation is too surreal for words. Trevor had gotten Sophie pregnant, Connor and I weren't the secret we thought we were, and I had the shittiest choice imaginable to make.

Not that either choice was an option. I certainly couldn't drop out; if I did, I'd lose my scholarship and be completely fucked. Not to mention that the boys are already enrolled in school here. I can't just pull them back out, whether they love it or not. And there's no way in hell I'm going to ruin Connor like that, either. I wouldn't. He'd be finished at Radleigh; maybe even finished teaching completely.

Or maybe not. I'm legal, age-wise at least. I know it's not *good*, but maybe it's not so bad?

"Stop trying to think; your brain will probably explode from the effort." She smiles cruelly. "So, which is it?"

"I don't know," I say flatly.

"Well, figure it out."

"Thanks, I'll just go ahead and do that." *Fucking psycho.*

I turn on my heel and walk away, my hands trembling as I clutch my prescription, "You have until tomorrow" ringing out after me in the otherwise empty hallway.

• • •

"She's full of shit," Frankie says decisively, raking a chip through the plastic tub of guac that sits in the middle of the table in the common room of the suite. "Sophie Springer has zero power. If she really had any, her boyfriend wouldn't have been able to screw around on her for months in the first place."

"It's so *not* that simple, Frank." Cait takes a sip from the water bottle at her side. "Just because Trevor has more doesn't mean Sophie has none. Anyway, it doesn't sound like it'd take much. All she has to do is get to your professor before Connor does and he's pretty fucked."

"I still can't believe you were banging Hottie Historian and you didn't even tell us," Frankie muses, popping the chip into her mouth. "I should've known when you messed with him at Delta, but I totally thought you were gonna hook up with that friend of his."

God, that night feels like a zillion years ago. "I told you, I *wasn't* banging anyone." I nip the edge off a chip. "He was just helping me out with some things, and it...happened. I don't even understand how she knows."

"Maybe she's just seen you flirt," Frankie suggests. "Maybe she doesn't really *know* anything for sure. I mean, it's not like she has pictures."

"Does she?" asks Cait.

"I have no freaking clue *what* she has," I admit grumpily. "For all I know, she's bluffing completely. But what if she isn't?"

"I think this is a sign." Cait forgoes the chips, dipping a baby carrot in the guac instead. Other than the Twizzlers, she eats like she's perpetually in training for the Olympics. "You need to get out of this while you can. It can't end well."

Both Frankie and I turn to glare at her. "No way. If she dumps him, Sophie wins," Frankie says firmly.

"Never mind Sophie," I add. "I don't *want* to break up with him. If it were that easy, I wouldn't have a dilemma to begin with."

"Okay, then you need to get Connor to tell the professor himself." Frankie snags one of the baby carrots and crunches into it. "It's gotta be worth *something* if he beats Sophie to the punch."

"She's right," says Cait. "The big issue is that he grades your tests and stuff, right? So he needs to tell your professor that he can't grade yours."

It makes sense, but still, the thought of asking Connor to do this makes me sick to my stomach. We'd agreed to put things on hold, and obviously we sort of sucked at it, but I did genuinely think we'd make it through the next few weeks without incident. This…it's going to embarrass the shit out of him—with Professor Ozgur, with the rest of the class, with the other grad students—if he's even willing to do it at all.

Both Cait and Frankie frown when I share my hesitations. "Lizzie B," says Frankie. "He's the one in the position of power. He needs to man up."

"That's all well and good," I say, drawing swirls in the guacamole with a chip, "but what if he won't?"

"Then he's not worth it," says Cait, ever blunt.

"This is, like, baseline, and it's what he should've done to start with."

"That's easy for us to say," I argue, "but what if he loses his teaching position over this? What if he can't stay at Radleigh if he loses it? He's supposed to lose his future over some chick?"

"You're not *some chick*." Frankie grasps my chin firmly in her palm, and I try to ignore the streaks of charcoal on her skin that are almost definitely transferring to mine. "You're Elizabeth fucking Brandt, and he's lucky to have you, no matter what it means giving up."

"Hear, hear," says Cait, lifting her water bottle.

I shake my head, laughing, and lift up a chip laden down with guac in a mock toast. If there's one thing I know for sure, it's that if I ever did make the decision to run back to Pomona instead of sticking it out here, I would miss the crap out of these girls.

• • •

It takes a shot of tequila, a bunch of deep breaths, and three pieces of nicotine gum before I can get up the nerve to call Connor. I'm dreading this conversation with every fiber of my being, but I know Cait and Frankie are right about this—it's the only thing we can do, and it's probably what we should've done to begin with.

It rings three times, and I wonder if he's screening

my calls, especially after I showed up this morning. But then his voice, or at least a gruff version of it, says, "Hey."

I know a time will come when that voice won't make my skin tingle down to my toes, even in my most anxious moments, but right now, I'm appreciating it while it still does. "Hey. I'm sorry to call."

"I should probably be sorry too, but it's been a really shitty day," he says, laughing bitterly. "It's nice to hear your voice."

Sophie. Shit. Has she already gotten to him in some way? "What's wrong?"

"Nothing you need to worry yourself with. Just dissertation crap. And family crap. With an awkward cherry on top."

I breathe a sigh of relief that none of that sounds Sophie-related, but then realize that doesn't actually help the fact that he's had a really lousy day. He sounds so miserable, and I hate that I'm not there to give him a hug right now, that I can't be. "Talk to me," I say, because it's all I can offer.

So he does. He tells me about how his advisor thinks he needs to take a portion of his dissertation in a different direction, and how a site he's supposed to visit in the spring is going to be closed due to construction. I have absolutely nothing of wisdom to say, and in fact know nothing about how any of this stuff works, but I vow to learn as soon as humanly possible.

"And what happened with your family?" I pry gently, because at least family I know a little bit about. "Your mom call again?"

"Oh, no, not this time," he says, anger so apparent in his voice that I wonder if his father's somehow come back into the picture, though it seems like that would've been his opener. "This time, it was finding out on my sister's fucking *blog* that she's getting married."

"I'm sorry, *what*?" I don't mean to blurt it out, but the image of Ty trying something like that makes a vein pop out in my forehead.

He sighs. "Yep. Apparently the wedding's in a month. In Mumbai. So, even if I wanted to attend, there'd be no chance in hell I could afford a ticket."

"Did you call her, at least?"

"To say what? Congratulations on the wedding you never even planned to tell me about?"

"Well," I say, searching for something to make this a little better, "I'm sure she thinks you read her blog. Which, actually, I thought you didn't."

He laughs shortly. "Well, after you asked me about it in my office, I felt bad that I don't read it more, given that it's pretty much our only connection other than the postcards she sends. So I started reading it regularly. I guess it's a good thing."

"It is," I say softly. "I know your family…leaves a lot to be desired, but you only get handed one. I'm not trying to play the 'dead parents' card, but cutting your ties while she's still around and walking the mortal plane seems less than optimal."

"How is that not playing the 'dead parents' card?"

"Fine. I played the 'dead parents' card. But you should call her. Hell, you can even tell her she's not the only Lawson sibling pairing off."

"That sounds like a great conversation," Connor says wryly. "Hey, sis, congratulations on the engagement I found out about online. I can't afford to come, not that I was invited, but if I could, I'd be bringing the student I'm sleeping with, who's almost young enough to be your daughter. Are you registered at Crate & Barrel?"

I suck in a deep breath through my teeth but it does nothing to calm the stabbing feeling of his words. "Wow, Connor. Fuck you. 'The student I'm sleeping with'? Really? That's what I am to you?"

"*Tabarnac.*" He sighs so deeply it seems to come from his bones. "I'm sorry. That was...I didn't mean that."

I don't answer. I won't say anything nice if I do.

"It's been a really shitty day," he continues softly, all the fight out of his voice, "and I just kept thinking about how all I wanted to do at the end of it was be with you. And then remembering I couldn't, that the only person in the world who could make this day better is *right fucking here* and I still can't have you—it just made me that much more bitter. Which is obviously a really dick thing to take out on you."

"Yep," I agree, though his apology has already thawed my anger and we both know it. "I guess learning you're apparently Radleigh's new most fuckable TA didn't help that?"

"Pretty sure my ego peaked the first time I made you come. Everything else is just sprinkles on the sundae."

"'Sprinkles on the sundae'? God, how do you make being such a dork so hot?"

"Years of practice, baby. Years of practice."

I snort, and he laughs, and it's really good to hear. "So, do I get to hear about the awkwardness?" I ask.

"Oh, it's nothing," he says. "I just bumped into Jess again and she tried to take me up on that whole 'raincheck' thing."

"Yikes."

"Yeah. 'I'm seeing someone' didn't go over so well considering I wasn't a couple of weeks ago when I told her I was too busy."

"Seeing someone?" I tease. "That's a cute way to put this whole thing."

"Hey, we've gone on actual dates. We've had dinner together—"

"At my house and apartment, with my family."

"And gone to the movies—"

"Again, with my family, and mostly because you

convinced me that I needed to chaperone Ty and his date from a distance."

"And gone bowling, and gotten ice cream—we are very much seeing each other, thank you very much. A date with tween boy chaperones is still a date."

"I suppose these outings *do* generally end in kissing," I concede.

"That's what makes a date?"

"That's what makes a *good* date."

He laughs. "Duly noted. I will keep that in mind when planning all future outings."

"If you need to remind yourself to kiss me, I'm definitely doing something wrong."

"There's no winning with you, is there?" he asks with a sigh.

"Not really."

We're both quiet for a moment, and then he says, "Thank you."

"For what?"

"For proving me right that just a few minutes with you can make my whole day better." I can hear the smile in his voice, and it's contagious. I like having proven him right on that front too. "Sorry I sorta blew that earlier."

"We're both gonna fuck up," I say, my stomach turning as I think about Sophie, about what I called to tell him but know I won't, not tonight. "But we'll figure it out, right?"

"Right." As if he knows all there is to figure out. As if he has all the information.

But he has enough on his plate today, and I definitely don't want to pile on any more relating to the whole teacher-student issue. Sophie drama can wait. I'll buy another day, and maybe by the time I can have this conversation with him, I'll have figured something else out.

Or maybe Sophie will transfer to the University of Guam.

A girl can dream.

chapter twenty-two

I'm no closer to figuring out what I'm gonna do about the whole mess when I leave for class the next day, but I figure as long as I avoid the coffee shop, Greek Row, or anywhere else Sophie Springer might be lurking, I'm probably okay.

I am wrong.

"So what'd you decide, Teacher's Pet?"

I whirl around at the entrance to Krieger Hall, home of my Russian class. Now that I'm no longer going to office hours with Connor, it's my only Friday class, and it's one I used to skip a decent amount.

Clearly I should've kept up that habit today.

"Are you stalking me?" I ask Sophie with a scowl.

"I don't need to stalk you," she says with that charming homecoming-queen-serial-killer smile of hers. "I know everything."

"I can't believe this is all coming from someone who called *me* delusional," I snap at her, stepping away from the door and giving her no choice but to follow me. "You don't even know what you're talking about, and you're going to ruin a good guy over it, and it's *still* not going to make you feel better about what happened."

She shrugs. "Won't make me feel worse."

I've wondered a few times over the past couple of months whether I'm a terrible human being. Now I know I'm clearly not, because this is what it looks like when someone really, truly sucks at life.

"Please tell me that you of all people are not actually bringing a baby into this world," I mutter, keeping an eye on the students walking past, hoping to spot someone in my Russian class who'll grab me away from this conversation.

She laughs. "You're kidding, right? Not that it's any of your business, but no, I'm not. So you can try and spread my little secret around, but after next weekend, it's just gonna be a lie anyway."

"Jesus, Sophie. If you're not even having it then why is this so fucking important to you?"

"Because I hate you," she says as coolly as if she'd just informed me she thinks cilantro tastes like soap. "And yet you're still here, so I take that to mean it's time I pay Professor Ozgur a visit, correct?"

"Burn in hell," I spit as kids behind me start dashing in, letting me know I'm about to be late. "I'm not responding to this stupid blackmail shit, and I'm glad you're not having this baby—you would've been a really fucking terrible mother. You have no idea what it's like to care about people."

"And you do?" she counters, eyebrows raised.

I do now, I think, but she doesn't deserve my response, doesn't deserve my attention, doesn't even deserve to make me late.

All I have is the fervent hope that she's bluffing, and sometime in the next hour and fifteen minutes, I'll figure out exactly what to do if I'm wrong.

• • •

I may as well have skipped Russian for all that I'm able to focus on poetry by Anna Akhmatova. All I can think about is Sophie out there in the world, planning my demise, and poor Connor, who knows nothing about it. And my brothers—oh, my brothers—who are probably going to get caught in some insane crossfire just because their sister's worst enemy is borderline deranged.

The second the bell rings, I bolt out of my seat, pulling my phone out of my bag with the intent to call Connor and have the conversation I should've forced last night. But then I see nine missed calls, from a combination of Cait and Frankie, neither of whom ever call when a text will do.

This cannot be good.

I do an about-face and head toward the dorm instead of my apartment, calling Cait back as I go. She answers on the first ring, and immediately puts me on speaker. "Where the hell have you been?" she demands.

"I was in class! What the hell happened?"

"In class?" Frankie sounds skeptical. "On a Friday?"

"Believe it or not, I was *supposed* to be going to Russian on Fridays in September, too," I say wryly. "Now, please tell me there's not an actual emergency."

"Depends on your definition," says Cait. "I assume your brothers are fine, but—"

"It's out there," Frankie jumps in. "You and Connor."

"She posted a picture of you guys," Cait adds. "Not...doing anything. But still. It looks bad."

My stomach bottoms out and I glance around; there are *definitely* people staring at me, staring at their phones, laughing. I speed up, practically running to the dorm. "Do I even want to know the caption?"

"Definitely not," says Cait, at the same time Frankie says, "Beware of Pedophile."

Rage, burning and infinite, works its way up from my insides until it's clawing at my throat, begging to be released in a scream that'll bring down the sky. Thankfully, I reach the dorm just then, and use my pent-up aggression to throw open the door, swipe my ID so hard I almost give the scanner a paper cut, and storm to the room.

"What the *fuck*?" I demand, slamming the door behind me. "I saw her an *hour* ago!"

Cait and Frankie come rushing out of my old room, eyes wide, arms open. "Oh, honey," says Frankie, crushing me against her and kissing the top of my head even though she's two inches shorter than me. "I'm so sorry."

I can feel Cait nearly exploding with the urge to say "I told you so," and I refuse to give her the satisfaction.

"He doesn't deserve this," I say, literally shaking with anger. "He didn't fucking do anything to her. Why would she do this to him?"

Neither of them answers, not that I really thought they'd have any insider info.

"There's no way he knows about this yet," I realize out loud. "I need to get over there. I need to tell him—"

"No," they say simultaneously, shoving me onto the couch. "Right now, Sophie has zero real evidence," says Cait. "She's just using the power of suggestion and a convenient shot she must've gotten after one of your tutoring sessions. You show up at Connor's office now, or, worse, his dorm, and you're just proving she's telling the truth. You need to give him some space. Find another way."

"I can't tell him shit like this over the phone," I protest. I look to Frankie for help, but she's nodding along with Cait. Then she glances at her watch.

"Shit, I have to get to the studio. But Cait's right. Sit tight, Lizzie B." She drops a kiss on my forehead, then grabs her flaming purple coat and faux fur earmuffs. "I'll call you later."

She flounces out, leaving me alone with Cait, who looks...pissed? "Do not give me an 'I told you so,' Caitlin."

"I wasn't going to," she says coolly. We're both quiet for a few moments, and I know she's got more to say.

"Out with it."

She exhales sharply. "I just think it would've been nice not to find all this shit out *after* Sophie. Why didn't you just tell us you were hooking up with him before this?"

"Because I *wasn't*. Not really."

"Is he the Top-Five kisser?"

Oh, right. I forgot I'd told them about that. "See?" I say sheepishly. "I did tell you about him."

She sighs. "I might've been able to help you out with things if I'd known sooner that *he* was the guy you've been obsessed with. Now I have no idea what the hell to do."

"There's nothing *to* do other than tell Connor. If Professor Ozgur finds this out from anyone but him, he's fucked."

"You're right about that," she concedes, nodding sharply. "Okay, yeah, call him."

I do, and there's no answer. I try again, hoping two calls in a row will make clear it's important, in case he's screening while he works, but no luck.

I leave a message to call me, and then I head home. There's nothing more I can do right now.

My life is falling apart, and I'm completely fucking powerless.

• • •

He's not the one who shows up at my door later that night, though; Cait is. She hasn't been back in my apartment since the night she came with me to check it out, so I suspect that whatever she's here to say…it isn't good. She's got a great poker face, though, and waits to open her mouth until I've closed my bedroom door behind us and she's made herself at home on my bed.

"Do I even want to know?" I ask, bracing myself against my desk. "It can't possibly be worse than what she's already done, can it?"

"Actually…." She cocks her head. "It's Trevor."

The groan that rises from my gut sounds a little like a dying animal. "Why, why, *why* does Trevor have to make this worse?"

"Actually," says Cait, a little smile playing on her lips, "he's been spreading the word that Sophie's full of shit, and making this up about you and the professor because she's jealous."

My jaw drops. "You're screwing with me."

"I screw you not. Don't ask me why he's doing it, but he's definitely doing it. Check online."

I rush to my computer—which I'd been avoiding, like I'd been avoiding everything other than my brothers, the TV, and the chocolate stash I hide from Max under my bed—and look at the very picture Cait and Frankie had mentioned before. My stomach roils at the sight of the "Pedophile" caption, but Cait was right—just below a couple of confused and amused comments, there's Trevor, with a surprisingly serious "Sophie, enough with the lies, and shut this down."

Dropping onto the bed, I try to figure out why the hell Trevor would do any of this. Does he genuinely think she's lying? Is he trying to protect me? "Of all people, why would Trevor Matlin stick up for me?" I ask Cait.

"No clue," she says, "but he definitely is. I've heard he's been spreading the word too, including to all the guys in the house, and he tweeted something about her spreading bullshit too."

"Meanwhile, poor Connor has no idea any of this is happening," I murmur. "At least, I don't think he does."

"I can't imagine he doesn't by now. This is *all* anyone's talking about." I shoot her a look, but she just shrugs. "What, you want me to lie?"

"I thought you hated drama."

"I do, but it's a little hard to stay out of it when your best friend is involved," she says wryly. "And you're damn good at finding it."

"You know I didn't mean to."

"I know." She wraps an arm around my shoulders and kisses the top of my head in a very un-Cait-like move. "But I have to admit, there's something sort of sweet about watching you fall so hard for someone. Even if it's sort of gross."

"Gross because it's me or gross because he's my TA?"

She taps her chin in thought. "Both."

"You're a sweetheart, Cait."

I can see her about to respond but then we both hear the doorbell ring and we silently lock eyes.

"Connor," she says. "It has to be."

"But what if it isn't? What if it's Sophie, here to tear me to shreds?"

I expect her to tell me I'm being ridiculous.

She doesn't.

The bell sounds again, and we both move to get up, then freeze when we hear the door open. One of the boys has answered the door. A few seconds later, Ty's voice calls, "Lizzie! Connor's here."

"Shit," I mutter.

"Um, isn't he who you *wanted* to see?"

"In theory, yes. Do I actually want to face him after everything Sophie's done? Hell no."

"Well, you have no choice now, so, get over it." She marches to the bedroom door and swings it open, leaving me no choice but to follow her out.

Connor blanches at the sight of Cait, and I know right then that he has no idea what Sophie's been up to. Which sucks in its own right, since I'll have to tell him now. I glance at Cait, and she squeezes my arm before walking right up to Connor and sticking out a hand. "Hey, I'm Cait. You must be Connor."

"You look familiar," he says, a crease forming in his forehead as he takes the hand she extends and shakes it. Then he smiles sheepishly. "You were at Delta that night."

"Guilty," she says, sounding equally sheepish. The entire thing is surreal. It's the weirdest "best friend meets boyfriend" I've ever experienced, though in fairness, it's also the only one. "I should go, leave you guys to talk. It was nice to officially meet you, Connor."

317

"You too," he says, polite but puzzled. She gives my arm another quick squeeze and lets herself out.

When the door closes behind her, Connor fixes me with a stare. "How long have your friends known? And how does she know we need to talk?"

I glance at Ty, who's still standing there, watching us, clearly eager for some dirt. "Come on," I say, rolling my eyes at my brother and leading Connor into my room. I close the door behind us and ignore Tyler's rude noises in response.

"She hasn't known for long," I tell him as he sits down on my bed, "but...shit. I don't even know how to tell you this. You really haven't heard anything?"

"I've been in meetings all day," he replies, a touch of...something in his tone. It's not quite anger, but it's definitely an edge.

"Is everything okay?"

"I'm not sure," he says, exhaling sharply. "But I told Professor Ozgur."

I blink. Then again. "I'm sorry, you told Professor Ozgur *what*?"

"That I'm in a relationship with one of our students."

Laughter pours out of me before I can stop it, positively bubbling. This was exactly what I'd wanted him to do, yesterday, when it might've made a huge difference. Now the word is out about us anyway, *and* he's confirmed Sophie's non-evidence. Though his way may have allowed him to keep his job—emphasis on *may have*—now his reputation's shot to hell because I didn't get to him in time.

If Professor Ozgur finds out that this information has gotten a whole lot further than his office, Connor is almost definitely fucked.

"This is funny?"

"No," I say, continuing to laugh miserably. "It's awful, actually."

He bites his lip, releases it. "I kind of thought you'd be happy to hear it."

"Connor, fuck, no, that's not—*no*." I take a deep breath, calm myself, and squeeze his hand, which he's balled into a fist. "Listen, I have to tell you something. And it's not actually funny. Like, at all."

"Okay, but just to be clear, you're scaring the shit out of me." He looks me in the eye and swallows hard. "I assume that since it's only been a few days, this isn't you telling me that you're pregnant—"

"You assume correctly." Though now of course I'm wondering what he'd say if that *were* the case, but this doesn't seem like the right time to make up false scenarios when we've got a very real one to deal with. "Unfortunately, Sophie Springer *is*, or at least will be for another few days, and it's made her hate me even more than she used to."

Connor blinks. "Sophie Springer? Why does that name sound familiar?"

"Because she's the one who was either handy with a can of spray paint or knew someone who was." I sigh, my stomach already tensing with nerves at his reaction. "She told people about us. I don't know how she knew, but she tried to blackmail me, and when I told her to go fuck herself, she went on a rampage."

"What does that mean, exactly?" he asks, his voice strained as he struggles to stay calm.

There's no point in sugarcoating it, so I bring my laptop over, show him everything, and fill him in on what I know. By the time I'm done, he looks like he's gonna be sick. Which is how I feel.

"She's psychotic," he utters when he can finally find his voice.

"Connor, I'm so, so sorry. I know that doesn't make up for any of this, but—"

He cups my cheeks in his palms and pulls me in for a long, slow kiss that's so warm and comforting, I think that if we could just stay exactly like this forever, I might be able to ignore all the other shit in my life. But of course, stupid human that I am, I actually need to breathe again; after a few minutes of losing myself in him, we part. "Stop apologizing," he says gruffly. "We're on the same side here. This isn't your fault."

"So now what?" I ask him, running my thumb along his scruffy jawline.

"Now you're stuck with a twenty-five-year-old disgraced history TA who can barely even dress himself. Lucky girl, you."

"Man, when you put it that way." I start to rise from the bed, then laugh when he grabs my arm and pulls me back, into an embrace.

"No way. I get at least one more day for my act of proud boyfriend chivalry." He pauses. "Don't I?"

"A week, even." I reach up and finger the collar of his dress shirt. "You know I'm lucky to be stuck with you, right? You take damn good care of me and my brothers. You teach me new things every day. You make me laugh." Dropping my voice, I lean in to suck at the skin just below his jaw. "Not to mention that you look hot as fuck in the height of nerdwear." I press a kiss to his full lower lip, nip it gently. "You make me come so hard they can probably hear me three towns over. You're pretty much the only thing I've done right since I got to Radleigh."

He swallows hard but doesn't respond. At least not with words. His arms circle my waist but I get the sense he didn't even realize he'd lifted them.

"You make me feel like so much more than I am." His voice sounds so raw, it hurts my throat. "What's gonna happen when you don't need my help anymore? When I can't teach you anything?"

"I'm not with you because I need you, Connor. I'm with you because I want you. And because you have a huge...heart."

He laughs softly into my hair. "God, I love you."

Like liquid warmth through my body, every damn time. "I love you too."

His voice drops to a murmur, soft and warm on the shell of my ear. "I really, really wish your brothers weren't home, because I'd like to do some pretty objectionable things to you right now."

Welp—bye, panties. You weren't that cute today anyway. "I really, really wish that too." I squeeze my eyes—and legs—shut, but I think the ship has sailed on finding any relief. "I'm guessing your place is off limits, huh?"

"I think it's best not to poke the dragon with pointy sticks while I'm still awaiting my fate," he says before pressing a kiss to my forehead. "Truthfully, I shouldn't be here now. It didn't even occur to me you'd have a friend over."

"Because it didn't occur to you I had friends?"

He rolls his eyes. "Because I've lost the ability to think like a fucking grown-up."

"You mean with your head instead of your dick?"

"I was thinking more along the lines of 'instead of my heart' but I suppose it's hard to argue with your version." Raking a hand through his hair, he exhales sharply and tears his eyes from mine. "I should go."

"And then what?" I press. "Will I see you in class on Tuesday, at least?"

"That's up to Professor Ozgur. He said he needed some time to think things over, speak with the disciplinary committee."

"The disciplinary committee? About what? You told Ozgur the truth. Enough of it, anyway."

He laughs bitterly. "Yeah, and the truth is that I'm sleeping with one of our students. Telling him myself just means I'm not *automatically* out on my ass, the way I would've been if he'd found out through one of Sophie's charming posts. I still may lose my fellowship."

My skin grows cold and clammy at his words. "And then what would happen?"

"I'm not sure." His shoulders drop, and my stomach drops with them. "I can't afford next semester without it."

"It won't come to that," I say with confidence I don't feel. Jesus, this is so messed up. "You told him. We'll be fine."

Connor just nods.

"What? What aren't you telling me?"

He sighs deeply. "Nothing. We'll worry about it if it comes down to it."

"You think I'm gonna let it go at that? No, thanks, I've seen enough shoes drop this year. Tell me."

When his gaze finally meets mine again, I can tell it's worse than I thought. "I need to be a student here to stay in the country, Lizzie. If not, I'm gonna have to go back to Canada eventually."

"No," I say before I can stop myself. "No, that's not possible. Not after all this." I sound stupid and childish, but I can't believe this could be it, after everything. "Who's gonna care that you're three fucking hours over the border, Connor? Seriously."

"I don't think we want to find out, given that taking part in illegal activity is just about the worst thing you can do for Ty and Max right now. This is all bad enough. If your social worker finds out, she might decide this in an 'unfit' environment for the boys, and then they'll be sent to foster care whether you feel capable or not."

I open my mouth to argue, then shut it. Goddammit, I hate when he's right. But I still refuse to give up. "We'll figure it out," I promise him. "I'm not going to let you or the boys get fucked over. Trust me."

Whatever he's about to respond, he's cut off by the ringing of his cell phone, and whether it's his mother or Professor Ozgur, I know he's going to take it. And he's going to walk out. And I don't know when I'll see him again. The realization rips me in two.

"I'll call you tomorrow," he promises as he pulls out his phone. Then he kisses my cheek and is out the door with an "*Allo, Maman.*"

I stare at the door for a long time after he leaves, until Max emerges from the boys' room and asks for a snack. It takes everything in me to shift back into parenting mode, and from there into studying mode. And it hits me, as I open up my Stats textbook and watch the words and graphs blur, that this may be all there is for me for the foreseeable future. That this— balancing parenting and work, alone—may be my entire life for the next eleven years.

There is no way I'm going to let that happen. Whatever I have to do, whomever I have to beg, I'm going to fix this. I'm going to make sure Connor stays. And I'm going to fix what's left of all of our shitty lives.

chapter twenty-three

I wake up genuinely determined to kick ass and take names, and stay that way for about three seconds until I glance at my phone. The whole thing is lit up with texts from Cait, which I worry is a sign of doom. Usually, Saturdays are filled with the joy that comes with no class, not having to drive the boys to school…not having to do much of anything.

But there's clearly not going to be anything relaxing about this one.

I can't handle whatever she has to say without coffee, so I slip out of my room and offer up a silent prayer of thanks that the boys are still asleep as I set about getting some caffeine into my system. As soon as my mug is full, I check.

How'd it go last night?? says the first one.

Then, *Was he mad??*

Oh, right. I'd never actually gotten back to Cait

after Connor left last night. Maybe there isn't anything new and terrible, then. Maybe—

I jump up as the ringer sounds and Connor's face lights up the screen. Immediately, I press a key to accept the call. "Hey."

"Have you checked your e-mail yet this morning?"

There's no missing the pain in his voice. "No." My own voice is barely a whisper, and I retreat from the small dining table into my room, start up my laptop, and log in to my e-mail. "Sophie?"

"Dummy e-mail account, but I can only imagine."

"How bad?" I ask, narrowing my eyes at my newest e-mail, which says "Open Me" and is from a none-too-flattering address I've never seen before.

"Bad."

"How can it be that bad? We've barely even done anything here, and she—" I freeze as the picture pops up. It's dark, and though it isn't obvious it's us, it isn't obvious it isn't. More importantly, I know exactly when and where this is. Because I recognize the grass outside my building. The grass where I sank to my knees in frustration that very first night Connor came for dinner.

The grass where Connor held me against a tree, stripped off my underwear, and made me come so hard I saw stars that had nothing to do with the clear night.

The picture is only a blurry still of us—the back of my dark head, the sleeve of Connor's shirt—but it's the two-line e-mail that has my entire body growing cold.

This is only one frame of the video. Now get the fuck out of Radleigh or the entire thing goes to your professor and your social worker.

"It's from my building's security camera," I say, touching a finger to the screen. "Holy shit. How did she even get this?"

"That video is gonna have a timestamp, Lizzie." Connor's voice is shaking, and it churns my stomach. "I told them we *just* got involved. If they see this, it won't help that I came clean about any of it."

I'm listening to him, but I can't stop staring at the words *your social worker.* Could she really have that information? Could she really do this? If this video were deemed evidence of the boys being in an unfit environment, I don't have a shot in hell at the guardianship proceedings coming up next month. Hell, I don't even know if I'd get to keep the boys through Christmas.

Either way, there's only one thing to do—I have to leave. "She won." My mouth is so dry I can barely get the words out. "I don't know how, or why she's pushing this so hard, but she won. I can't stay here and risk this getting out. I have to go home."

"And who's to say that if you do, she won't just release it anyway?"

"What else can I *do*, Connor? Seriously, if you have any other ideas—"

"I don't," he bites out, and I know his rage isn't at

me, but it stings all the same. "You need to reason with this girl. That's all there is. Please."

I nod, then realize he can't see me, and say okay even though the idea of going another round with Sophie is about as desirable as walking into my Byzantine final naked. Neither of us is in the mood to chat, and we quietly promise to call each other later before hanging up.

Max wakes up while I'm still trying to decide on an outfit that combines "Feel bad enough for me to stop this psychotic crap" and "Shove it up your ass and die." Of course he decides he doesn't like any of our breakfast options, which makes me snap, which makes him cry, which wakes up Tyler, which puts him in Maximum Asshole Mode, which makes me stalk back into my room and throw on the first pair of jeans and sweatshirt my hands land on, just so I can get the hell out of here. I childishly tell the boys I don't care whether they eat or not, grab my puffy coat, and storm out like I'm actually the youngest Brandt sibling.

But as I turn toward the direction of the parking lot, I realize there's somewhere I should be stopping before I deal with Sophie.

And it makes me sick that that somewhere is in a place my brothers and I have been calling home.

I do an about-face and walk to the security office, my stomach turning at the thought of finding the person inside who not only watched a tape of me fooling around with Connor, but put it into the hands of my worst enemy. It's hard to imagine the heavyset woman who answers my knock has had anything to do with any of this, but I'm still wary when I ask if I can come in to discuss some security footage from the month of October.

"We only save footage for a month," she says, her voice tinged with impatience as she blocks my entry into the office. "If you were robbed—"

"I wasn't. I...can we please discuss this in private?"

She takes the longest minute of my life to decide, and then finally steps aside to let me in.

No point beating around the bush, so I wait until she closes the door behind us and say, "There's footage of me, from October, doing...things."

"Things?"

I'm not easily embarrassed, but the way her eyebrow rises like it's being pulled up by a fishhook is definitely doing flame-y things to my face. Then I think of Sophie's e-mail, of Connor's shaky voice, and I push forward. "Someone turned security footage from this building into a sex tape, starring me, and I'd really like to speak to that person." The word "*Now*" lingers on the tip of my tongue, but I swallow it back into the lump in my throat.

I expect her to fire questions at me—how I know it came from here, how I know about it at all, why I was doing sex-tape-worthy things in full view of the security camera—but she just sighs. I guess all the answers are obvious, and this woman doesn't seem dumb. Instead, she asks me for the date of the night in question and pulls out a binder as I give it to her.

"One of the new guys was on that night," she says in a way that might be intended to sound apologetic; I'm not really sure. "I'll talk to him."

"Ma'am, with all due respect, this is the literal definition of an emergency. I can't wait for you to set up a meeting with this guy and then get back to me."

"What would you have me do, *ma'am*? Give you his name and phone number? That would be a huge violation."

"As opposed to handing out a tape of me, taken outside my own home? Are you kidding me right now?"

"Correct me if I'm wrong, but the only way this tape could've caught you is if you were already out in public," she says, narrowing her eyes. "So pardon me if I don't understand why you suddenly care about propriety."

The words are a slap in the face. She's right, but that isn't the point. Making a mistake in the past shouldn't mean you deserve to have it haunt you forever. Not when there are things that can be done to fix them. "Because a career and the custody of my two little brothers depends on it. *Please*."

331

There go those eyebrows again, and she studies my face as if trying to tell whether I'm making this all up. Finally, she sighs again and says to sit tight. Then she picks up the phone and places a call. For a moment, I'm terrified no one will pick up on the other end, but then she's telling someone to come in to the office ASAP, and when she hangs up, she says he'll be here in half an hour.

"What am I supposed to do until then?"

"Go home," she says. "Leave me your phone number, and I'll call you once I've spoken with him."

"Wait. I can't even be here?"

She gives me a look like I'm an idiot, and I suppose I should've seen that coming. I leave her my number, ask her to please get in touch with me as soon as possible, and then let myself out.

I don't want to go home yet, but I don't want to be far when the guy shows up, so I busy myself by going grocery shopping at the corner store. As I toss bacon, frozen waffles, and other things it probably makes me a terrible guardian to be feeding the boys into my basket, I check my phone obsessively, waiting for the screen to light up.

It doesn't. I text Cait back while I check out, then slide my phone into my pocket so I'll stop staring at it.

It's not even 10:00 a.m. and I already know it's gonna be a *very* long day.

• • •

Unsurprisingly, when I do get the call from security as I'm frying bacon and eggs for Ty and Max with jittery hands, it's not particularly informative. "He swears he didn't hand off that footage," she says.

I keep my voice low, though Ty and Max are distracted by the TV anyway. "Does it feed to anywhere else?" I ask.

"No, just to this office."

"Does anyone else go over it after the livefeed?"

"Not unless someone's reported an incident."

"And did anyone?"

"Let me check."

You didn't already? I want to scream as my knuckles whiten around the phone while I listen to her flip pages. Resisting the urge to go off on this lady is seriously draining the last of my reserves of grace.

"Hmm, actually, it looks like someone *did* report an incident—a possible break-in. Suspect a Caucasian male about six feet, a hundred and sixty pounds, brown hair…"

Connor. "Can you tell me the name of the person who reported the incident?"

"Now, you know I couldn't—oh."

"Oh? What's 'oh?'"

"You've never made any inquiries about this before today?"

"No, I haven't; I didn't know there was anything to inquire *about* until today. Why?"

She takes a deep breath. "Because according to this, the incident was reported by one Elizabeth Brandt."

• • •

I run out of the house so fast I actually have to dash back in to shut off the stove and grab my coat and gloves, then yell back to Ty to serve himself and Max. By the time I reach the Epsilon Rho house, I'm sweating in the puffy down, despite the fact that it's below freezing outside.

I rap on the door so hard I think my knuckles might bleed.

And I'm not at all prepared for Sophie being the one to answer the door.

Her lips curl into a smirk the second she registers who's darkening her doorstep. "Come to say goodbye in person?"

I yank her outside, ignoring the fact that she's not remotely dressed for the weather, and pull the door closed behind us. "What the—"

"You fucking psychopath!"

She stops. Freezes. Shivers. I could not give less of a shit. For once, Sophie actually looks a little frightened. And she should. She quickly tries to mask it with bold irreverence, but there was no missing it, and it fucking feeds me right now.

The fact that when she opens her mouth, no sound

comes out, doesn't hurt.

"Don't. Say. A word," I seethe, spit flying. "You called the security office at my *home* and pretended to be me so you could illegally obtain footage of me and turn it into a *sex tape*? I realize you have extremely limited brain capacity, Springer, but you do understand that custody of my orphan brothers is at stake, right? And your stupid petty shit over a guy who obviously never liked you that much to begin with isn't even a drop in the fucking relevance bucket compared to that."

"Oh, enough with the martyred orphan act." She rolls her eyes. "As if you're such a victim. If you care so much about your brothers, maybe you shouldn't have been screwing a teacher in the first place, outside, where *anyone* could see you."

"Except only one person *did* see, and that would've been the end of it if you weren't so intent on destroying my life. Don't put this on me. I tried to apologize to you."

She barks out a seal-like laugh, but she's so cold it comes out in shaky puffs of air. "Please! As if that meant shit."

"What the hell else could I possibly have offered you at that point?" I demand. "What could I have done to make it better? Nothing would've been good enough for you except destroying my life, and let's be honest, Soph—you're not worth it."

Her eyes flash with sparks, but my entire body is

brimming with flames of rage, and I'm not stepping back, not for a second. "I don't know how you knew to get that tape, or how you got a copy of it, but if you even think of doing anything with it other than destroying it, I will uncover every detail and have you afuckingrrested."

"Oh, please, like you're in any position to threaten *me*. This is insane, and I'm going inside."

She turns back to the door, but I yank her back around and hold her there, my fingertips digging into the soft, cold flesh of her arms. "Delete the tape, Sophie. Obliterate it. Now."

"If you had any shot of me doing you any favors before, you've certainly blown that now," she says through chattering teeth. "You know how I knew to ask for that tape, you slut? I came to your complex that night. I was stupid enough to let Trevor talk me into thinking maybe you were lying about everything you said at the diner. I wanted the truth, from you, with no one else around. And then what do I see when I pull up but you waving goodbye to your TA, who's sporting wood like a thirteen-year-old kid with a Victoria's Secret catalog.

"So yeah, I knew you were just enough of a stupid skank to have done something right there, and saw outdoor security cameras, and I took a shot there might be a recording. And I was right. And maybe if you didn't live in such a shithole, you'd have security guards who aren't both painfully stupid and hard up for cash. I wasn't even sure what I was gonna do with it until that day I saw you at the doctor, but now? I sure as hell do."

She pulls her arm back, and this time, I let her. "So. All your mysteries solved, except for the big one: How do you even live with yourself?"

Then she lets herself back into her big, fancy house, leaving me alone in the cold.

• • •

Connor's going to kill me. He asked me to do *one* thing—to talk to Sophie like a freaking human—and I couldn't even do it. But it's not my fault that she's *not* human.

All I can do is pray that someone who can get to her is.

When I ring the bell a few doors down at the SigPsi house, I'm not sure who I expect to answer, but I'm beyond relieved when it turns out to be Doug Leach. "Lizzie," he says, puzzled but not unkind. "Did not expect to see you here."

"Did not expect to see me here either. Trust me. Is Trevor here?"

"Up in his room."

Doug steps back to let me in, but the thought of being back up there, of reliving that night, gives me pause, and I linger on the doorstep, even though it's freezing as balls and I've already been out way too long, with Sophie. Finally, I take a cautious step over the threshold, more to escape the wind than anything else, but I don't move beyond that, even when Doug closes the door behind me.

"Do you want me to get him?" he offers, and the nice gesture snaps me out of my weirdness.

I'm about to tell him not to bother, but I'm not exactly dying to walk through that house, let alone revisit the exact scene of...everything. "That'd be great, if you wouldn't mind."

He smiles briefly and heads up, and a couple of uncomfortable minutes later, Trevor's familiar form trudges downstairs. "Just that attached to this house, huh?" He's trying to sound like an asshole, but the rest of his face hasn't caught up; there's a trace of concern there, and it's...weird.

"Why are you out there defending me?" I ask plainly, because I'm not interested in getting caught up in Trevor's cutesy bullshit. If he's setting me up for another fall, I need to know. There are too many people at stake in everything that happens to me now.

He exhales a sigh. "Because you were right," he says, scratching the back of his neck. "I was a dick and you deserved better than that. You happy now?"

"I'm...shocked, actually. I mean, you're right, but—"

"Don't push it," he snaps, but there's no fire

behind it. His shoulders even slump a little, a pose I have never, ever seen on Trevor Matlin. "Look," he says, softer now. "I really am sorry. I didn't know what to do that night. Everything went fucking crazy, and Sophie was going nuts, and you were...I didn't know how to get in touch with you after that."

"You lost my number?" I ask wryly.

"Not...I don't mean literally. We weren't exactly *friends*, Lizzie. Our texts weren't the 'come weep on my shoulder' type."

I can't really argue with that. The truth is, Trevor was an asshole, but so was I. I like to think I'd have been a better person if the situations were reversed, but I honestly have no clue. I only know that I'd be better now, because someone was better to me, and I see how much it matters. "Well, I appreciate it now, anyway," I say finally. "I don't know if it's doing anything, but it was nice to see."

He nods, and it's obvious we're both pretty uncomfortable with and embarrassed by this conversation. I feel about two minutes past my welcome. So I'm surprised when he speaks up again. "I don't know what's gonna happen, but if you need me as an alibi for whatever Sophie says...I owe you one."

"Actually...." I take a deep breath. "I might need more from you than that."

He crosses his arms. "Such as?"

I can't believe how many times I'm being forced to

have this conversation. The mere fact that this recording existed without my knowledge for almost two months feels so violating I want to hurl. "I need you to get Sophie out of her house, now, and then I need you to destroy something on her computer. A video."

Trev quirks an eyebrow. "A video. Of you fucking this professor guy? Seriously?"

I choose not to correct the finer points. "I swear it's the last thing I'll ever ask of you, Trevor. And like you said—you owe me. You fucked up my *car*, for Christ's sake."

"That's wasn't—" He sighs. "I can't make any promises, okay? I'll try."

"Thank you," I say, because it's really all I can. "You know I wouldn't ask if I weren't desperate. She's threatening to send it to my social worker and my professor and...." I am definitely sharing too much information with someone I trust very little. "Please, Trev."

He nods, once, and I'm relieved to see that somewhere in there is the Trevor Matlin I actually used to have fun with on occasion. I rise up on my toes and give him a peck on the cheek.

When I walk out, I don't look back.

chapter twenty-four

Well, that was a tremendous fucking failure of a day. I suppose I should be grateful I kept my dress on that night. Having my tits on the internet really would be the icing on top of today's shit cake.

At least there's no yelling or crying coming from the other side of my apartment's door. I desperately need to study for my Stats final, and if the boys are actually chill tonight, I should still have a good few hours for that, even if I make dinner. Which I probably should, given I left them alone all day without even cash for pizza.

Christ, I'm a terrible parent.

The quiet that greets me when I walk inside is welcome, but only for a minute.

Then I realize it's unnatural.

"Ty?" I call out, glancing into their room. Empty. "Max?"

No response, and they're not in my room, either. The bathroom door is wide open; no one inside. An icy vine of fear starts to creep its way up my spine, but I realize I'm being ridiculous. There are way too many possible explanations behind their absence for me to start freaking out right now.

I give myself five minutes to look for a note, check my texts and emails, and listen to voicemails. I call Tyler's cell, but it just rings. I leave him as calm a message as I can, asking him to call me back, and leave a text asking the same.

Twenty minutes of no response later, though, I'm starting to panic.

Deep breaths. They're both gone, which means they're probably somewhere they're both welcome, rather than at just one of their friends. Not that I know any of their friends, anyway. Max does know where Connor lives from that one time he played video games there after therapy, but there's no chance he would've taken them in without calling me. I look up the numbers for all the restaurants we go to near our apartment and call, but no one's seen them.

Then it hits me: they must've gone to a movie.

I laugh at myself for my overreaction when the answer was so obvious, and push aside the niggling little feeling that I still don't know for sure. I can't stress about made-up scenarios right now. I have too many very real, very shitty ones to deal with. And I know I should tell Connor how badly I fucked up, but I just can't right now. It's too much.

I settle myself down at the dining table instead, Stats book wide open, highlighter in hand, cell at my side. For an hour, I force myself to focus on problem sets and graphs, one eye on the little screen of my phone that never lights up.

Finally, I call Lauren—with the snow coming down, the boys would probably have asked for a ride rather than walking anywhere, right? When she greets me, I hear boys in the background, and my breath hitches in my throat at the hope that maybe I've found them after all. "How are you?" she tacks on to her hello.

Lauren always asks this. I'm tempted to answer with the truth—that I'm a complete and total mess—but we're not friends. No one wants that truth, except for maybe Cait and Frankie.

"I'm good, thanks. I was just wondering—did Max call you, by any chance?"

She laughs. "Nope, don't remember chatting with any seven-year-olds today, other than my own. Why?"

"No reason." It definitely won't do me any favors for her to realize what a shitty parent I am, especially if I want to keep up our carpool situation. "Thanks, Lauren." I hang up before she can say anything.

I'm officially starting to worry again.

I leave another message for Ty, then grab my coat. Only as I'm sliding it on do I realize something I didn't when I first came home and hung it up.

The coat closet is noticeably emptier than usual.

I double back to the boys' room and throw on the light, and suddenly it's glaring—Max's favorite stuffed dinosaur, Ty's little collection of Yankee caps…they're all gone.

The boys didn't leave for a movie.

They *left*. Period.

I run out to my car like a bat out of hell, clutching my phone like a lifeline, and jump into the driver's seat. The snow is coming down harder now, and I have no idea where they could've gone. I try to remember if Ty's bike was still on the patio when I left, and curse myself for being too stupid to check.

Once I'm on the road, I realize I don't even know where I'm going. I check the movie theater, but no one recognizes the pictures I hold up on my phone. I don't know any of their friends, and they're obviously not at Lauren's. I go to every place I can think of, but other than the college bars, clubs, and restaurants they'd never go to, it's pretty dead around Radleigh.

I have no idea what else to do.

"What the *fuck*, Tyler?" I scream to the inside of my car as I frantically dial him one more time, to no avail. "I spend so much time trying to keep this stupid family together, and you just—"

I break off when I realize I was about to hurl my phone at the window, and drop it onto the passenger seat instead. My throat burns from all the screaming I still want to release, though, so I do—for a good, solid minute.

I scream for my brothers, for Sophie's shit, for Trevor putting me on her shit list in the first place, for Connor's job, for all the finals I should be studying for, and for my parents, my parents, my parents.

And then I stop, because my throat hurts, and screaming isn't getting me anywhere, and my brothers are still out there somewhere.

What the hell would my mother do in this situation? Or my father? How did they handle all three of us? I can't even handle two.

They had each other, the more rational part of my brain points out. *Call Connor—he'll help you.*

He will; I know that. But I'm not ready to tell him how badly I screwed up today. I can't bear to tell him I've probably gone ahead and gotten him fired, and then ask for his help on top of it.

I can lie, though.

"It went surprisingly well with Sophie," I practice saying in the quiet of the car. "She promised not to send the video, and I promised not to tell the police how she illegally obtained it. So, not to worry—everything will be fine."

Yeah, there's no way I can pull that off.

I pull back out into the street and drive around, my headlights bright and eyes peeled for signs of two tweens in puffy parkas. An hour passes with no sign of them, and no return call. Meanwhile, I've gained zero ground, the snow is making it nearly impossible to see anything at all, and I know that if the boys have indeed been roaming around this whole time, there's no way they're okay.

The thought of something happening to one—or both—of them chills me to the bone, and I realize I'm such an idiot, I completely forgot to check the very first place I should have: the hospital.

I yank the wheel into a U-turn instinctively, then promptly regret it as my car skids, narrowly missing two others and the divider. My heart pounds as the drivers shake their fists and give me the finger, and I right the wheel and catch my breath. *Do you want to die exactly how your parents did?* my brain screams at me. *What the fuck is wrong with you?*

My knuckles tighten on the wheel as I speed up in the direction of the hospital, and I grit my teeth and glare at the road with unblinking eyes.

Because the truth is, the answer to the second question is *Everything*, and the answer to the first one suddenly feels a whole lot like *Maybe*.

• • •

It's a mixed bag of feelings when it turns out they're not at the hospital, either. Obviously I'm glad they're not hurt, but that was my last best shot. I still have no texts from Tyler, no calls, and no clue how to proceed.

Finally, I suck it up and call Connor.

He picks up on the third ring, sounding every bit as weary as this morning. "Hey. I'm guessing it didn't go well with Sophie."

My stomach clenches. "What makes you say that?"

"E-mail from the head of the History department. He wants to talk to me personally about whether I have a future at a school where professors are receiving pictures of their TAs *in flagrante*. Apparently Ozgur isn't pissed enough for his liking."

I close my eyes and lean against the wall of the hospital lobby. Operation Trevor was my last hope, and apparently it was a huge failure. I don't know if he couldn't manage to get Sophie out of her room or if he never even tried, but I should've known the odds of Trevor Matlin saving the day were zero to none. "Fuck. I'm sorry, Connor. This is my fault."

"It's—is that a siren? Where are you?"

"I'm at the hospital. I—"

"You're *what*? Are you okay?"

"Sort of." I'm suddenly exhausted beyond belief. I'd do anything for a nap in one of the uncomfortable-looking beds being rolled around. "I'm not hurt or anything, but I came here looking for the boys. They're gone."

"What do you mean, the boys are *gone*?"

"I mean they took off—no note—with a bunch of their things, and disappeared. Tyler's not answering his cell phone, and I've been looking for them for hours—"

"Why the hell didn't you call me? Jesus, Elizabeth. Sit tight. I'm coming over there, and we'll figure this out. We'll find them. I promise."

God, it's nice to have someone on my team. Though it makes me feel extra guilty that I didn't get to fully confess about today's events. "No point in your coming here," I tell him, already striding outside. "They're not here, and staff has called the three closest hospitals; no sign of them anywhere. I don't really know what I can do now."

"Then go back home, in case they show up. I'll meet you at your apartment." I can hear the jangle of his keys, one of those cute French-Canadian swears as I'm guessing he stubs his toe in his rush to leave his room. He has so much to stress about right now, and he's shoving it all aside to help me, which is such a Connor move I don't even know what to do with myself except fall even harder for him.

"Thank you."

"You don't have to thank me. I'll see you in ten minutes." He hangs up, and his voice lingering in my ear is the night's first bright spot.

348

I really hope it isn't its last.

• • •

He really must've left his room the minute I called, because he's sitting on my living room couch when I return. I have to bite my tongue not to comment about the fact that he's wearing an extremely un-Connor-in-public-like outfit of a hoodie and sweatpants, his appearance as disguised as humanly possible. He's radiating paranoia, as if there are security cameras inside my apartment, too. As if there's really any more damage they can do beyond what they've already done.

"Sorry, I let myself in with the extra key," is the first thing he says. "Just seemed like a bad idea to stand outside."

"Yeah, it's also fucking freezing out." I accept the quick kiss on the forehead he offers, but anxiety is radiating off both of us in waves. "They must be *miserable* out there. If they're even out there." I nibble on a thumbnail and walk over to the French doors that open to the patio.

I don't even know how to feel about the fact that Tyler's bike is still here.

"Where could they possibly go?" he asks, pacing the room. We run down everywhere I've been, and then Connor suggests calling Lauren again, asking her if she has any ideas. The thought of admitting to her that I've lost my own brothers makes me wanna puke, but the thought of actually losing them makes me wanna puke more.

I pull out my phone to make the call, but a knock sounds at the door, startling me into dropping it. I don't even care. I'm so happy to hear that knock I think my heart is gonna explode. "They're back. Oh thank fuck, they're back." I dash to the door and grab the knob, yanking it open. "Boys, I am gonna—"

The words die on my lips.

It isn't the boys who are standing behind the door.

It's the social worker.

chapter twenty-five

"Hi, Elizabeth. It's nice to see you again."

I nod dumbly as Karen cranes her neck to look past me into the apartment, no doubt taking in an eyeful of Connor. At least we're fully clothed. Not that it really matters at this point.

"Can I come in?"

I step back to let her in, glancing at Connor, who looks completely confused. "Connor, this is Karen, our social worker." His eyes widen, and I narrow mine so he'll take the hint. "Karen, this is…" There's really no good way to introduce him. "Connor."

"Your Teaching Assistant, correct?" She raises an eyebrow and opens the folder I hadn't realized she was holding. "Yes, I've been…made aware."

Sophie. Of fucking course. Instinctively, I step away from Connor, which is such a joke. This whole thing is such a fucking joke. My brothers are missing, wandering out in the freezing-ass cold on their own, and the social worker is here for a fucking *sex tape* between two consenting adults that shouldn't even exist in the first place. "Karen—"

"Where are the boys?" she asks stiffly, pasting a smile on her face that could cut glass.

"They're with friends." The lie is instinctive, and I pray it's actually the truth…somehow. "We weren't expecting a visit," I add with a weak smile.

"I'd imagine not." She glances at Connor. "I'd really like to speak with the boys, Elizabeth. Could you bring them home? It's important. I'd like to talk to the three of you as a family."

The implication that Connor is not welcome here hangs heavy in the apartment, which suddenly feels impossibly small for three adults. "Karen, maybe we could talk first. You've obviously heard things. And maybe…seen things?"

Her expression betrays nothing, but there's no denial, either.

"I realize how it looks, but I assure you, it's…not how it looks. We're…." I sneak a look back at Connor. "The university knows. My professor knows."

"That's all well and good, Elizabeth, but there's still the matter of having tween boys living in an environment where pornography is being made."

Connor sucks in a sharp breath. "Miss…Karen. There is no one making pornography here. Yes, we got carried away somewhere we shouldn't have, and I apologize for that, but the boys were nowhere in sight."

"And that tape was obtained illegally," I add. "I mean, does it *look* like we were filming ourselves? Someone with a vendetta against me impersonated me and then bribed a security guard for the tape. It's not like that's a thing we *do*."

"So the boys are in an environment where someone has enough of a vendetta against you to do those things?"

Of course I'm digging myself into a hole. That seems to be all I'm able to do these days. I open my mouth to respond, but the phone rings, and I jump for it, praying it'll be Tyler.

It's Nancy.

"I'm sorry," I say to Karen, "but I really need to take this. It's our godmother. She's the financial guardian."

Karen makes a "go ahead" gesture, but I can tell she's growing impatient. Hard to blame her. It's a lousy way to spend a Saturday night.

"Hey, Nancy. It's not a great time—"

"The boys are here."

I blink. "I'm sorry?"

"Tyler and Max just showed up at my door. Apparently they took a bus down here, unattended." She sighs. "Lizzie, what's going on?"

I dart my eyes back to Karen, who's watching me closely, and my relief at hearing the boys are okay is swirling around in a mix of fear of her finding out what happened and anger at the boys for being so stupid and putting me in this position. I have no idea what the hell to do.

Thankfully, Connor seems to realize neither of these conversations can be paused right now. "Lizzie, why don't you talk to Nancy in your room, and I'll make Karen some coffee? Or tea?"

Karen sniffs but accepts the offer of some decaf. Unfortunately, I don't have any decaf, because I think it's stupid, but what she doesn't know won't hurt her. I leave her with Connor and take the phone into my room, closing the door tightly behind me.

"They're with you?" I whisper fiercely. "I don't understand. I had a billion fires to put out around here today, *and* studying to do for finals, and when I came back, they were just…gone. I called Tyler a thousand times, and he didn't pick up once. He was on a *bus*? With *Max*?"

"You should talk to him, Lizzie. Here—"

"No, wait, not yet. I have another problem." I quickly fill her in on Karen's surprise visit. "What do I do?"

"Oh, sweetheart. How do you get yourself into so much trouble?"

"I don't even know, but please, please help me fix this mess tonight because I swear, Nancy, I am on the verge of a nervous breakdown." I can already feel tears filling my eyes, needles prickling my skin. "I just need her to get out of here or I am seriously going to lose it."

"What did you tell her?"

"That the boys are at friends' houses. I panicked. It was the first thing I thought of."

"Well, that's gonna be a little tricky now. Okay, hand me off to her."

I walk back out, and am relieved to see that Karen looks a little more relaxed now, and is even smiling at whatever charm Connor is working. God, he's so cute. I wish I could just take a minute to appreciate his rumpled hair and facial scruff, but we have waaaay more important matters to tend to right now. "Sorry to interrupt," I say, trying to project sweet calm—two things that don't come naturally to me in the slightest—"but Nancy was hoping to talk to you. She picked the boys up from their friends' houses." I say this last bit with my mouth as close to the phone as possible.

Both Connor and Karen's eyebrows shoot up, though he's quicker to recover from the surprise he shouldn't be exhibiting. "Doesn't your financial guardian live in your hometown?" she asks. "I thought your brothers were at friends."

"Yes, they were. They were, um, at friends in Pomona. They're staying with Nancy this weekend."

She obviously wants to ask me a million more questions, but I thrust the phone at her, and she has no choice but to take it. Instead, I'm forced to listen awkwardly to the only half of the conversation I can hear. "They traveled to you by themselves...? I see...And they were at friends...? And they'll be coming back when...?"

As Karen continues to give Nancy the third degree, I bite the inside of my cheek and exchange nervous glances with Connor, who looks like he wants to disappear. I should probably let him, but I can't bring myself to. Not when I'm barely holding myself together as it is.

A couple of minutes later, Karen hangs up and sighs, then hands me back the phone. "I can't say I approve of your decision to let the boys travel alone, or at this time in the school year, but thankfully it seems your financial guardian has been taking good care of them, and I trust you will be picking them up from the bus at a reasonable hour tomorrow."

"Of course."

"I'll have to return at another point when they're here, before the guardianship proceedings, and I expect that there will be no more solo out-of-town ventures before then."

I give her a jerky nod. "Of course not."

"Good." She nods at me, then at Connor. "As for this...." She shakes her head. "I certainly hope you use more discretion around the two of them then you do around security cameras."

There's no venom in her voice when she says it, though, and whether it's because Connor charmed her over coffee or she's simply exhausted, I don't know. But I'll take it. "Of course." I sound like a robot at this point, but she's so close to leaving, I can practically feel the rush of relief I know will engulf me as soon as she does.

I take my rebuke for another minute, and then, *finally*, she's gone.

"Well," I say once I can no longer hear her footsteps. "That...sucked."

Connor lets out a huge sigh, dropping his head in his hands and rubbing his eyes. "That's one way of putting it." He stretches out his legs, then stands. "Well, at least everything worked out, for now. I should get back."

Wait, what? "You're going back? Why?" I finally have the place to myself, and while granted, I'm not happy about how that happened, nor am I particularly in the mood to do anything other than drink and pass out, it seems crazy not to take advantage of the rare privacy.

"Because the last thing we need are some more creepy paparazzi photos getting out if someone spots me here while the department's still making their decision. Things are already pretty awful. I think it's time we stop tempting fate. At least until we get our respective sentences handed down."

I want to argue with him, but I can't—not after my day of disasters. Having let down everyone humanly possible in the last twenty-four hours, it's probably appropriate I defer to someone else's judgment for a change. So I walk him to the door, my hands jammed in my pockets to stop myself from reaching out to him, and then accept a perfunctory peck before he pulls up his hood and walks out.

He closes the door quietly, considerately, as he always does, but it still feels like the loudest, loneliest sound in the world.

• • •

As promised, the boys return the next night, looking tired, cranky, and wary. Well, Tyler looks wary; Max doesn't seem to realize they've done anything wrong at all. The entire ride home from the bus stop, he chatters to me about Pete, and Nancy's tacos, and how he made a snow angel on the lawn, with no clue I'm so tense and angry in the driver's seat that I'm literally shaking.

Next to me, Tyler is silent, his eyes fixed on the darkness beyond his window. His jaw is set like he's gearing up for a fight, which is just as well, since he's sure as hell gonna get one.

I don't want to argue in front of Max, though. I know I need to explain to him that this was wrong, and why, and that he can never, ever do it again, but there'll be time for that when I'm calmer.

Right now, I just want answers from the tween criminal mastermind I've apparently been harboring for the past three months.

Nancy'd put them on the bus with enough sandwiches and snacks to last them the week, so at least I don't have deal with feeding them. I send Max straight to the shower, but when Tyler tries to creep off to his room, I snap.

"Don't even think about it, little brother." I flick an index finger at the couch. "Sit."

"I'm *tired*—"

"And whose fault is that? Did *I* tell you to sit on a five-hour bus ride today? *Or* yesterday? No, no I definitely didn't. And I certainly didn't say it was okay. What the hell were you thinking, getting on that bus by yourself?"

He crosses his arms over his sweatshirt. "I wasn't by myself."

"You realize that's even worse, don't you?" I curl my hands into fists at my sides so I won't reach out and shake him. "Max is *seven*, Tyler! What would you have done if he'd gotten hurt? Or lost? How did you even get on the bus in the first place?"

"I'm not a baby, you know."

"Are you sure about that? Because this was incredibly childish of you." I can hear myself channeling my father at his angriest, but I can't make myself stop. "You know what responsible adults do, Tyler? They talk things out. They leave notes if they want to go somewhere. They *answer their damn phones.*"

"Oh, right, like you never just disappear," he says with a snort. "You were gone that entire day, just like you are *every* Saturday, and every Sunday, and every Friday night."

"Are you kidding me?" I throw up my hands. "You think I was gone all day yesterday because I was out at the mall with my friends? You think I disappear to have fun? I have to *study*, Tyler. I have to go grocery shopping, and deal with the car, and pick you guys up from school, and buy you school supplies, and keep this house running." *And clean up the messes I've made by sleeping with my TA.* "Do you think suddenly becoming an eighteen-year-old parent of two is easy?"

"You're *not* our parent," Ty says fiercely.

"Oh, grow up, Tyler," I snap. "You know full well I'm not trying to say I'm Mom, or take her place. But I'm responsible for you in every way a parent is, and that means you can't pull shit like running off on me whenever you feel like it. And you sure as hell can't take Max with you."

"So what *can* I do?" he demands. "Because it doesn't seem like anyone here is allowed to have a life except for you. Do you know how much time I spend babysitting Max? Do you realize I haven't gone to a single party, or basketball game, or even movie since I got here? How am I supposed to do anything but think about Mom and Dad when I can't even leave the house?"

His voice cracks on "Mom," and just like that, all the anger building in my gut dissipates.

"You have Connor," he says, his voice rough. "You have somebody here. But everyone I have left is in Pomona. And being alone here sucks."

My heart aches as I finally understand how he must've been feeling these past few months, not making friends, not having anything to distract him from the pain at all. Not that losing my parents doesn't still hurt like hell every damn day, but he's right—I have Connor to help me soothe the pain. I have someone whose shoulder I can bury myself in when I wanna cry about it. Hell, I even have the distraction of all the messes I've created.

Tyler has nothing but memories and therapy sessions.

I think back to Thanksgiving, and how happy he was after spending time with Jake, and with Amy. How happy Max was being doted on by Nancy and playing

361

with Pete. They were happy for those few days, in a way I realize now I've never seen them here.

I know I should tell him that he's not alone here, that he has me and Max, but it's not what he wants to hear; I don't want him to think I'm missing his point. Because I'm not. I get that this may never be a place that makes him happy. And even if I took him to the movies next week, or let him throw a party here, it wouldn't change the fact that he was ripped away from everything he knows to be inserted into my fucked-up life.

"Tell me what I can do to make this better, Ty," I say softly.

He just shrugs, refusing to meet my gaze. "Nothing. It is what it is." His heavy sigh makes him sound twice as old as he is, and it cracks my heart. "Look, I'm sorry I ran away with Max. I won't do it again."

"Okay."

"Can I go to bed now?"

I nod. I don't know what else to say. I don't know what else to do.

He turns on his heel, walks into his room, and closes the door behind him, leaving me standing alone in the living room, struggling to breathe.

• • •

I don't sleep much that night. I don't talk much, either. Not to Connor, not to Ty or Max, not even to Nancy. I don't answer Trevor's texts, which apologize for the fact that he didn't get to Sophie's room in time to delete the video. All I do is study. Dinner is pizza I order in and leave on the table while I lock myself in my room.

But Monday, I have to talk—to Professor Ozgur, as per an ominous e-mail he sent me over the weekend, "requesting" that I meet him to reevaluate my work for the semester. I've been anxiously tapping my foot on the floor of his office for almost ten minutes now, waiting for him to show up even though I'd be perfectly happy if he bailed.

"Miss Brandt." No such luck on the bailing, I guess. He steps inside, wearing his usual stiff suit, and takes a seat at his desk. I notice he leaves his door slightly ajar, which I guess is the thing you have to do with sluts who've proven they can't be alone with teachers without manhandling them, or something. "Thank you for coming."

Definitely did not *have a choice.* I literally have to bite my tongue to stop those words from coming out, and opt to silently hand over a folder with all my work from this semester instead.

He accepts it and places it on his desk. "I hope you've already reviewed anything in here you'll need to study for your final—"

"I have. And I have copies of all of them at home, anyway," I say dismissively. "I *did* this work, Professor Ozgur, and I did it well. I *know* this work. Honestly and truly. I'm not worried about what you'll find when you look through those papers. Hell, you can quiz me now, if you like."

"That won't be necessary," he says wryly. "Miss Brandt...." He sighs. "Can I speak candidly with you?"

"I'd appreciate if you would."

"Yes, I should have known." He rests a hand on the folder and meets my gaze with his. "I'm not particularly concerned about the contents of this folder. I've seen your attendance improve one hundred percent since your parents' accident, and your participation improve as well. I'm certain you are a very capable student, and the fact is, many would have crumbled under the pressures and trauma you've faced this past semester. You, however, rose to the occasion. Quite mightily, I might add."

I have no idea what to say in response to this. Not only is it completely unexpected, but other than Connor and Nancy, he's the first person to say what I've been desperate to hear: that I'm actually doing sort of okay, all things considered.

Fortunately, he doesn't require an answer before continuing. "The fact is, Mr. Lawson—Connor—is an excellent TA, and, in my experience, quite a solid human being as well. It goes without saying that I in no way approve of the relationship between the two of you. There are rules against that sort of fraternization here, and for good reason."

There's a "but" coming. I know it. I can feel it. I just can't quite believe it.

"But, I can understand that with everything that's happened in your personal life this semester, there may have been extenuating circumstances. And, though I clearly don't know Mr. Lawson's character quite as well as I thought I did"—ouch—"I must concede that if ever there were a teaching assistant capable of...romantic involvement with a student without compromising any academic integrity, I do believe he would be it."

Oh. My. God. "You're not going to fire him."

"I am not going to recommend his termination, no. It's not entirely my say to have, and as chair of the department, Professor Rostov is extremely displeased, but that said, it's extremely rare for a graduate student to be dismissed from the program without such a recommendation from his supervising professor."

It's been so long since I've heard good news that I'm not even sure this is it, but it sure as hell sounds like it. I could kiss Professor Ozgur right now, if that weren't the massive problem behind this whole epic disaster in the first place. "Professor, *thank you*. Really, thank you. I promise, you will not be sorry for supporting Conn—Mr. Lawson."

He smiles thinly. "A video of the two of you was e-mailed to me, Miss Brandt. I did not watch it, but I think it's safe to say I'm aware you're on a first-name basis."

My cheeks blaze, but he doesn't seem to be raging, and Connor is almost definitely safe, and we are going to be okay. I know it. I feel it, with a certainty I haven't felt about anything since...I don't even know. "Yes, sir." I jump up, because it's just way too awkward to sit there anymore after that comment, and gather my things. "I'll see you at the final. Thank you, sir."

He nods. "I'll see you at the final, and return this folder to you then."

I nod back, then scramble out of his office as if Constantinople itself were burning to ashes at my feet.

chapter twenty-six

I still have some time before I have to pick the boys up from school, so I take the long way back to my apartment, past Nijkamp Hall. I know I have to give Connor his space right now, but I feel like just seeing his building will make me feel the tiniest bit better.

Love is fucking weird.

I scan the third-floor windows of his building, as if I'll catch him watching me like some creeper. And then I hear a laugh, followed by "Lizzie, right?" and nearly fall on my ass on a patch of ice.

More laughter as I straighten myself up and dust myself off. I pick my head up, prepared to face Sophie Springer minions, but I freeze when I realize why the voice that called my name sounded vaguely familiar.

Jess.

She's standing with a guy in a peacoat and bright-red scarf and a Japanese girl wearing such high stiletto boots I'm not entirely sure how she's still vertical. They're both holding cigarettes, though Jess isn't, and my fingers itch to pull one out of my bag, but I don't carry them around anymore. "Right," I say tightly.

"You all right there?" the guy asks, smirking as he blows out a stream of smoke.

I will be once I get away from you, I think but don't say. It's obvious all of them know Connor—know everything—and the last thing I need is to make things worse by letting them spread that I'm a childish brat.

Dammit, I really want a cigarette.

"Fine. Just a little ice."

"You want one?" the other girl asks, and I realize I've been staring at the cherry of her cigarette glowing in the dusk.

So, so, badly, but considering Connor risked his job for me, and the boys gave up their home to come here, actually making an effort at quitting smoking seems like the very least I can do for them. "Yes," I admit, "but I'm on the gum. Thanks."

"Good girl," Peacoat says approvingly before taking another drag.

"Well, not *so* good," says Jess, and they all crack up again.

Okay, there's a limit to how much of this shit I have to let myself be put through. I roll my eyes and resume my walk, but Jess quickly rushes over and puts a hand on my arm. "Oh, God, Lizzie, I'm totally kidding. I'm sorry. We're just having a little fun at Connor's expense."

"Well, Connor's not here right now, so actually, it's at my expense," I point out dryly.

"Touché." The guy grins and sticks out a black-leather-gloved hand. "I'm Bryan, you know Jess, and that's Cyn."

I shake it warily. "Apparently, everyone on the Radleigh campus knows who I am, so."

"Oh, you make it sound so bad," says Cyn. "Trust me—most of us are just fascinated that there was a decent personality under there somewhere. He's so much...."

"Nicer?" Bryan fills in.

"I was gonna say funnier," she says. "Also, hotter. I don't know what you did, but thanks. Nice to finally get some eye candy around the history department."

"Hey!"

"Eye candy who wants to fuck my gender," Cyn amends.

"Oh." Bryan sniffs. "Fine then."

"And we all know Jess is a fan," Cyn says slyly, and Jess whacks her on the arm. I can't help snorting, and I don't feel particularly bad about it, after she laughed at me.

"Guess he told you," Jess says to me, her cheeks pinking up from more than the cold.

"Apparently, Radleigh's not a great place for keeping secrets," I reply, though now I *do* feel a little bad.

She smiles sheepishly. "No kidding. Though he definitely had me fooled. I never would've picked him for the type."

"He isn't." I reach into my bag for a piece of gum, because I'm craving nicotine like my next breath all of a sudden. "It just...happened." My fingers close around the package, and I free a piece and slip it into my mouth. "You guys are all in the history department?"

"Yup," Bryan confirms.

"Do you...um....do you know—"

"If your boyfriend is completely fucked?"

I wince, nearly swallowing my gum. "Well, not the most delicate way to put it, but yeah, I guess. Has this happened before?"

"A few years ago, there were rumors about one of Rostov's TAs, but there was never any proof," says Cyn. She takes one last puff on her cigarette, then drops it to the ground and grinds it under the toe of her boot. "And he certainly didn't confess."

"So completely Connor-like to be noble even when he's breaking the rules." Bryan rolls his eyes, and then his cigarette joins hers on the pavement. "For real, though, it's been cool to see him happy. Even with all the stress and stuff, he's...different. In a good way. Less like he's dragging his feet through life."

"Oooh, good way to put it," says Cyn, pulling lip gloss out her bag and dabbing it on. "That's totally it."

"Well, I guess that's…good?"

"It's good," Jess assures me, putting a hand on my arm, her voice surprisingly quiet and serious. "I've seen him smile more in the past couple months than in the last three years of this program."

"Oh." My stomach flutters at the knowledge that I have that power, that I'm not just this…wrecking ball in the life of Connor Lawson. "Well." Words seem to have failed me. Mostly, I just want to see him now.

"Man, it's cold as balls out here," Bryan mutters. "Let's go in." I watch them start toward Nijkamp Hall, then Jess stops and turns.

"Aren't you coming to see Connor?"

The word "No" dances on my lips, but it seems silly to say. I'm dying to see him. They know we're together. They obviously expected me to be going up to his apartment, because that's what girlfriends do. So…what exactly is the point of saying no?

"I guess I can stop in and say hi." He might be pissed as hell when I do, but that doesn't seem like something they need to know. I shrug and follow them inside, trying not to smile at the irony of Jess being the one to sign me in, and then say my goodbyes upstairs as they leave me at Connor's door.

I wait until Jess's door closes behind her before knocking. This is either going to go really well or really poorly, and I don't think I want her hearing either one.

• • •

Connor answers after a couple of knocks, clearly not having expected any company. "Elizabeth. What are you doing here?" He looks mildly alarmed to see me. He also looks like crap. Well, more like he *feels* like crap. Actually, the scruffy, messy-haired, faded-old-pajamas look is working on him something fierce.

"Nice to see you too, sweetheart," I say with a grin. "Can I come in?"

He steps back, scratching the nape of his neck. "I thought we talked about seeing each other being a bad idea. How'd you even get up here?"

"Do you want me to go?"

"You know I don't." He sighs and steps back to let me in. "Water?"

"No, thanks." I slip off my coat and toss it on one of the stools at the counter. "I just met some of your friends. Cyn, Bryan, and Jess say hi."

"Lizzie—"

"And before that, I was at the History department. I met with Professor Ozgur."

"You…what?"

"Yup." I lean back against the breakfast bar. "And you know what, Connor? They all know."

"Well, yeah, of course. I—"

"No, Connor." I fix him with a hard stare. "They all know. Everyone knows. This entire campus knows we're together. Sophie even sent the fucking video to Ozgur, and you know what? *He refused to watch it.* Every classmate, every teacher, probably every cafeteria server knows about us. And you know what's gonna change that? Nothing. So you know the point of us staying apart right now? Nothing."

His lips twitch. "You make things sound so simple."

"They aren't. But here's the thing. We're not gonna survive handling this apart. We have to have each other's backs. If we're not approaching this that way, what are we even doing?"

He closes his eyes, and I'm afraid he'll have some great counterargument I hadn't considered, even though this very speech has been building since I first showed up at Ozgur's office. But when he opens then, they're deep-blue calm.

Then he walks up to me, cups my face in his hands, and kisses me long and slow and deep. By the time he pulls back, I'm holding the countertop for dear life.

"You're right. And I'm sorry." He rakes a hand through his hair. "I'm trying not to make my problems your problems, but I guess that ship has sailed."

"That ship has Bermuda Triangle'd."

He brushes a hand over the top of my head, stroking my hair, my cheek. "So now what?"

I rise on my toes as if to kiss him again, but graze his ear with my lips instead. "Now you bend me over this counter, or throw me on your bed—I don't care—and fuck me." He groans as I reach down and wrap my hand around the rapidly forming tent in his sweatpants. "You have a hot, young girlfriend who gets wet at the mere sight of you. Who's your partner for as long as you'll have her. Stop feeling bad about it and fucking *own* it, Connor."

"Sounds pretty damn miraculous when you put it that way," he murmurs, his hands coasting up my skin as he slides my sweater up and over my head, taking care not to knock off my glasses.

"Exactly. Which is why fucking said girlfriend's brains out is of the utmost importance right now."

"I like those brains, though," he says between hot, sucking kisses on my neck.

"I'll grow new ones." I pull his shirt up and off while he attacks the button of my jeans, and all I can think is how stupid we are for not having been doing this every minute humanly possible. He kisses me breathless, then dashes away, but he's back with a condom before I can even voice a coherent protest.

"Always the responsible adult," I tease through heavy breaths as I watch him roll it on.

He raises an eyebrow at the irony, then spins me around, braces me against the counter, and presses up against me. "Ready?"

"God, yes."

He slides in with one thrust, which might've been painful if I hadn't been hoping for it, expecting it, needing it. He fucks me hard and fast, and even as his breathing and moaning suggests just how rapidly he's losing control, I know this is probably the only time we'll do it like this. I'm not all that sorry about it. I used to prefer it quick and rough, when I was with Trevor or some random guy at a party.

I used to like a lot of things that don't fit into my lifestyle anymore.

He realizes too late that I'm not gonna come as quickly as he is, but I don't care. This feels like the first day of...I don't even know what, but I know we have plenty of time ahead for perfect sex and perfect words. Or not.

Honestly, perfection's always seemed sort of boring.

When he does come, and I don't, he immediately apologizes, which makes me laugh. "You'll make it up to me," I tell him with a grin, swatting his hand away and pulling my jeans back up from where he abandoned them mid-thigh. "I need to get back. I hadn't actually planned to stop by here at all."

"I'm glad you did." He disposes of the condom and slips back in to his boxers and pants, though he leaves his shirt lying on the floor where I carelessly discarded it and possibly even ripped it. Oops. "Especially given the next time I'll see you will probably be at your final. If I'm still allowed," he adds wryly.

I want to assure him he will be, but obviously I have no clue, so I just give him as reassuring a kiss as I can before sliding my sweater back on and wrapping myself back up in my coat and scarf to head out into the bitter December wind. "Call me when you know more," I say as he walks me to the door.

"I will." We kiss once more, and then I head back home, forcing myself to put all of this out of my head. There's nothing more I can do for him. I need to get my brothers now. And I need to study. Because none of this will matter if I get tossed out on my ass.

And as much as I've been playing with fire lately, that's just one burn I cannot risk.

chapter twenty-seven

Things have been strained with the boys since they came back, but when I pick them up today, there's an extra layer of nervousness surrounding them that sets me on edge. Even when we get home, there's no fighting over the TV, or the fact that we're having takeout again so I can study, or *anything*. In fact, they're creepy quiet, sitting docilely on the couch with books I can't imagine they're really reading, and it's freaking me out. "What?" I demand, coming out of my room after an hour of waiting for a bomb to go off.

"Nothing," says Ty with a shrug. "We're reading."

I resist the urge to say "Bullshit" with Max in the room. "What are you two up to? If you're thinking of disappearing again—"

"We're not," Ty insists flatly, and I know Nancy must've given them an earful, because Lord knows I haven't had the strength to.

Max is suspiciously quiet.

"What am I missing here?"

I watch Ty and Max exchange a glance, and it is so, so weird. What's with the constant conspiracies? When did my brothers even get old enough to conspire? What the hell is going on here?

Finally, Ty says, "Um, Nancy wants you to call her."

"Why didn't she just call my cell?"

"Just…call her, okay?"

Max's head is bent so far over his book I doubt he can even see words at this point.

I really, really have to study, but it's obvious I'm not going to get anything done until I make this mysterious call. "Fine." I pull out my cell phone and start to dial Nancy when I see the boys sliding off the couch and going into their room. I don't even have time to ask what the hell is happening before I'm greeted by her familiar friendly voice.

"Apparently, you have something urgent to discuss with me," I say as I take a seat on the couch and curl my legs up underneath me. "Is everything okay?"

"Everything is fine," she assures me, and I breathe a little easier. "But yes, I did just talk to the boys about something, and I want to talk to you about it too." She sighs. "I wasn't sure which order to have the conversation in, so I'm hoping I did this correctly. The last thing I want is for you to be upset with me. Or with the boys."

"Now you're just making me nervous, Nancy." I squeeze the cushion beneath me and then release it, squeeze then release—a makeshift stress ball. "Out with it, please."

"I think it's become clear that this is not the best arrangement for everybody. For anybody, really," she says softly. "Not that you haven't done great with the boys," she adds quickly, which only slightly soothes the sting of her words, "but obviously, they miss being home and seeing their friends. And you…you clearly have so much going on right now, and your new relationship, and you're getting back on track with school…. This can't be good for you."

"We never really thought this would be *good* for me," I remind her, taking care to keep my voice low so the boys can't hear. "But there's no alternative."

"Well, that's the thing. I think there might be." I hear her shifting on the other end. "It's true that both boys would probably be too much for me, but I bumped into Linda Markson—Jake's mother—at the supermarket last week, and she was telling me how nice it's been to see Tyler lately. One thing led to another, and she offered to let Tyler stay with her next semester."

Tyler. In Pomona. Back at the old school he actually liked. Living with his best friend and a mother who actually knows what the hell she's doing. It's crazy to think about, but God, that does sound so much better than anything I have to offer. "What about Max?"

"Max would stay with me," says Nancy, and I can hear the smile in her voice at the thought. "He and Pete would both love it, and I could certainly use the company. I may not be able to chase after kids like I used to, but with only one…I think I could. I really think I could. And I'm sure his friends' parents would be happy to help too. So would your parents' old friends, of course."

"And…they want this?"

"It does seem like they do." Her tone is careful, and I know she's still worried about upsetting me. I also know I shouldn't be upset, that this makes sense, that it's what they were trying to tell me all along with their idiotic caper. That it's actually kind of a reprieve.

But I can't help feeling like it means I've failed them.

And I can't help feeling a little jealous that they'll both have parents around, and I'll just be here. Floating. Little Orphan Lizzie.

"If it's what they want," I say slowly, "and everyone's on board, and their old school will take them back…then what else is there to talk about, really?"

"You know you'll be welcome to stay here anytime too, right, Lizzie? You'll never be without a home, even after you sell the house."

Something I have to do soon, I know. I can't even think about it without tearing up, and now isn't the time. "Thanks, Nancy." I want it to be enough, but of course it isn't; what possibly could be, after everything? "And thank you, for working this out for the boys, and taking Max."

"Well, this still depends on you, too, Lizzie. Are you okay with this? I assumed it would make life easier for you."

It will. I know it will. But it sounds so lonely now, especially since I've already forfeited my spot in my old dorm room for next semester. I'll be stuck in a two-bedroom apartment by myself, and as for whether Connor will even still be here with me...yet another thing I can't afford to think about right now. "Yes," I say, because there isn't any other answer. I can't be a mother right now. I suck at it. I'm turning nineteen, and finally just barely starting to figure myself out in this place. Nancy's right—this *is* the best thing for everyone. "You're right. It's sad, and I'll miss the hell out of them, but...."

Even as I agree with her, tears prick at my eyes as I contemplate being on my own again. The thought of the entire Brandt family being dispersed breaks my heart.

But nothing's gonna bring us all back together at this point. There's nothing we *can* do but make the most of the loved ones willing to take us in.

I just really, really hope mine is still here when I need him the most.

"You should talk to the boys," Nancy says gently. "Make this decision together. And study, of course—I don't want to take up any more of your time. I'm sure your head's about to explode."

I nod, then realize she can't see me, and offer a weak "Yeah" before promising to call her again later that week. Arrangements will need to be made to transfer the boys back, and we'll need to figure out some sort of financial arrangement with the Marksons, not to mention the house sale. My head is swimming, and I haven't even opened my books yet.

"Ty! Max! Get out here!" I call, dropping my head into my hands and rubbing my temples.

The door opens slowly, and I don't even have to turn around to know that Ty is peeking out first. "Are you mad?" Max asks, sounding legitimately scared as they return to the living room.

"Of course I'm not mad," I say with a sigh. "I'm sorry I was a sucky replacement for Mom and Dad. I'm sorry I couldn't make this place home."

"You didn't suck, Lizzie," says Ty. "You can't make this place home because it *isn't* home. It's college. You should be…college-ing stuff. With Connor."

I look at both him and Max, and my heart breaks at the realization that we all genuinely want each other to just *be happy*.

We just have to figure out how the hell that can still be possible now.

"So we'll try this." I give the couch cushion another stress-ball squeeze. "You boys split up in Pomona, and me up here. Are you sure you're gonna be okay being in different houses?"

"We'll see each other," Ty says firmly, and it's obvious they've already discussed this.

"You better. I'm gonna talk to Nancy more soon, but Ty, I expect you over there for dinner at least once a week. Assuming that's okay with Nancy," I add hastily.

He nods.

"Okay then." I should probably have more words of wisdom, but I got nothin'. I'm fried. I'm sad. I'm scared. And I need to study Russian verbs like a freaking machine. "I'll work it out with Nancy. Meanwhile"—I push myself up from the couch—"I have stuff to do." Never mind that all I want to do right now is call up Connor and beg him to come over so I can curl up in his arms and have him convince me that they're not leaving because I was a shitty parental substitute. Never mind that all of this feels so incredibly, infuriatingly unfair. Never mind that I would do anything—*anything*—to know if this is the right move, and to know if I screwed things up for Connor this morning as badly as I clearly have my guardianship.

Without another word to the boys, I walk into my bedroom and lock myself in with my books for the rest of the night.

• • •

My Byzantine History final is my very last one, which seems like a cruel joke, since all I want to do is be done with this class already. I talked to Connor first thing after his meeting on Monday, and I know he'll be there; the board mercifully decided on probation instead of kicking his ass out of the program, thanks to his personal confession and Professor Ozgur's support. Apparently everyone was convinced this wasn't likely a repeat occurrence. Connor said he heard something mumbled about how they imagined I'd castrate him if it were.

I haven't seen him since we fucked in his dorm, since neither of us wanted to give the impression he was helping me study. We've barely even talked, except for me filling him in on the situation with my brothers, and him telling me about the meeting. Mostly we just send cute little texts throughout the day, and I realize that despite everything, I'm actually pretty damn lucky.

It's important to remind myself of this when I walk into the room, because holy shit is everyone staring at me when I do. And at Connor. And at the fact that we're not even making eye contact. Because I want a good luck kiss like nothing else, and I'm pretty sure if I so much as glance at those eyes I'm not gonna be able to take this test without one.

Forcing myself to ignore all the stares and whispers—not to mention Professor Ozgur's annoyed coughs and calls to attention—I take a seat behind a pole, obstructing my view of Connor's head. My entire body is prickling with heat and anxiety, but Ozgur's already been over my work; he knows I've earned my grades. And I know I've worked my ass off for this class, both with Connor and without him.

I can do this.

The guy on my right passes me a blue book with a smirk, and it takes all my restraint not to try to claw off his face. And then the test comes, and I look at it, and I smile.

Yes, I really, really can.

An hour and a half later, I file out with the rest of the class, taking care to hand my exam to Professor Ozgur and not Connor like everybody else, because I know that stupid little bit of shame is the last thing I have to endure.

And then I walk up to Connor, hand him a note that says *6:00 p.m., and I promise extra bacon*, accept the little squeeze of my fingers in return while I mentally flip off everyone watching, and walk out into next semester.

epilogue

"Wow. The place looks...wow."

"Thank you," Frankie says proudly, and I'm not actually sure whether she's genuinely oblivious to the dryness in Connor's tone or just chooses to ignore it. Either way, I know she loves how the apartment looks, with her art splashed all over the place, and so do I. Plus, it was by far the best financial solution for me after the boys moved out. Cait's tied to the dorm as part of her lacrosse scholarship, but Frankie was thrilled for the opportunity to get her own room and a patio where she can put up an easel. Plus, she doesn't mind in the slightest when Connor and I get a little...noisy. "The kitchen could still use a little more color, but we've got time. The semester hasn't even started yet."

Then she dances off to her bedroom and closes her door behind her.

Connor shakes his head, laughing, and wraps his arms around my waist to pull me in for a kiss. It's been a long winter break, and after spending Christmas—aka my birthday—apart, so he could be with his mother, it was nice to have him visit for a little while before coming back here. "Your roommate's really into nudes, huh?"

"Hey, they're classier than the nudes *your* friend had up in here," I remind him. "I have to admit, though, I kinda miss having Max's toys and books everywhere."

"I know." He kisses the top of my head, then leads me to the couch. "But he seemed happy to be with Nancy, and Pete. Didn't he?"

"He did," I grudgingly acknowledge. "And the fact that Ty and Amy are now 'official' probably means moving back was the right move for him too. I'm just...I don't know. It's not like I'm lonely, exactly— they weren't supposed to be up here in the first place. But—"

"You feel like you failed," Connor says gently, which isn't so much brilliant wisdom as the fact that I've said it a bajillion times and he actually listens. "You didn't, Lizzie. At all. The only reason they got through the past few months is because of you. They needed to get away from there for a while. This all helps acknowledge that it's a new reality—for all of you."

"And you're still cool being part of that weird new reality?" I ask wryly. "Dating the slutty orphan girl?"

He snorts. "The disgraced TA who's still getting a combo of dirty looks and high fives all around is opting not to call the kettle black, here." He laces his fingers through mine. "Anyway, I'd prefer if you didn't refer to my girlfriend that way. I'm pretty serious about her, so."

"Serious, huh?" I bring our hands to my mouth and nip his thumb. "How serious?"

"Thinking about asking her to go down to New York City with me for a couple of days over Spring Break to meet my mother and sister serious," he says without missing a beat.

"Your sister?"

"I called her," he admits. "Obviously I couldn't make her wedding, but she said she'd hit the states on their whirlwind honeymoon and schedule it around my break. So. Up for it?"

Spring Break feels like forever from now, but I can't imagine a way I'd rather spend it. "Definitely up for it. Especially since I imagine I'll be asking you to log a little more sibling time during Spring Break too."

"You don't even need to ask."

I know he means it, which blows my mind every time, and I wrap my arms around his neck and pull him into a long, slow kiss. Or it would've been long if a knock hadn't sounded at the door.

I instinctively leap out of his arms as Frankie's door comes flying open. "It's just Cait!" she calls back over her shoulder, not even glancing at us as she lets her in.

"Jumpy much?" Connor murmurs in my ear, laughing.

I stick my tongue out at him, but settle back into his embrace as Cait steps in and proceeds to remove the four hundred layers of clothing necessary to brave the brutal snowstorm outside. The truth is, since that night at Trevor's, the knock of an unexpected visitor always makes me jumpy.

I miss the boys. And I miss my parents. And I can't help wondering how they'd feel about how we ended up, all split apart. But I think they'd be happy, knowing we're all happy. I think that's what they'd want for us more than anything. It's the most bitter irony that I'm only figuring out the whole adulthood thing they wanted for me because they're gone, but at least I did it, and I'm here, and I love and am loved.

I can't think of anything better to give them—and anything better they could've given me—than that.

As I wave hi to Cait and direct her toward the mugs and hot cocoa powder in the kitchen, Connor squeezes me around the waist and kisses the top of my head. I may not have my brothers, or parents, or a house up here, but I do have family, and I do have a home, and I think I might even have a handle on this "adult" thing.

Maybe.

Eventually.

Whatever—I'm getting there.

acknowledgments

It feels ironic that a book that started so defiantly as a solo project ended up with such a village behind it, but I wouldn't have it any other way. Endless thanks first and foremost to the fabulous readers whose copious notes helped shape this book into what it is—Maggie Hall, Sara Taylor Woods, Gina Ciocca, Rebecca Coffindaffer, Katie Locke, and Lana Popovic. Much love and thanks as well to Marieke Nijkamp, Cait Greer, Candice Montgomery, Patricia Riley, and Michelle Smith for reading and supporting it along the way. In case you didn't all know from me telling you pretty much every day, you are the most wonderful, thoughtful, insightful, inspiring, kind (but not in a boring way), and talented women on the planet, and I'm lucky to call you friends, betas, CPs, the world's greatest houseguests, drinking buddies past and present, doppelgangers with benefits, and other things that aren't really acceptable for public consumption.

I'm extremely grateful to have friends who helped with the finer points of the procedural aspects along the way—thank you to Tamar Warburg Gross, Yael

Schlenger, Yael Merkin, and Andrea Hannah for sharing your knowledge and experiences. Anything amiss in these areas is definitely my error, not theirs. And thank you to Cait Greer and Frankie Brown for lending me your names; I had no idea who Cait and Frankie would become when I asked for them, but I like to think they're awesome in large part because of their namesakes.

Huge thanks to my copy editor, Sarah Henning; my cover designer, Maggie Hall; my proofreader, Sara Taylor Woods; and my formatter, Cait Greer, for turning this manuscript into a book, with style, attentiveness, and endless patience for my stupid questions. And speaking of stupid questions, big, grateful hugs to Liz Briggs and Riley Edgewood for answering about a billion of them, to KK Hendin for talking things out with me in the early days, and to Lindsay Lewis for helpful notes. Thanks also to Meagan Rivers, Stephanie Kuehn, and Whitney Fletcher for their help with the cover copy, and to Christina Franke for her last-minute eagle eye.

To Lindsay Smith, thank you for spending months kicking my butt into gear, and pushing me to go above and beyond what I thought I could. I am absurdly lucky to have an accountabilibuddy in my corner, and even luckier that it's you. To Rick Lipman and Kelly Fiore, thank you for being the kinds of sounding boards that make me laugh on days I wouldn't think it possible; it would be my secret dream to see a gif war between you two, if I didn't think it would make the world implode.

I have so much appreciation for all the amazing work that bloggers do, and want to express my gratitude to all the amazing ones who helped me promote this book leading up to its release. Thank you so much for all the support you've shown me and this book, and for being such such great encouragement along the way.

To my family, for everything, always. I cannot imagine a more supportive group in my corner, no matter what I'm writing, no matter how I put it out into the world. As much as I hope you've all listened to me when I said not to read this book, if you didn't, I hope it comes through that I was only able to write a book so heavily about family because of how much I love and appreciate mine.

To Yoni, the Connor to my Lizzie. (Except we're totally not like them, obviously.) I hope they're as happy eleven years from now as you've made me for the last eleven, and since I created them, that feels like a pretty safe bet. I'm a big fan of Happily Ever Afters, and I love you more every day for giving me mine.

Finally, to the NA authors out there who made this category a Thing years ago, who took chances on self-publishing when it didn't even occur to me to try— thank you for refusing to give up, so the rest of us could know we didn't have to.

about the author

Dahlia Adler is an Associate Editor of Mathematics by day, a Copy Editor by night, and an author and blogger of YA and NA at every spare moment in between. She lives in New York City with her husband and their overstuffed bookshelves. If you give her a macaron, she just might fall in love with you.

More often than not, you can find her on Twitter as @MissDahlELama, and on her blog, The Daily Dahlia: http://dailydahlia.wordpress.com.

Turn the page for a sneak peek at the first chapter of book #2 in the Radleigh University series,

right of first
REFUSAL

chapter one

The stream of profanity that rings through my dorm room is made a thousand times funnier by the fact that it's in French. Inexplicably so, since my Filipina-American former roommate is the one yelping it. It's hard to run and help her when all I wanna do is laugh, *but*, it is my stuff I'm pretty sure she just dropped on her foot, so.

"You all right there, Queen B?" I slide off my bed, where I got distracted trying to decide where to store my shin guards now that I have to go back to taking up only half my room. Not sure how I used to do this back when Lizzie and I were cohabitating, but right now, it seems impossible to store my stuff in the allotted space.

"How do you have so much *crap*, Cait?" Lizzie calls back from where she's buried in what used to be her closet. As of today, that closet now belongs to one Andrea Nelson, a girl I've never met but who's apparently a sophomore—same as me and Lizzie—who was thrilled to get in off the Radleigh University housing waitlist. My suite was a no-brainer, given it had not one but two open spots, since Lizzie not only ditched me for an off-campus apartment, but took our best friend and suitemate, Frankie Bellisario, with her.

"I know, right?" As if on cue, Frankie pops up in the doorway, cracking a piece of gum so huge I can smell the artificial watermelon flavor from here. "You'd think I'd be the mess around here, but my room's alllll clean and ready for Samantha What's-her-face."

"I'm pretty sure it's Samara," says Lizzie, climbing over the heap of clothing she dropped and hopping onto her old bed to nurse her foot. Such a drama queen. "But sounds like you'll be making a great first impression."

"Hey, I have no impression to make," Frankie reminds us, perching on Lizzie's old desk, which is unfortunately still piled high with my old notebooks and test papers from last semester. "These newbies are Cait's problem."

She grins, flipping her long, dark, purple-tipped hair, and I glare at her. "Sure. Make light of the fact that you two ditched me. Bitches."

"You were invited to join us," says Lizzie, picking up a pair of gym shorts between her fingers and wrinkling her nose. "Though I don't know how the hell we thought we were ever gonna have room for your stuff."

"Ha ha." There's no point in rehashing the conversation. Lizzie only got the new apartment in the first place because she'd gotten custody of her little brothers when her parents were killed in an accident a few weeks into the school year. She'd relinquished custody to her godmother after a few months, but that didn't relieve her of the apartment. Her brothers leaving meant the room they'd shared was now free, but my lacrosse scholarship requires me to stay in campus housing. Frankie, on the other hand, had no such ties, and is a total whore for a little outdoor space.

That leaves me, my generally absentee suitemate—a pre-med named Stamatina—and two new strangers who are likely arriving today, given classes start tomorrow and neither's shown up yet.

God, I hope they don't suck.

"You need to either throw some of this shit out," says Lizzie, holding up a handful of...I'm actually not sure what, "or ship it back to your Mom's, because that new girl is gonna drown in here."

I sigh and join Lizzie in the closet, and we spend the next half hour splitting my stuff up by playing "Fuck/Marry/Kill."

"Definitely marry that sequin top," Frankie says authoritatively, blowing a bubble. "I love that thing."

"That's because it's *yours*." Lizzie plucks it off the

pile and tosses it at her. "Guess you were only actually fucking it."

I snort with laughter at that, at least until both Lizzie and Frankie declare that I need to Kill my favorite Celtics T-shirt.

"Are you kidding me?" I hug it to my chest and inhale, somehow expecting it to carry the scent of the games I used to go to with my dad and older brother, a billion years pre-divorce. But it doesn't smell like hot dogs or beer; just the dust it's been gathering for months. "No. This stays."

"There is no *way* that thing fits you, you Amazon," says Lizzie. "It's at least two sizes too small. How many years pre-growth spurt is that thing, anyway?"

"The shirt stays!"

"I think she wants to fuck the shirt," Frankie stage-whispers to Lizzie.

"Are you kidding? Did you hear that determination in her voice? *That's* marriage, Frank. Cait is going to *marry* that shirt. And we are going to wear some hot-as-fuck co-maid of honor dresses. It'll be glorious."

"Does this mean she's gonna finally get some ass?" Frankie gasps. "Hell, I'll wear a gown made out of that nasty-ass shirt if it does."

"Fuck you both," I sing-song, snapping the shirt at Frankie's ass. She cracks up and whips me back with the sequined thing, and in no more than ten seconds, we've spread out in an all-out war, with my clothing as the weapons. I nearly twist my ankle on my desk chair dodging the wrath of the button-down Lizzie's wielding—a shirt I'm pretty sure I've worn exactly zero times in the year and a half I've been at Radleigh—but quickly recover and nail her on the leg with my Celtic Pride.

We're having so much fun being back together like this, just the three of us, that we're all startled as hell when an unfamiliar fourth voice cuts in.

"Um, am I in the right place?"

Immediately, I toss the shirt onto my bed and dust my hands off on my sweats. "Andrea?"

"Andi," she says quickly. "Are you Caitlin?"

"Cait." She looks so terrified of the three of us, I almost laugh again, but I'm pretty sure laughing in your roommate's face on her first day in a new room isn't considered polite. "This is Lizzie and Frankie. They used to live here. They don't anymore."

"Oh." She glances at her new bed and desk, both of which are still piled high with my crap. "Um, am I…I mean, are these…?"

"Right, sorry!" I start snatching the piles and tossing them onto my own bed and desk, feeling a little like an asshole now. "They were just helping me clear space for you."

She glances from closet to closet, both of which are obviously busting at the seams with my stuff. "Uh huh."

Frankie snort-laughs, and then Lizzie's phone pings with a text. "Ooh, it's Connor. We're grabbing dinner at the Mexican place that opened up over break. You guys wanna join?"

I'm kinda desperate to say yes—I'm sick of the inside of these walls, and I'm *starving*—but I need to clean this place up, and leaving Andi alone on her first day seems like kind of a dick move. I open my mouth to tell them to go on ahead, when another new voice— this one much deeper and decidedly male—floats into the room. "Andi, which one is it?"

"On the right!" she calls over her shoulder.

A moment later, the source of the voice steps into the doorway, and any words that might've formed in my brain disintegrate completely. Just…vaporize into nothing.

My roommate may be new to me, but her boyfriend isn't.

In fact, I know Lawrence Mason quite well. Or at least I did when we were teenagers at sports camp.

But I left him behind—along with my virginity. And trust me when I say I expected to see the former again about as realistically as the latter.

Holy. Shit.

"Mexican sounds perfect," I squeak back to Lizzie. "Let's go." Before anyone can say another word, I'm out of the suite like a bat out of hell.

I can always pick up shoes from Lizzie's on the

way.

• • •

"What the hell was that?" Lizzie demands as soon as we're all seated. "I wish you would've seen that poor girl's face when you bolted out of there."

"Not to mention the guy's!" Frankie laughs. "Christ, I thought he was gonna pass out from, like, proximity to your insanity."

"I said I'd explain later," I mutter, mentally begging a waitress to come over so I can hide my burning face in a menu. As the member of our trio— well, quartet, I guess, now that Lizzie's boyfriend Connor's a permanent fixture—who *doesn't* thrive on drama, I'm not enjoying this nearly as much as they are. At least Connor has the grace not to ask what the hell we're all talking about.

"Yeah, and it's later," says Lizzie. "So spill."

"You'd think you'd wanna spend more time around that guy," Frankie adds. "He was pretty fucking hot. I mean, taken, obviously, but..." She whistles. Badly.

A waiter does indeed come over then to distribute menus and drop off a basket of tortilla chips, but it doesn't distract anyone for a second. Not even when Connor pointedly says, "Hey, will you look at how many kinds of burritos there are on the menu that have nothing to do with harassing Cait about her private life!"

Connor may be twenty-freaking-five and waaaay too old to be dating my best friend—especially considering he used to be her TA—but right now, he's my favorite person at this table.

"Connor," says Lizzie, squeezing his hand on the table. "You don't understand. Cait *never* has drama. Cait's favorite thing in life is giving *us* shit for our drama. I basically need whatever information she's withholding in order to live. And I need to live in order for you to get laid tonight, so, take that into consideration."

Connor pauses, nabs a chip from the basket, and takes a thoughtful bite. "So, Cait, are you gonna spill, or...?"

Men. Such traitors the second sex becomes part of the equation.

I sigh. A year and a half of living with these girls is long enough to know they won't be shaking this anytime soon. "Fine." I take a long sip from my water glass. "Let's just say that wasn't the first time I've met Andrea's—Andi's—boyfriend."

Three pairs of eyebrows shoot up. Well, two pairs: Connor's not quite as skilled in eyebrow acrobatics as the girls are. "Do tell." Frankie props her chin up on her hands, dark eyes shining.

"We went to camp together, like, a billion years ago. Sports camp. He's a basketball guy, I think." I don't know why I add the "I think" part. Of course Lawrence Mason is a basketball guy. At Stone Lake, he was *the* basketball guy. And I was *the* lacrosse girl. We made one hell of a power couple, as far as those things went.

"So that's it?" Connor asks. "You know the guy from summer camp?"

"Hmm." Now Lizzie pops a chip into her mouth with one hand, using the other to twirl a long black strand of hair around her finger. "I think she more than 'knows' him. I think maybe she knows him…biblically. Am I getting warmer, Caitlin?"

If I ate tortilla chips, I'd be stuffing a handful into my face right now. As it is, I really wish they'd brought some healthier foods out to snack on. *Some* of us are in training year round.

"Wait, what's this guy's name?" asks Frankie.

I pointedly ignore the question, but that doesn't stop Lizzie. "Let's see who we can remember from The Caitlin Johannssen diaries. Cait's prom date was… Mike?"

"Matt," says Frankie, making clear I've told these girls way too much about my life. "And the guy from the boat was Hector. That guy didn't look to me like a Hector. We *have* heard about a guy from sports camp, though—"

"Oh my God," I blurt. "Just stop. It's Mase, okay? The name you're thinking of is Mase. His last name's

Mason, and kids in camp used to call him Mase."

Both of their mouths drop open, and suddenly, I want to crawl under the table and die. "Mase!" they say excitedly in unison. "Mase!"

"So, we know the name Mase?" Connor asks.

Lizzie smirks. "We *definitely* know the name Mase. Mase took Cait's ladyflower under the stars during a *very* romantic evening."

"Good job, Cait-Cait!" Frankie throws an arm around my shoulders. "I had no idea Star Boy was so hot!"

"Star Boy?" With every word out of Connor's mouth, he sounds more and more confused, and I want to disappear that much more.

"He charmed her with his knowledge of the constellations," Frankie says dreamily. "Man—athletic skills, brainy, *and* that ass! No wonder you gave it up."

Fuck it. I grab a handful of greasy, fatty chips and stuff them in my face; I'll run it off in laps tomorrow anyway. "I hate you guys. So much."

"You love us and you know it." Lizzie reaches across the table and squeezes my hand. "So that's Mase! He *is* hot. And I don't remember things ending really badly, so why'd you run out?"

"Are you kidding me? What part of 'My new roommate is dating the guy I lost my virginity to' sounds like I should've stuck around?"

"She has a point," says Connor.

"It's in the past!" Frankie argues. "Have a good laugh, reminisce for five minutes, done."

"I...think that's more your style than Cait's, Frank," says Lizzie. "Some people get a little more...attached."

"Attached" is one word for it. One might also say that I didn't get over him quite as quickly as I'd thought I would when we mutually parted with the understanding it was our last summer at camp and it'd be too hard to try to make it work.

One might say it was kinda startling to see that I found him even more attractive now, in the two seconds I saw him, than I had back then. And I'd found him *quite* attractive then.

One might say I suspected it would be a very, very slippery slope back into wanting him—liking him—if I spent more than two seconds alone with him.

One might say that for all the details I'd shared with Lizzie and Frankie about my love life, the one I hadn't was this: I'd been in love with Lawrence Mason.

And I'm pretty sure he'd been in love with me, too.

But before I can utter any of this to them—before I can even decide if I want to—the waiter reappears.

"Have you made any decisions yet?"

So far, only bad ones. Really, really bad ones.

CPSIA information can be obtained at www.ICGtesting.com
Printed in the USA
LVOW11s1819061115

461433LV00005B/367/P